A DEADLY PROMISE

A DETECTIVE KAY HUNTER CRIME THRILLER

RACHEL AMPHLETT

SAXON
PUBLISHING

ONE

Estelle Hastings-Jones winced as the end of a low tree branch smacked against the sports car's bodywork, the sharp slap resonating through the rain that hammered the windscreen.

Beside her, her husband Mark gripped the leather steering wheel, the powerful engine keen to surge forward despite the narrowing lane in front of them.

Just as she thought it couldn't get any more precarious, the front left wheel lurched into a deep pothole with a spine-juddering thump, and Mark cursed under his breath.

'The bloody website didn't say anything about the road to this place being non-existent,' he muttered. 'Who was last along here, the fucking Romans?'

'William the Conqueror, according to…'

'Don't be facetious.' Despite his words, she saw the faint smile that passed his lips in the glow from the dashboard lights. 'How much further along is it?'

She squinted at her mobile phone, careful to shield the screen from Mark so as not to ruin his night vision. 'About quarter of a mile. The instructions they emailed to me said to look out for a new set of gates and a green metal post box fixed to one of the pillars. There's a security panel below the post box for the entry code.'

'Okay.'

Lowering her phone, Estelle eyed the deep puddles lining the road, her gaze then travelling to the thick foliage that curved above the car like a tunnel far below the earth, and shivered despite the car's heater warming her toes.

'Maybe we should've booked into that hotel further along the A20 rather than here,' she said.

'They were fully booked, I told you. No room at the inn,' said Mark, glancing across at her. 'Besides, I don't see anywhere to turn around, do you?'

She pursed her lips, and instead tried to relax.

His hand found her thigh. 'I'm sure the place is worth all this. It'll give us a chance to recharge and relax before driving home tomorrow, right?'

'We'll soon find out – this is it, on the left.'

A pair of thick steel-framed gates reared out from the vegetation under the glare from the car's headlights, blocking their path. The wooden slats resembled that of a castle keep, giving the impression of an impenetrable fortress that only a select few could pass through safely.

Mark slowed the car to a crawl, easing its nose towards the gates. 'What's the code?'

'5371.'

He lowered the window, swore as the wind lashed rain against his face, and reached out for the security panel.

Estelle heard the soft *beep* of the keypad, and then a

faint whirring sound as the gate mechanism eased into action.

As Mark steered the car between the gaping slats, the road changed from decades-old asphalt to freshly laid gravel that crackled under the tyres and spat up into the wheel arches.

He automatically slowed to avoid chipping the paintwork.

The driveway widened, and Estelle saw his hands relax as a stunning Tudor property came into view.

Spotlights sprang to life when he was a few hundred metres away, bathing the parking area and front of the house in a soft hue that welcomed them forward, and she felt some of the tension in her shoulders ebb away.

The curtains had been left open downstairs, so she could see the warm light from lamps in the rooms illuminating the walls, and she wiggled her toes in anticipation.

'I'm getting in the spa bath before I do anything else tonight,' she murmured.

'Sounds good, but first you can help me with the bags.' Mark grinned, turned off the engine and leaned over to kiss her. 'It's not the South of France anymore, but I think it's going to be a perfect end to the holiday before we head back to Cumbria.'

She smiled, her hand on the door release. 'Shall I bring some of the champagne in with us?'

'Good idea. We don't have to leave until eleven tomorrow, so bring two.'

With that, they dived out into the rain, laughing as it pelted down while they retrieved their suitcases from the back of the car and ran towards the front door, their shoes sending up spray from the soaked gravel.

Mark entered the same code into the security panel beside the door, and then Estelle found herself in a wide hallway, with a crimson and white tiled floor that had been polished to a high sheen.

Her heels clacking across the surface, she dropped her suitcase at the base of an oak staircase and lifted her head to marvel at the chandelier that sparkled above their heads.

'There's a note over there,' said Mark, jerking his chin towards an antique pair of occasional chairs and a matching table.

An envelope was propped against a reading lamp, and when Estelle opened it, she sighed. 'Oh, this is lovely. It's from Penelope and Stephen who own the place. It says "Help yourself to the wine and soft drinks in the fridge, as well as the treats and snacks we've left out for you on the kitchen table. Our cleaner, Katrina, will have been in a few hours before your arrival so you should find everything in order", and then she's left her phone number in case there're any problems.'

'Sounds fabulous. We'll have to use that booking website again.' Mark skim-read the note over her shoulder, then nuzzled her neck. 'Let's go and put that champagne in the fridge, and then we can explore.'

Kicking off her shoes, she followed him in bare feet through a doorway at the back of the hallway, gasping as she walked into a modernised kitchen with a gleaming stainless steel eight-burner gas hob set into a central worktop.

The perimeter of the space had been designed with a

mixture of work surfaces and cleverly disguised cupboards. A vase of lilacs gave off a subtle scent from its position on an enormous dining table set for twelve, and fresh fruit had been arranged in a crystal bowl beside packets of different snacks on the central worktop.

When Estelle opened the fridge, her eyes widened in amazement. 'They've even left us fresh steaks and vegetables. And cheeses, and…'

'Well, we *are* paying six hundred quid for one night,' Mark replied. 'Nice touch though, I have to admit.'

While Mark deposited the champagne in the fridge and retrieved a complimentary bottle of wine originating from the Loire Valley, she searched for a corkscrew, marvelling at the cabinetry workmanship as the drawers swished closed silently.

Finding a pair of crystal glasses, she turned to him and grinned. 'How about we find that spa bath?'

'Lead the way.' His eyes sparkled. 'We'll worry about the bags later.'

Estelle insisted on exploring the downstairs rooms before heading upstairs, marvelling at the floor-to-ceiling bookshelves in the library, and then cooing over the luxurious furnishings in the living room before threading her fingers through Mark's and taking the stairs up to an expansive landing.

She wrinkled her nose and paused under an oil painting depicting a bucolic landscape. 'It smells funny up here.'

Sniffing, Mark's brow furrowed. 'I thought the note said their cleaner had been in earlier?'

'It did. Y-you don't think the place has been burgled do you?' Estelle's grip on his hand tightened. 'I mean, you hear all sorts of things about what burglars do apart from stealing things, don't you?'

'I don't think there's been a break-in. I didn't notice any broken windows or anything like that downstairs, did you? And the front door was locked because we had to use the access code.'

She bit her lip. 'We assumed it was – I didn't try pushing it open until after you'd entered the code.'

'But it clicked. The lock clicked, I'm sure it did.' Mark squeezed her hand, then let go and handed her the wine bottle. 'I'll check out the rooms first. Wait here.'

'No – I'll go with you.' Clutching the bottle by the neck, she squared her shoulders. 'Let's start at the front of the house.'

Turning right at the top of the stairs, she followed him around the landing overlooking the tiled hallway below, the chandelier lights twinkling at her, taunting.

The smell didn't linger this side, and when Mark opened the first bedroom door, she heard him breathe a sigh of relief at the sight of an immaculate bedroom complete with matching bunk beds and an action figure mural covering one wall. A laptop had been left on a child-sized desk with its password and the family's wi-fi code scrawled across a note stuck to its screen along with an invitation to guests to use it if needed.

'I don't think they've been burgled,' he said. 'That's just the sort of thing that would've been taken otherwise.'

'Then where's that smell coming from?' Estelle walked along the landing to the next room and again found a tidy bedroom with two single beds. A plain decor had been applied to the walls, complemented by brightly coloured curtains that she swished closed before shutting the door.

'No idea. Maybe there's a leak in the bathroom.'

'Christ, we'd best check. If we have to get a plumber out at this time of the night…'

She sniffed as they crossed back to the other side of the landing. 'It's definitely stronger this side.'

Mark opened another door. 'This is the main bathroom.'

Switching on the lights, Estelle blinked as the bright LEDs shone off freshly wiped tiles, a faint aroma of citrus emanating from the room-width waterfall shower at one end and the gleaming bath tub.

No water pooled around the base of the bidet or toilet, and when she lifted the lid, a similar lemony scent rose into the air.

'Okay, so no leaks in here.'

'Maybe it's coming from the en suite then.' Mark was already walking to the far end of the house before she caught up with him. 'Failing that, it could be one of the sewer pipes under the floorboards.'

Despite her worry, Estelle smiled at his words. 'Once a builder, always a builder.'

'I might run the company these days, but I still remember some of the issues we used to have on site.' He pushed open the door into the master bedroom, then stopped suddenly, emitting a gagging noise. 'Jesus Christ.'

'Mark? What's the matter?'

He didn't reply, and instead staggered a few steps backward. 'Oh my God.'

Estelle frowned, and brushed past him.

Then she saw the woman sprawled on the bed, the soiled sheets twisted beneath her prone body, and the blood stains splattering the plush cushions that had been arranged along the headboard.

A cavernous wound split the woman's alabaster throat from side to side, leaving a dark pool of congealed blood that covered her sweatshirt. Her eyes were wide open in terror as her mouth had gasped its last breath.

Estelle screamed.

TWO

Detective Inspector Kay Hunter pulled up the hood of her waterproof jacket and emerged from the warmth of the pool car, her eyes scanning the scene before her.

Floodlights had been erected on the driveway, highlighting a demarcated path that led from the cluster of vehicles clogging the waterlogged gravel across to the front steps of the imposing Tudor-style residence.

The traffic division had set up a roadblock farther up the lane, diverting any wayward traffic that missed the warning signs on the Faversham road and sending vehicles on a convoluted route that would ensure an in-depth knowledge of the Kentish countryside by the time they reached the end of it.

Kay shoved her hands in her pockets and tried to ignore the fact that one of her ankle boots had sprung a leak since the last downpour.

Instead, she took in the sight of a murder investigation in its early throes, her gaze resting on two uniformed constables at the fringes of the taped-off boundary.

The broader of the two – Kyle Walker – had returned to work full-time twelve weeks ago following a period of ill health, something which Kay knew too well was a direct result of him being present when a colleague had been shot and Kyle almost lost his own life in the process. He stood with his head lowered to his radio underneath a canopy that had been set up to provide a modicum of shelter, the canvas roof flapping in the breeze.

Beside him, Aaron Stewart towered over his colleague, his imposing frame belying a man who was a devoted father and husband. He was speaking with a couple in their fifties, both of them bundled within warm blankets.

Two vans belonging to the team of lead CSI Harriet Baker were parked directly in front of the front steps of the property, the side doors open and a steady stream of technicians moving equipment and empty sample boxes into the house.

Kay glanced over her shoulder at the sound of footsteps crunching across the gravel to see Detective Sergeant Ian Barnes hurrying over, a set of protective coveralls cocooning his bulky form.

Her older colleague's face was grim, his eyes betraying the horror he had witnessed inside the house.

'Guv. Harriet's ready when you are.' He slicked a hand over wet hair, flicking the water to the ground. 'I thought you might want to see what we've got before you speak to the couple who found her. Kyle's managed to book them into a hotel down the road for a night – his sister knows someone there, so they'll be in staff accommodation but...'

'Out of this and in the warm.'

'Exactly, and on hand if we need to speak to them again in the morning before they head home to Cumbria.'

'Okay, let's take a look.' Kay squared her shoulders, then followed him across to the tape separating them from the crime scene. After signing in, she handed back the clipboard to Kyle with a brief nod of thanks. 'Good to see you, PC Walker.'

'Good to be back, guv.' He lowered his voice. 'Shame about the circumstances, though.'

'Indeed.'

Barnes handed her a sealed plastic bag containing a clean set of biohazard coveralls, then gestured to a large white tent beside the front steps. 'Pop them on in here, guv.'

Thankful that one of Harriet's team had thought to lay a blue tarpaulin on the wet ground inside the tent, Kay pulled on the protective clothing, tugged the matching booties over her shoes and took a pair of gloves from Barnes.

'What do you know so far?' she said while she got changed, raising her voice over the thrumming of rain on the thin polyester roof.

'Mark and Estelle Hastings-Jones – the couple talking to Aaron – booked into this place a couple of months ago as a stopping-off point on their way back from a driving holiday in France. The owners, Penelope and Stephen Brassick, spend a lot of time in New York – Stephen works as an actuary for an international investment company so they rent out this place through one of those exclusive sites. When Mark and Estelle arrived, they noticed a smell while they were exploring upstairs. They found the victim in the master bedroom. On the bed.'

Barnes pulled the protective hood of his overalls back over his head, then held open the tent flap for Kay and made his way up the front steps. He paused in the hallway to let a pair of CSIs come down the stairs with a laden evidence box. 'It's not pretty, guv.'

'Injuries?'

'Where to start?' He sighed. 'She's got bruising to her face, one eye is completely closed up, and whoever did all that to her then sliced open her throat.'

'Jesus. Is Lucas here?'

'Been and gone – he got a call-out to another scene at Rochester five minutes before you got here, but he said he'll phone with a time for the post mortem when he's back in the office tomorrow.'

'Thanks.' Kay took a deep breath, then pulled up her mask as the two technicians passed her. 'Lead the way.'

She took in the ostentatious decor as they went up the stairs, the bright chandelier bulbs almost blinding her as they climbed. She wondered if the owners would ever return after this, her mind then turning to the tasks she would set for her team, and potential witnesses that would have to be tracked down and interviewed as quickly as possible.

'What about neighbours?' she asked when they reached the landing. 'Who's speaking to them?'

Barnes shook his head, the movement crinkling the hood that covered his hair. 'There's not enough manpower, guv. Aaron's waiting for another patrol to get here from Sevenoaks, and then they'll divvy up the interviews between them. There're only three other properties along here, so it won't take long.'

'Still, it's a delay we could do without...' Kay bit back the frustration, and looked around her.

The artwork on the walls wasn't to her taste, but it looked as expensive as the rest of her surroundings, and her covered boots sank into the thick plush carpet that lined the floor in every direction.

Despite the mask, she could smell the unmistakable stench of death.

They fell silent as Barnes led her towards a door at the far end of the landing, and she felt her plastic booties slide when her feet found the raised protective pathway that Harriet's technicians had set up so no one trod on the carpet this close to the murder victim.

Every fibre below the pathway would be analysed before their work here was done, and nothing was being left to chance by way of cross-contamination.

The stench of urine and shit penetrated Kay's mask when she entered the room, and she began to take shallower breaths, attempting to offset the assault. Even then, she had to prevent a gasp escaping her lips when Barnes stood to one side, and she saw the woman's body sprawled across the super king-sized bed.

A mop of dark brown hair mottled with grey roots obscured most of the victim's face but even from the doorway Kay could see the ugly welts that covered her eye sockets and cheekbones.

Her jeans had been tugged down to her knees, and a criss-cross of scratches covered her thighs and abdomen, some deeper than others.

A shudder wracked her shoulders when she took in the deep slash wound that had obliterated the woman's throat, her pale-coloured sweatshirt barely visible through the congealed blood that had pooled from her broken body.

'Evening, Kay.'

Her head jerked up at the familiar voice to see one of the suit-clad technicians watching her from beside the bed.

'Harriet.'

The CSI lead was the only person who Kay would defer to during her time here, and she held the expert in high regard.

'If you walk between the yellow flags, you can join me here. We're nearly done processing her, and then we'll get her moved so we can do swabs of the bedclothes.'

Barnes gestured for Kay to go ahead. 'I've already seen enough, guv. I'll wait here.'

Resisting the urge to take a deep breath, Kay trod carefully between the plastic flags Harriet had indicated, nodding her thanks to a technician who moved his equipment box out of the way, then turned her attention to the CSI lead.

'You've been busy.'

'We were having a quiet night until this,' said Harriet. 'Just as well, because I think we're going to be here for a while yet.'

'I won't keep you too long then. What can you tell me so far?'

'Well, once we pulled the sheet from her, we discovered all these scratches to her legs and abdomen too.' Harriet paused and traced the patterns with her gloved fingers.

'Any DNA?'

'We've swabbed everything, but I believe these were done with a knife, the blade going deeper as the attack went on. Lucas will confirm at the post mortem if this was done with the same knife that ended her life.'

Kay swallowed. 'She was tortured, and then had her throat slit, you mean?'

'I think so but of course Lucas will have the final view on that. I can only report it as I see the wounds here. Look at the way her fingernails dig into the sheet underneath her as well.'

'Are those ligature marks around her wrists?'

'Caused by thin rope, a cord – we're still looking for that, don't worry,' Harriet added, then placed her hand on Kay's arm. 'Look at her feet.'

They shuffled to the end of the bed, and Kay's eyes widened.

'What the hell…?'

'Someone used the hair straighteners over there to burn the soles of her feet and her toes.'

'Jesus Christ.'

'Interestingly, she wasn't gagged or silenced in any way. Lucas and I took a look before he left here, and there's no indication of material being forced into her mouth. She's bitten through her tongue at some point.'

'Shit…'

Harriet sighed. 'This is a bad one, Kay. God knows what else Lucas will find during the post mortem.'

Kay ran her gaze over all the injuries once more. 'And no one heard this?'

'Apparently not – the nearest neighbours are back

along the lane, about quarter of a mile, and control received no calls about a disturbance prior to Mark Hastings-Jones phoning it in,' said Barnes from his position on the demarcated pathway. 'The owners of this place told Aaron they wanted somewhere private, off the beaten track.'

'He managed to get hold of them?'

'They left a contact phone number for the guests to call in case there were any problems.' His eyes clouded. 'Although I'm not sure they expected something like this.'

'We'll still need to formally interview them. Do they know the victim?'

'She's their cleaner, Katrina Hovat.'

'We found her coat and handbag downstairs in a scullery off the kitchen,' said Harriet, seeing Kay's surprise. 'Driving licence, house keys, the lot.'

'Home address?'

'Got it written down,' said Barnes, and patted his breast pocket under the coveralls. 'I've radioed through to control to get a patrol over there as soon as possible.'

'How did she get here?'

'Her car's parked round the back, probably because it's easier to access the scullery from there – that's where all the cleaning stuff's kept, like the vacuum cleaner.'

'I've got a pair of technicians analysing her car at the moment,' Harriet said. 'I'll let you know if we find anything of use.'

'Thanks. Did she have her own set of keys to this place as well?'

'No need,' said Barnes. 'The back door uses the same

security code as the front door and the owners confirmed that's what she would've used.'

'And whoever did this to her? How did they get in?' Kay's eyes rested on the broken form on the bed. 'Any signs of a break-in?'

'None,' said Harriet.

'Guv, I'm wondering if she knew her attacker, and so let them in through the driveway gates, then answered the front door to them,' said Barnes.

'We've taken fingerprints off the keypad system, so I'll let you have the results from those in due course,' Harriet added.

'There is one thing,' Barnes said. 'We haven't located a mobile phone for her anywhere yet.'

'Not in her bag?'

'No, and nowhere in the rooms we've searched so far,' said Harriet. 'We'll do a more thorough search in here once her body's been moved, so I'll let you know if that changes anything.'

'Okay.' Kay felt condensation forming on her mask and forced down the urge to pull it from her face. 'Can you show me the scullery, Ian? I'd like to see where her things were found, and her car.'

'I'll give you a call with an update about my findings sometime tomorrow,' Harriet said. 'And I'll arrange for two of my people to go to her flat first thing in the morning.'

'Thanks.'

While she followed Barnes back downstairs, Kay's thoughts returned to the number of phone calls she would need to make before the night was over.

So much of her role as Senior Investigating Officer was given to organising a large team of people, many of whom held specialist roles and were therefore not based at the Maidstone police station. Even more were now private contractors, the police force giving up in-house expertise to that of outsourced help to save costs.

And then there were the political manoeuvrings that would take place out of necessity – obtaining more officers to join her investigation, even though most of them were already thinly spread throughout West Division and overworked.

Reaching the kitchen, she paused for a moment beside the central worktop, unable to tear her gaze away from the expensive cabinetry and sleek design.

'Ignore the footprints,' said Barnes, tearing her away from her thoughts. 'We've already established those belong to Mark and Estelle.'

'What about Katrina and her attacker? Any footprints belonging to them?'

He shook his head. 'Penelope Brassick told Kyle when he phoned her that Katrina was due to start here at seven this evening. It didn't start raining until eight.'

Kay took in the otherwise spotless worktops and polished tiles. 'And she would've cleaned up after herself if she made a mess.'

'When I interview the Brassicks in the morning, I'll get a better idea of Katrina's usual routine if they know it. I've already sent them a quick email to request a note of times to set up a video conference call.'

Taking one last look through the back door at the CSIs

working their way around the victim's car, Kay shook her head sadly, then turned to her colleague.

'Harriet's right, Ian. Whoever did this to her is evil.'

'And dangerous, guv.' His eyes hardened. 'If this is what they're capable of and we haven't seen it before, then they could've been doing this a long time.'

'That's what I'm afraid of.'

THREE

Kay paced the worn carpet in front of the whiteboard, her gaze taking in the threadbare pattern evidencing the numerous murder enquiries that had tested her team's investigative skills in the past.

Six hours after returning home from last night's crime scene, her alarm had gone off and she'd emerged into a rain-soaked morning, the streets of Maidstone awash with muddy puddles and debris-clogged gutters.

Clutching a steaming takeout cup of coffee, she raised her head at the sound of her colleagues walking across to where she waited, the telltale squeak from DC Gavin Piper's worn-out chair cutting through the chatter and general hubbub.

She managed a smile as DC Laura Hanway hurried to catch up with him while tying her hair into a messy bun. The younger detective had only returned from holiday the day before but had insisted on being rostered in to the investigation as soon as she'd heard the news. Dark circles betrayed her earlier insistence that she was ready to contribute to the team, and Kay had no doubt that the woman would come to regret the decision by mid-afternoon.

'Best make sure the vending machine's topped up with coffee pods,' she murmured to a uniformed constable nearest the whiteboard. 'I think Laura's going to need them.'

PC Debbie West grinned. 'Don't worry, guv, Barnes has already asked about that. And there're energy drinks for Gavin, too.'

'Fuelled and ready, guv.' Gavin held up a can as he sank into his chair and balanced a notebook on his knee.

'Great, so I'll have two hyperactive detectives to deal with by eleven o'clock,' said Kay. 'Good job you're going to be busy.'

A flitter of polite laughter peppered the incident room, and then she gestured to Barnes to join her.

'Okay, to work,' she said. 'For those of you who haven't met Detective Sergeant Ian Barnes, he'll be acting as my deputy SIO on this case. Ian, do you want to give us a quick update before I divvy out this morning's tasks?'

'Guv.' Barnes unbuttoned his jacket and waited until Kay had moved to a spare chair. 'Thanks to Debbie and the admin team for getting these photographs printed out and last night's witness statements into HOLMES2 so quickly this morning. What we know so far is that the victim is Katrina Hovat. She was forty-three years old and worked part-time as a cleaner for Penelope and Stephen Brassick, the owners of the house where she was found murdered last night. The couple who found her, Mark and Estelle Hastings-Jones, rented the house through a website specialising in short-term lets of executive homes and were due to stay for just one night on their way back up north after a driving holiday to the south of France. They're now staying in staff accommodation at the hotel on the A20 between here and Charing while we crosscheck their statements against what we glean from the rental company, et cetera.'

He paused to take a sip of coffee, then grimaced. 'Shit, I thought the new supplier was meant to be an improvement, Debs?'

'It is. They're cheaper,' she responded without missing a beat.

Rueful laughter passed among the gathered officers, then Barnes turned to the photographs and they fell silent.

'Lucas confirms he'll do the post mortem this morning, but we know that after Katrina was tortured her killer attempted to strangle her before slicing open her throat. The weapon hasn't yet been retrieved. He's also told me that the marks to her neck suggest someone wore gloves and used their hands rather than a ligature like her wrists were tied with. The full extent of her injuries is horrific – and that's before Lucas tells us what else she endured. In the meantime, Harriet's team finished processing the house at three o'clock this morning so don't expect a full report until much later today. What Harriet has been able to tell us is that whoever did this was professional – she believes they wore protective clothing similar to what we wear to crime scenes. She's got sets of fingerprints to test but we believe – given the sorts of places they were found – that they belong to Mark and Estelle, the Brassicks or Katrina. The Brassicks are providing us with prints via an agency in

New York in order to eliminate them as soon as possible. If anything doesn't match, then we'll pursue that as a valid lead. Harriet's team have just arrived at Katrina's flat this morning and she'll let us have an update once that's been processed.' He turned to Kay and raised an eyebrow. 'I think that's it so far, guv.'

'Thanks, Ian.' Kay swapped places with him and eyed each of her team members in turn. 'Whoever did this to Katrina seems to be well-practised in torture methods. The cuts and scratches to her legs and abdomen would have caused her an incredible amount of pain, but none were near a major artery. She wasn't gagged – so they intended her to talk. The question is, what about? Why was she attacked at the Brassicks' house and not at her flat? What did she know that was so important to them?'

'That demonstrates a hell of a lot of confidence by whoever murdered her, guv,' said Gavin. 'And a knowledge of her routine.'

'Not that she had much of a routine,' Kay said. 'She only went and cleaned for the Brassicks while they were away if the house was booked out. If they were at home, then she went once a week.'

'How long have they been in New York?' said Laura.

Kay peered over the heads of her colleagues until she found Kyle Walker. 'Kyle? Can you fill us in?'

'Sure, guv.' The uniformed constable rose from his seat. 'When I spoke to Stephen Brassick last night, he said this was a three-month visit for them – he typically has to go there to work two to four times a year. When he isn't in New York, his employers can either send him to their offices in Zurich, or he works from home and takes the train into London twice a week. It depends a lot on what their clients need.'

'When did the Brassicks leave for New York this time around?'

'About ten weeks ago, so they're due home in two weeks.' He grimaced. 'He did say they'll probably go to his parents' when they get back and sell the house though.'

'Thanks. What about Mark and Estelle Hastings-Jones? Do they have any alibis for their time prior to their arrival at the house so we can rule them out?'

'Mr Hastings-Jones topped up with petrol at the garage just off the M20 fifteen minutes before they got to the house, guv,' said Kyle. 'And he had the receipt to prove it. I've requested CCTV from the garage to double check though.'

'Good, thanks.'

'Do you think the Brassicks might've been the intended target, not Katrina?' said Gavin.

'It's a possibility,' Kay replied, scrawling his suggestion on the board. 'I'd like you and Laura to do the video interview that Debbie is setting up with them later today. Find out if they've received any threats over the past year or so, and what they know about Katrina's background. Aaron, where are you up to with the neighbours' statements?'

The constable raised his voice so he could be heard. 'They're all complete, guv, and we'll get those into HOLMES2 after the briefing. As we suspected with the Brassicks' house being so secluded, none of them heard anything and they were extremely shocked by the news of Katrina's death. That said, only one neighbour ever saw her, and that was only when her car got a flat tyre in the lane about four weeks ago. None of the neighbours use Katrina's cleaning services though, and none of them know the Brassicks other than in passing.'

'Okay, thanks. Laura, when you and Gavin speak to the Brassicks, can you ask them why Katrina was there four weeks ago? If they had guests renting the house then, I'd like their details.'

'Will do, guv.'

'On to Katrina's car – Laura, again, can you follow up with Harriet's team about that and get onto the DVLA to see what her driving record's like? Aaron said a neighbour mentioned a flat tyre so see if you can find out where she got that fixed too.'

Kay turned her attention to Gavin. 'I'd like you to attend the post mortem this morning. Take Laura with you. Lucas has confirmed it'll be at eleven fifteen, so that gives you both time to get on with these other tasks before you head over to Darent Valley hospital.'

The detective constable's brow furrowed, but he turned his attention to his notebook.

She sympathised with him – a post mortem was never an easy part of any investigation to witness, but even less so when a victim had been tortured. Yet she knew both he and Laura would gain a lot from the experience, and take what they learned into future investigations.

'Right, before I head over to Katrina's flat with Ian, where's Nadine?' Kay waited until a petite uniformed constable rose from a chair on the fringes of the group, her cheeks flaming. 'Everyone, meet PC Nadine Fenning, who joins us today from Tonbridge.'

She waited until a smattering of polite greetings subsided, then continued. 'Kyle, I'd like you to work with Nadine and Debbie to go through Katrina's social media profiles. First of all, we need next of kin details as a matter of urgency. I don't want her family finding out about her murder via the news or anything else until we've had a chance to speak with them. After that, look for the obvious – anything to show potential arguments that turned nasty, or incidents where she was threatened. Get a feel for what sort of person she was when she wasn't working. We also need to find out what else she was doing work-wise. She managed to run a car and rent a flat, so she must've had quite a few clients for her cleaning services. Hopefully Dave Morrison's found something to help us searching the flat, but the social media angle's important too.'

'Any news about her mobile phone?' Laura asked.

'Not yet – Harriet confirmed just before this briefing that they didn't find it during the search of the Brassicks' property, or in Katrina's handbag or car.' Kay tapped her pen against the board, then spun on her heel. 'Aaron, can you organise an urgent search of the lane from the Brassicks' house out to the main road? Maybe her killer disposed of the phone after they left the scene.'

'I'll make a start as soon as we're finished here, guv.'

Kay ran her gaze over the swirling notes that now criss-crossed the whiteboard and felt a renewed energy surge through her as she faced her team.

'Okay, everyone, that's it for now. Let's find a killer.'

FOUR

Ian Barnes cursed under his breath while a small beat-up hatchback reversed into the sole remaining space on Katrina Hovat's street, then glared at the driver as he drove past.

Beside him, Kay grinned. 'You'll have to get used to this walking malarkey soon, you know. Where are you and Pia off to?'

'The Pyrenees.'

'Lots of walking there. Lots of fresh air, healthy food…'

'Stop it, guv.' He shook his head, unable to stop the smile forming. 'I take it you and Pia have been gossiping again?'

'We might have had coffee the other day,' she replied nonchalantly. 'And she *might* have dropped a hint I need to stop buying you lunches for a while.'

'Did you see the concoction I had to bring into work yesterday? I mean, since when do walnuts and bits of melon belong in salad?'

His colleague laughed at his indignity. 'Walnuts are good for protein. And there's another five months to go yet...'

He groaned in response, then sat up straighter as an SUV pulled out from a space near the junction with the next row of red-brick terraced houses. 'Bingo.'

Leading the way back to the subdivided house where Katrina's flat was located, Barnes dodged around piles of dog shit and noted the potholed pavement was pockmarked with patch-worked areas by utilities companies, leaving an uneven surface that caused Kay to curse several times before they reached the property.

He paused at the low decrepit brick wall that separated the three-storey house from the road and took in the overgrown front lawn.

Movement at the communal front door caught his eye, and then PC Dave Morrison peered out.

'Sarge, guv. Want to come up?'

'Morning, Dave. Who's here with you?'

'A newbie – Sean Gastrell,' said the constable. 'Just finished probation and knows what he's doing so I've left him upstairs with Harriet's lot to learn more.'

Barnes smiled. Not many experienced constables would choose to manage a cordon and let someone else be in the thick of an investigation, but that wasn't Dave's style.

'How's he getting on?'

'Good. Seems to have actually listened to what he was taught for a start, and he's been asking some intelligent questions compared to some of the other youngsters HQ have sent us in the past.' Dave winked. 'I reckon he's a keeper, Sarge.'

'Noted. We'll have to see what we can do.'

Kay scrawled her signature under Barnes's and pulled protective gloves from her bag, handing him a spare pair. 'Will these be enough, Dave, or do they want us in full noddy suits?'

'Gloves are fine, guv.'

'What about the other two residents?' Barnes said. 'Had a chance to speak to them?'

'The one through there on this floor is at work at the moment – I spoke with the bloke upstairs who's just back from a night shift in Ashford. Luckily he's also the landlord so he gave me the other tenant's phone number. I'll give him a call again later to arrange taking a statement. I also mentioned to the landlord – Harry Knowles – that you'd probably want a word too.'

'Great, thanks. Right, guv – after you.' Barnes gestured to Kay to go ahead, trudging up the stairs in her wake, and trying not to sound too out of breath by the time they reached the top.

She grinned over her shoulder at him, but said nothing.

In reply, he rolled his eyes, brushed past her and stuck his head through the open doorway to flat three.

'Hello?'

A young constable with sandy-coloured hair cropped short and startling green eyes ducked out of a room off to the right of the narrow hallway, a notebook and pen in his hands. 'Sarge?'

'DS Ian Barnes, and this is the SIO for this investigation, DI Kay Hunter.'

The constable's eyes widened slightly. 'It's an honour to be on your team, guv.'

'Oh, I wouldn't go that far just yet.' Kay smiled. 'You haven't worked with me before.'

'Still…' The constable's cheeks flamed red.

'What have you observed so far – Sean, isn't it?'

'Yes, guv. Well, Gareth and Patrick here – the CSIs – got here two hours ago, and have processed the living room, bathroom and bedroom so far. It's a poky place, so it's not taking them long…' He gestured for them to step over the threshold and led the way into a living area that merged into a small kitchenette.

A bare plain wooden table stood near to the oven accompanied by two chipped mismatched chairs, while the living room consisted of a pair of armchairs, a bookshelf, and not much else.

'No TV?' Barnes said.

'There used to be one until recently,' said Sean. He pointed to the faded paintwork on the wall opposite the armchairs, and then a line of dust on a cabinet below that. 'Looks like it's gone.'

'Stolen?'

'No sign of a break-in, Ian.' One of the CSIs emerged from the bedroom farther along the hallway and pulled down his mask. 'Reckon she pawned it. We found a receipt for it and a laptop computer in the bedroom.'

He handed over a pair of plastic evidence bags, and Barnes looked at the names at the top of the receipt.

'Thanks, Gareth. I know this place. They're legit, which will help.' He handed them over to Kay and pulled out his mobile phone. 'We should get someone to head over there and retrieve the laptop for evidence.'

Sean cleared his throat. 'I've done that, Sarge, just before you got up here. I thought it might be important.'

'Good work, constable. Do you know who was sent over?'

'No – control didn't provide a name, they just said they'd get someone over there ASAP.'

'Fair enough.' Barnes handed back the bags so the CSIs could log them into evidence properly. 'Anything else?'

'Not really.' The CSI shrugged. 'She certainly wasn't attacked here – there was no sign of a break-in, and there's dust everywhere.'

Kay frowned. 'She was employed as a cleaner. I'm surprised at that.'

'You know what they say about builders, guv,' Barnes grinned. 'Too busy to work on their own places half the time. It could have been the same for Katrina. I mean, cleaning doesn't pay much – she must've had more than one job I reckon.'

'Anything to suggest that?' Kay turned her attention back to the CSI technician.

'Yes, hang on.' The CSI disappeared back into the bedroom then emerged with a bulkier evidence bag. 'We've got a folder with all her utilities bills and bank statements so we'll send that over later. I had a quick look at the bank statements, and there are regular cash deposits. This appointments diary was on the bedside table too.'

'So she sells the laptop and switches to a paper

system,' Barnes murmured as Kay flicked through the pages.

'And only in the past four weeks,' she said. 'No names in here, though. Just initials.'

'We need to find that mobile phone.' Barnes glanced at the CSI. 'I don't suppose...'

The man shook his head. 'Sorry. We've nearly finished here, and we've found nothing.'

'Not hidden anywhere like the toilet cistern?'

'Nothing like that, no.' He pointed to the various socket points around the flat. 'We even checked behind those as a matter of course.'

'We'll need this diary sent over to the incident room as quickly as possible,' said Kay.

'As soon as we're done here, we'll make sure the evidence logs are completed and you can have the lot.'

'Okay if we have a look around for ourselves?'

'Be my guest. Just give us five minutes to tidy up in the bedroom.'

While Sean walked away to stand by the front door, Barnes moved over to the kitchen cupboards, opening one after the other with an increasing sense of unease.

'Even Emma ate better than this while she was at uni,' he said, closing another door. 'Katrina wasn't living on much more than cereal and canned stuff by the look of it.'

'The fridge isn't much better,' came Kay's muffled response. She slammed shut the freezer compartment and straightened. 'Just half a pint of milk, a loaf of bread that's way past its sale date, and half a bag of frozen peas.'

'Nothing's shown up on the system in relation to social services, guv.' Barnes rubbed his chin. 'Laura did a quick check this morning, and Katrina wasn't receiving anything by way of benefits.'

'Which suggests she perhaps had another job apart from the part-time cleaning. But why sell her television? You don't get much for those second-hand these days, not with all the stores having sales of new stock every month. And why sell that and the laptop to a pawnbroker rather than online? She'd have made a bit more money that way.'

'Maybe she needed the money in a rush, especially if she needed to buy food. And maybe she hoped to be able to afford to buy them back at some point.' He sighed. 'Well, apart from that diary and the bank statements, we haven't got much to go on, have we?'

Kay turned for the door. 'We'd better hope that Kyle and Nadine have better luck with the social media accounts.'

FIVE

Gavin shoved his hands in his trouser pockets and squinted up at the imposing large windows of the Gravesend hospital, trying to ignore the queasy sensation that seized him.

No matter how hard he tried, he could never greet the prospect of a post mortem with the stoicism that Kay did, despite the knowledge that what they would learn during the process could be integral to the investigation.

'We're going to be late if you stand there much longer,' Laura grumbled, peering over the roof of the car at him. 'And you're making me more nervous.'

He loosened his tie, cleared his throat, then led the way over to a tinted glass door off to the left of the massive structure, holding it open for her.

The soles of their shoes squeaked across the highly polished tiles, echoing off plasterwork walls that were bare save for an obligatory notice board covered in safety posters and a fire extinguisher fixed to a bracket underneath it.

A flight of stairs took them up to the second floor, and they followed the corridor past the X-ray and MRI departments to a single door at the far end of the corridor.

Gavin could almost feel a chill caress his shoulders when he pushed open the door into the mortuary suite.

A thin wan figure hovered behind a single desk, his eyebrows lifting in welcome. 'Thought you weren't going to make it. Was the parking a bitch as usual?'

'Something like that. Has he already started, Simon?'

'No he hasn't,' said a harried voice behind him.

Gavin turned to see the Home Office pathologist, Lucas Anderson, in the doorway balancing two takeout cups of coffee and a tablet computer.

Handing one of the drinks to his assistant, he jerked his chin towards a darkened corridor off to one side. 'The pair of you, go and get changed. I'll see you in there.' Lucas paused to take a sip of his coffee. 'And I'll warn you now, it's not an easy one.'

Laura paled. 'That bad?'

'Go and get ready.' The pathologist's eyes softened. 'The sooner we start, the sooner you can get back to Maidstone and let Kay know what we find.'

'That's not reassuring,' Gavin muttered as he traipsed after Laura, then headed into the men's locker room.

While he pulled a protective bonnet over his hair and tied the baggy trousers at his waist, he tried to concentrate on his breathing, desperately attempting to lower his heart rate. Kay had told him in the past that his reaction was normal, that it was a sign he cared about the victims they sought justice for, but right now it did little to resolve the nervous energy coursing through his veins.

He caught sight of his reflection in the mirror above a small basin in the corner of the room and paused, noting he was as pale as Laura had been.

Katrina Hovat had been brutally assaulted, and then killed, alone and terrified.

He owed it to her to do his job to the best of his abilities.

Squaring his shoulders, he swung open the door and pulled up his mask as Laura emerged from the other locker room, her long hair hidden under her bonnet, her features deathly white.

'Ready?' he said.

She nodded, but said nothing in response, then fell into step beside him.

Pushing through the double doors at the end of the short corridor, Gavin entered the examination room and immediately took in the sorrowful sight of Katrina's body laid bare, the damage to her slight frame all the more stark for being illuminated by the powerful lights above.

Lucas was bending over her abdomen, a scalpel in his hand, and peered over his mask as they drew closer. 'Hope you don't mind but I've made a start – I've got eight of these to do today, including two for Essex.'

'Understaffed again?' Laura asked.

'As always.' Simon Winter moved across from his position next to a laptop and prepared an electric saw for Lucas. 'We haven't had a weekend off in over a month.'

'Still, it is what it is.' Lucas took the saw from him and flicked a switch. 'Stand back a moment, you two, I won't be a moment.'

Gavin averted his eyes, noticing that Laura turned

around and suddenly seemed interested in a stack of medical files on Simon's desk while the saw's blade ground away.

Finally the awful sound abated, and he looked back to the examination table while Lucas began extracting vital organs and passing them to Simon to be weighed.

'Okay, so apart from the injuries she sustained during the attack, I'd say our victim was underweight for her age with considerable wastage to her abdomen. You can see where the skin hangs loose here.'

'Kay and Barnes messaged earlier and said there was hardly any food in her flat.' Gavin moved closer, braver now that the worst seemed to be over. 'Was she malnourished?'

'Heading that way. This loose skin would suggest rapid weight loss, certainly.' Lucas moved to Katrina's shoulders and gently turned her skull in his hands. 'Whoever tried to strangle her before using a knife had reasonably long fingers, strong too. Look at the way the bruising marks her skin here. Then we have the blows to her face.'

'Was she punched?' Laura asked, her interest piqued.

'I would say so, yes. But then she was also hit *with* something. So you'll need to check with the evidence Harriet's lot found to see if you can find a weapon. Look – you can see deep indentations here where something sharp embedded itself in her skin each time.'

'An ornament perhaps?' said Gavin.

'Perhaps. I haven't found any traces of wood or metal, so that might help you narrow it down. And the way her throat has been slashed open... to me, it suggests frustration by her killer that strangulation didn't work. Look at how deep the initial entry wound is here.'

Lucas placed Katrina's head gently back on a supporting block and worked his way down her body, listing each and every injury so Gavin could note them down.

'Here we have significant bruising and scratches to her thighs, and here…' Lucas paused, and blinked. 'Well, like I said, it's one of the worst murders I've seen in a while.'

'Was she raped?' Laura whispered.

The pathologist nodded.

'Any semen we could use for DNA analysis?' Gavin asked.

'She wasn't penetrated in the… normal… way.' Lucas held his gaze. 'Whoever did this to her used a blunt instrument. I've asked Harriet to return to the house to see what she can find.'

Gavin heard Laura's sharp intake of breath, bile rising in his throat, and looked away from Katrina's body for a moment, his fists clenching.

'Jesus Christ,' Laura murmured.

Blinking, he tried to refocus on the questions the woman's injuries raised. 'Have there been any other attacks like this recently? I mean, outside of the Maidstone area. I can't recall anything like this on our patch.'

'Nothing that I've had to deal with since Kay put Jozef Demiri away,' Lucas replied. 'I'll enquire with my colleagues though, and I'll let you know.'

'Thanks.'

Shaken, Gavin followed Laura out of the examination

room, and paused outside the men's locker room when he heard her sniff loudly.

'Hey, do you want to stop somewhere quiet for a drink on the way back?'

She turned then, and he saw the redness in her eyes as she held back tears. She sniffed again, then nodded. 'Yeah. Good idea, thanks.'

'We'll get them, don't worry.' He tore off the protective mask and loosened the overalls at the collar, suddenly too hot in the narrow corridor. 'We'll find the bastard that did that to her.'

Laura wiped her eyes, then kicked open the women's locker room door. 'Damn right we will, Piper.'

SIX

Laura leaned over and adjusted the webcam fixed to the top of the computer screen, glaring at the image reflecting back at her.

She had dived into the ladies' toilet at the pub Gavin had found off the M2 on their way back to Maidstone, fixing the smudges of mascara under her eyes and reapplying lipstick, but couldn't do anything about the haunted expression in her eyes that added to an already jet-lagged complexion.

By the time she had returned to the table Gavin had found in a secluded corner, he'd dispatched half his coffee already and was staring into space.

He had called Leanne, his girlfriend, as soon as they reached the police station, telling her that he'd be working late, and said nothing more about the post mortem until Dave Morrison had enquired.

They'd shared the scantest details with the uniformed constable, and he'd wandered off shaking his head.

Now, she tried to put the memory of Lucas's

examination room to the back of her mind and instead ran her eyes down the list of questions she and Gavin had prepared for their video conference call with Penelope and Stephen Brassick.

Due to the five-hour time difference, the sun was already dipping below the buildings outside when Gavin walked in, his hair freshly washed and a distinct sandalwood fragrance accompanying him.

'You showered?' she teased gently as he took the seat beside her. 'You do realise they can't smell you?'

'I can still smell that bloody mortuary,' he said.

'Sorry.'

He exhaled. 'Me too. Didn't mean to bite your head off. How're you doing?'

'I think I'm going to have a stiff drink when I get home. A large one.'

'You got anyone there you can talk to?'

'I split up with Tyler last month.'

'Sorry to hear that.'

'Don't be.' She smiled. 'You were right, he's a dickhead.'

Gavin choked out a laugh, then jerked his head towards the screen as the connection was made, and a raven-haired woman in her forties appeared on screen.

She wore a light grey suit jacket over a pale blue shirt; the wall behind her was a series of small cream-coloured square tiles.

'Detectives Piper and Hanway? I'm Detective Adrienne DaCosta, with the 10th Precinct. We're the local precinct for the Brassicks, so I thought I'd take a moment to introduce myself,' she said, then held up a thin manila folder. 'I'm also the one who's liaising with your agent to obtain their fingerprints for elimination purposes so I'll have these emailed over while you're talking with them.'

Laura raised her voice a little to counteract the slippery internet connection. 'Thanks for your help with that, and for helping to arrange this interview, Detective DaCosta.'

'Not at all.' The woman raised her eyebrows at voices beyond her screen, then glanced back. 'Mr and Mrs Brassick are here, so I'll hand you over to them. They know they can call me if there are any technical issues or if you need further help from this end.'

'Thanks.' Laura waited while the detective snatched up the folder and made way for a couple in their late fifties, their faces bleak.

Penelope Brassick was dressed impeccably, a string of pearls accentuating a tailored navy dress that unfortunately did nothing for the dark circles under her eyes, while her husband wore a black suit jacket over jeans and a white shirt. Stubble covered his chin, and not in a fashionable way.

Laura realised neither of them had probably had much sleep since Aaron Stewart called them with news of Katrina's murder the night before.

'Mr and Mrs Brassick, thank you for making time to speak with us today,' she began.

'Please, it's Stephen and Penelope.' The man ran a hand over thinning brown hair, then gestured at his wife. 'I'm sorry, we're still in shock. I-I can't believe something like this happened to Katrina. In our home...'

Laura gave them a moment, then glanced at her questions. 'How long had you employed Katrina?'

'We didn't employ her – she came to us through an agency in Maidstone,' Penelope explained, her voice betraying the slightest hint of an adopted American accent. 'We weren't happy with the service we were getting from the previous agency we were using so I called around to find someone else, and they sent Katrina over.'

'We could tell straight away she was a conscientious worker,' Stephen added. 'She was the sort of person that didn't need telling anything twice and wasn't afraid to use her initiative.'

'Hovat doesn't sound like an English name – where was she from originally?'

'The Czech Republic.'

'How long had she been cleaning for you?'

'On and off for six months. She started in the new year.' The man reached over and squeezed his wife's hand. 'Feels like it's been longer than that – in a good way.'

'She was fun to have around,' said Penelope, dabbing at her eyes with a handkerchief. 'I was so impressed that first time that I had her come and clean on a weekly basis while we were at home. It was peace of mind for us having her available to clean when we let out the house too.'

'You said you never had any problems with her or her work,' said Gavin. 'But was there ever a time you felt that she was worried about something?'

'Not at all. Like Stephen said, she was conscientious.'

'And I'd hope that she knew she could've talked to us if she was worried about anything,' added her husband.

'The officers who were first on scene noticed that you have security cameras on the outside of your house...' Laura broke off as Penelope held up her hand.

'Anything you need, anything at all, we're happy to provide it. Stephen's got access to the camera feed on his laptop so if you let us have an email address, we'll grant you administrative access rather than try to download the files from here.'

'They can get quite big, especially as they run all night if the local fox is around,' her husband added.

'That'd be appreciated, thanks. You said that Katrina didn't mention any concerns to you when you last saw her, but did she seem distracted at all, perhaps checking her phone more often, or taking calls in private?'

The couple looked at each other, then back to Laura.

'Not that I can recall,' said Stephen.

'Me neither,' Penelope added.

'One last question – could you give me the contact details for the agency you got Katrina through?'

'Sure.' The other woman retrieved her mobile phone from her bag and recited the number. 'I used to speak to someone there called Madeleine when I wanted Katrina to clean while we were away.'

'Thanks, and thanks for your time today, especially in such difficult circumstances,' said Laura, closing her notebook. 'Do you have anyone you need us to call, perhaps a local locksmith to reset your security system?'

'Don't worry, I can do that online through a different system to the cameras and set a new key code,' said Stephen. He gave a rueful smile. 'Technology, huh?'

SEVEN

A bright sunny June morning greeted Kay the next day when she parked at the Palace Avenue police station.

Hoisting her handbag over her shoulder and clipping her security ID to her trouser waistband, she balanced a stainless steel travel mug in one hand and passed through the back door into a beige-painted corridor, nodding to Ellis Hughes at the front desk.

'Quiet night?' she said, looking through a thick glass window in a door that separated them from the cell block.

'For a change.' The uniformed sergeant peered over his glasses at her. 'You might want to have a word with Gavin and Laura when you go upstairs, guv – if you don't mind me saying so.'

Kay frowned. 'The post mortem?'

'The pair of them looked shell-shocked when they got back yesterday afternoon.' Hughes shook his head sadly. 'And they've got enough experience under their belts these days that it takes a lot to shake them.'

'Thanks. I appreciate the heads-up.' She managed a

small smile. 'Hopefully by now most of the team know they can talk to me about anything, but a reminder now and again doesn't hurt.'

'Exactly my thoughts, guv.' He winked. 'Now you'd best get upstairs before that coffee goes cold.'

'See you later.'

Kay pushed through an inner secure door leading through to the stairwell and looked down to the car park below.

All the cars belonging to her team members who had allocated spaces were present, and the rest were filled with police vehicles of varying shapes and sizes. She picked up her pace when she spotted a familiar motorbike parked beside Barnes's car, its rider waiting beside an open-top box, and reached the landing as Laura emerged from the second-floor corridor, determination in her stride.

'Morning, guv.'

'Morning. What's the rush?'

In response, Laura held up an evidence bag containing an old laptop computer. 'Kyle Walker found this at a pawnbroker's shop in town late yesterday.'

'Is that Katrina's?'

'Yes – the owner still has her TV as well. Apparently she was happy for him to sell that, but was planning on coming back for this.'

'Ah, that explains why I saw Andy Grey outside.'

'He's come over to collect it – none of us can get over to Northfleet until this afternoon, and I guessed you'd want him to take a look at this as soon as possible.'

'You'd be right. Thanks.' Kay moved to one side to let the other woman pass. 'Laura?'

The younger detective paused a few steps down the staircase and looked over her shoulder. 'Yes, guv?'

'Come and see me if you need to offload about yesterday's post mortem, all right? It can't have been an easy one to deal with.'

'You'd be right there, guv.' She flipped a strand of hair behind her ear. 'And thanks, I may well do that. Me and Gavin stopped for coffee on the way back, but...'

'Sometimes it's good to chat to someone different, right?'

'Yeah. Especially with one like that. You'll talk to Gavin too though?'

'I will. I'll also make sure Barnes knows in case he's more comfortable talking about it with another bloke.'

'Thanks.' Laura held up the laptop. 'I should go.'

'I'll wait until you get back before I start the briefing.'

When she entered the incident room, the fine hairs on the back of her neck prickled with anticipation. There were already a number of officers sitting at desks, heads bowed to computer screens or phones to their ears, their voices competing with the whirr of the overworked printer and photocopier and the noise of team members calling across the room to each other with urgent requests.

Everything was urgent now.

Placing her bag under her desk, Kay crossed to the whiteboard where Barnes stood, his jaw set.

'I bumped into Laura on the way up here,' she said.

'Kyle did well to secure the laptop so quickly. Was Andy downstairs?'

'In the car park, waiting for her. Hopefully, given the age of that laptop, it won't take him long to access it once he's back at HQ.' She slurped her coffee. 'Do me a favour? Have a word with Gavin this morning and make sure he's okay after the post mortem. I took a look at Lucas's report last night, and it made for a harrowing read.'

He nodded. 'I read it when I got here, and don't worry – I'll speak to him.'

'Thanks.' She turned as the door to the incident room opened and Laura reappeared, her cheeks flushed from running up the two flights of stairs. 'Everything okay with Andy?'

'He says he'll give you a call as soon as he has anything, guv.'

'Right-o. Let's make a start then.' She gave her team a moment to settle on chairs or lean against the desks nearest to the board, and then turned her attention to Kyle. 'Good work with the laptop. How are you and Nadine getting on with Katrina's diary?'

The tall officer deferred to his colleague, waving her forward.

Nadine gave him a nervous smile of thanks. 'So far we've had no luck gleaning names from it, guv, just a system of initials Katrina used, but what we did establish is her work patterns. She never had any appointments between eight in the morning and six at night between Sunday and Thursday, which to us suggests she was doing the work around a main job to earn extra money.'

'Anything in there to suggest what that main job might be?'

'Not in the diary, guv. If we're right and she was working two jobs then she kept them separated.' Nadine blushed. 'We even tried that old trick of rubbing a pencil over some tracing paper to try and read any indentations on the pages, but there was nothing.'

'Worth a shot anyway, thanks.' Kay finished writing on the board and then tapped the end of the pen against her chin. 'How did you get on with the social media profiles?'

Nadine beckoned to Kyle, then sat down.

'We found a couple of profiles for Katrina but although she used to post regularly she hasn't been active on either of them for about fourteen weeks, guv,' Kyle began, handing over some printed-out pages. 'We haven't found any next of kin, either. I've cross-checked with local obituaries against some posts she shared a few years ago and it appears that both of her parents are dead, and she didn't have any siblings. Her employment status was last updated two years ago and I've traced that to an aged care facility on the outskirts of town here. I didn't find anything on either of her profiles to suggest she'd been threatened or intimidated by anyone.'

Kay sifted through the print-outs while she listened. 'And yet she went from posting at least twice a week about fun things she was doing or seeing to suddenly retreating completely.'

'People are falling out of love with some of the social media platforms over privacy issues,' Barnes suggested.

'True. Good work finding the employer's details though, Kyle – are they local?'

'They are, and I took the liberty of arranging for you to meet them in the morning, guv. Hope that's okay.'

'Perfect, thanks. What about friends listed on these profiles?'

'We're still tracing and contacting as many of them as

possible with a view to making appointments for interviews from this afternoon, guv. We're concentrating on the people she seemed to interact with the most before going quiet.'

'Okay. Work with Debbie to task three other officers to help you with the interviews. The sooner we get those done, the better. Onto the bank statements – Gavin?'

'Guv, I don't think all of the cleaning jobs in Katrina's diary were paid into her bank account,' said the detective. 'There are two semi-regular payments into her account, one from Maid By Us, which is the agency contracted to clean Penelope and Stephen Brassick's house, and another regular payment that only has a reference number and no company name. The amounts from that second payment remain the same although they're larger than the Maid By Us amounts, and are paid in every two weeks—'

Kay frowned. 'That suggests it's coming from her main job, then.'

'That's what we thought,' said Laura. 'But it's like Nadine said – Katrina was doing a lot of extra work on the side if that diary's anything to go by, and so me and Gavin thought they'd probably be cash jobs.'

A collective groan passed through the incident room.

'If she was being paid in cash, then there's not a lot of hope we're going to find out who paid her,' said Barnes.

'And that's assuming it was all cleaning jobs,' Nadine added, then blushed.

Kay added their suggestions to the board. 'Let's not rule out anything at the moment. Hopefully once Andy's managed to crack that laptop open he'll be able to find access to a cloud-based diary with more information, or at least a contacts list.'

'Guv, the other thing about the bank accounts is the lack of expenses going out,' said Laura. 'It's all day-to-day living costs, food, rent, utilities bills – no discretionary spending, no treats, nothing.'

'That ties in with what we saw at her flat – most of the cupboards were bare, and of course the television was missing.' Kay sighed, running her gaze over her notes. 'So, we have a woman who works more than two jobs, spends no money except on essentials… has she withdrawn from her social circle due to embarrassment, or fear? Why the subterfuge with the initials in the diary? And did anyone else have access to her flat?'

'Guv, if those appointments in her diary were cash in hand then she probably doesn't want the tax man to find out about them,' said Barnes. 'Especially if, as Nadine suggested, those might not have been cleaning jobs but something else.'

Kay paused, huffing her fringe from her eyes. 'Okay, that's a good point. Let's get on with the tasks we've got today, interview her friends, and then see what her employers say tomorrow. Dismissed, everyone.'

EIGHT

Kay stared up at the four-storey block of flats, squinting as early afternoon sunshine sparkled off the windows on the top floor.

Each flat had a small balcony overlooking the street, with some residents arranging colourful pots filled with various leafy plants. One enterprising resident had erected a trellis, and she spotted the large tomatoes hanging from the vines covering its framework. Other residents simply chose to hang out their washing, no doubt making the most of the westerly aspect.

A steady hum of traffic carried from the one-way system circling the suburb, at odds with the happy shouts from kids playing an impromptu game of football in the small park behind her.

She looked down at movement beside her.

'Which one is hers?' said Barnes, shielding his eyes. 'Please tell me it's not on the top floor unless there's a lift.'

Kay smiled. 'Flat 3, one floor up. You should be okay. I thought you were going to the gym with Pia now?'

'I am. I'm still hurting from Thursday night's session so the less I have to do today, the better.'

He stomped off towards the communal front door to the building, holding it open for her and then jerking his chin towards the back of the building. 'Two flats on each floor then. They must be a decent size.'

'Lots of light, too,' Kay said, peering up the stairwell that glowed from spotlights sunk into the plasterwork walls. 'Although I think I'd prefer one of the ones overlooking the river. More to watch.'

'More to pay, too. I remember when these were built.' Barnes began climbing the stairs. 'This block was the cheapest out of the three.'

When they reached the next floor, he stepped aside to let her pass. 'How did this woman know Katrina?'

'Kyle says it looks like they used to work together at a pub in town until a few years ago.' Kay paused outside the solid wooden door for number three, and lowered her voice. 'Annabelle Menzies was divorced and bringing up her son on her own at the time. From the photos Kyle printed out from social media it looked like she and Katrina were quite close, and then when Katrina left the pub to work at the care home they caught up now and again socially. Nothing in the past three months though.'

She knocked, reached into her bag for her warrant card and exhaled.

Being the bearer of bad news was never easy, let alone in such horrific circumstances.

Moments later, a woman with deep lines criss-crossing her forehead and her hair tied back in a messy bun answered, her eyes narrowing at the sight of them.

'What's going on?'

'Annabelle Menzies? My name's Detective Inspector Kay Hunter, and this is my colleague Detective Sergeant Ian Barnes. I wondered if we could have a word please?'

'What about?'

Kay lowered her warrant card. 'It's probably best if we speak inside.'

'I'll decide that. What do you want to talk to me about?'

'It's about your friend, Katrina Hovat. I'm sorry, we have some bad news.'

Annabelle's eyes widened, her hand gripping the door harder. 'Is she okay?'

'Can we come in? Please.'

The woman stepped aside before wandering along a short hallway and into a living area that – as Kay had predicted – overlooked the park and the football game below.

It was tidy and functional, with flatpack bookshelves from a well-known department store filling one wall on either side of a small television. A pair of sofas occupied the space in the middle with a glass coffee table taking up most of a white and grey shaggy rug.

She heard Barnes close the front door softly before he joined her, and then gestured to one of the sofas. 'Is it okay if we sit down, Annabelle?'

The woman nodded, curling her feet up under her as she sat at the far end of one with her back to the window and nibbled at a fingernail while Barnes extracted his notebook.

'There's no easy way to break news like this,' Kay

began. 'I'm sorry to have to tell you that Katrina was found dead on Friday night, and that we're treating her death as suspicious.'

The woman's jaw dropped, her face paling. 'Dead? How?'

'I'm afraid I can't share the details with you at the moment, but I would like to ask for your help in finding whoever's responsible.'

'Are you saying she was murdered?' Tears streaked down Annabelle's cheeks, and she wiped at them with the heel of her hand. 'Why?'

'We're going to do all we can to find out why, but would you mind answering some questions about Katrina?' Kay softened her voice. 'It would really help us.'

In response, Annabelle uncurled herself from the sofa and dashed out of the living room, her sobs audible through the thin walls.

'God, I hate this part of the job,' Barnes muttered.

'Me too.'

Kay heard the toilet flush, then the sound of Annabelle blowing her nose before the woman padded back into the living room and collapsed on the sofa, hugging her knees while she stared at the carpet.

'Sorry.'

'It's okay. It's a perfectly normal reaction in the circumstances.' Kay gave her a moment to settle, and waited until the woman's eyes found hers. 'We found your details on social media – it looked as if you and Katrina were quite close. Would that be right?'

Annabelle nodded. 'We used to work at a pub in town in the evenings a couple of nights a week, just to earn some extra money after our divorces. The landlord liked having us work there because we had more experience than some of the youngsters, and we took less crap from the customers than younger staff would. We used to have such a laugh…'

She shook her head sadly, then unravelled a paper tissue and dabbed at her eyes.

'Did you keep in touch when you both left the pub?'

'Yes, on and off. She got a job at a supermarket that offered more hours and a bit more pay two years ago, and then I got the job I'm in now working as an admin assistant for an insurance broker so it wasn't like we could catch up regularly.' She gave a watery smile. 'When we did though, we'd always just pick up the conversation where we left off. We could talk about anything to each other.'

'Did Katrina ever say, or did you get the impression, that she was worried about something or someone?' Kay asked.

'No, not that I remember.' Annabelle frowned. 'Mind you, I haven't – hadn't – seen her for about four months now. I was only thinking last week I should send her a message, try to catch up. I wish…'

Fresh sobs wracked her shoulders, and Kay paused while the woman composed herself.

'I wish I knew if she was scared of something, or someone.' She bit her lip. 'The only thing she was worried about was money. She was working all hours, which is why it took months to organise something, and when we did she didn't want to go to a fancy bar or anything like that.'

'Was that unusual for her? To be worried about money?'

'Only since her job at the supermarket ended in January. They put in more of those self-service checkouts and decided to get rid of anyone working more than a certain amount of hours every week so they didn't have to pay out so much in wages. Katrina was doing some cleaning work here and there to make ends meet anyway, and then she found some other part-time work but it wasn't enough.' Annabelle sighed. 'Just before I last saw her, she'd got a new job at one of the retail shops in the centre of town but she wasn't making as much as she had before. She was still doing three jobs. I was worried about her, and told her so – she looked knackered.'

'When was this, the last time you saw her?' said Kay.

'Early March. I did text her at the end of April to see if she wanted to meet up for coffee, but she just said she couldn't. I offered to pay, thinking perhaps she was still struggling, but I never heard back from her.' Annabelle's shoulders slumped. 'I wondered if I'd accidentally insulted her by offering to pay, but I didn't know what else to do.'

'You said that Katrina was divorced,' said Barnes. 'Are you aware of any problems there? Was she still in touch with her ex?'

'No – he lives up near Sheffield somewhere,' said Annabelle. 'As far as I'm aware, once the divorce was through they never spoke again. She said it was amicable though – I think they married young and just drifted apart. He works in marketing, I think – or did, when me and Katrina worked in the pub together. I think that was the last time she ever mentioned him.'

'We're aware she's been doing cleaning work part-time, but you mentioned she had a third job on top of the retail work,' Barnes asked. 'Any idea what that job was?'

'No, sorry. She only mentioned it in passing. I don't think it was paying much either, but I assumed doing all that work brought in enough to get by.' Annabelle sniffed. 'She always said she just needed a big break, something to give her a financial boost to get ahead.'

'We noticed that she didn't have a television anymore when we visited her flat yesterday, and there wasn't much food in the cupboards. Had she mentioned whether she'd been selling her belongings?'

'What? No – I didn't hear from her after texting her in April. God, now I feel rotten that I haven't called her since. I should've done. I should've insisted on helping her somehow.' Annabelle's gaze roamed around her living room. 'Even if she wanted to stay here for a bit, I would've let her. I mean, I don't have a lot of space here, but...'

'One last question,' said Kay. 'Do you know if Katrina has any close family members that we can contact? We tried to locate her parents, but—'

'They died a few years ago,' Annabelle said. 'I went to the funeral with her. And she hasn't got any brothers or sisters – there wasn't anyone else at the funeral apart from a handful of her parents' friends, and she and her ex didn't have kids.'

'Thank you.' Kay stood, and passed one of her cards to Annabelle. 'All my contact details are on there, so if you recall anything that might help us, don't hesitate to give me a call, please.'

'Okay.' The woman's hand trembled as she took the card. 'I will.'

'And if you've got a friend or family member you can call, perhaps spend some time with today, do,' Barnes added. 'Hearing news like this is never easy.'

Annabelle wiped away fresh tears. 'Can you see yourselves out?'

NINE

Gavin's stomach rumbled as he locked the pool car and glanced across the narrow street towards a row of terraced houses, the brickwork painted a mixture of pastel colours interspersed with an occasional ugly pebbledash render.

He moved out of the way as a twenty-something on a skateboard zipped past, the man leaving a trail of cigarette smoke in his wake while farther along at the junction an independent takeaway shop with a battered façade conducted a busy trade in fried food, the fatty aromas wafting on the breeze towards him.

Laura followed his gaze and wrinkled her nose. 'You're not seriously thinking of getting something to eat there, are you?'

'No,' he said quickly, then turned his back and ignored the hunger pangs that pinched his abdomen. 'But maybe I'll stop on the way back to the station and get a sandwich.'

His colleague grinned before jerking her chin at a pale

blue-painted house in the middle of the terrace. 'That's the one. Number forty-seven.'

They crossed the road, their footsteps sending a large ginger and white tabby cat scooting out from under a worn-out SUV and onto a low brick wall beside the neighbouring property.

Gavin reached out to ruffle its fur, then changed his mind when it glared at him with narrowed yellow eyes. Instead, he turned his attention to the weather-beaten door of number forty-seven and rang the bell, its chirp resonating through the thin wood.

'Do you want to lead this one?' he said under his breath. 'In the circumstances, she might appreciate talking to another woman.'

'No problem.' Laura pursed her lips as a chain rattled against the woodwork and then a woman in her late thirties blinked against the bright sunshine.

'Yes?'

Laura held out her warrant card and made the introductions. 'Are you Carissa Margoyles?'

'Yes.'

'We understand you're a friend of Katrina Hovat. May we come in please?'

'What's going on?' The woman looked from Laura to Gavin. 'Is Kat okay?'

'If we could come inside?' Laura looked over her shoulder as an old man walked past with a terrier on a lead, his eyes agog at the two suited detectives. 'It'll give us some privacy from your neighbours.'

'I'm not sure. I mean, I know you're the police an' all but…'

'I understand. I'm sorry, but we have some bad news and I think you might prefer to hear it indoors.'

Carissa gulped, and her hand fluttered to her chest. 'Oh, my God. She's been hurt, hasn't she? That's why she hasn't been answering my calls.'

Gavin stepped forward as the woman staggered against the door frame and cupped her elbow in his hand. 'Let's go and sit down, Carissa. I'll pop the kettle on.'

He led the woman over the threshold, finding himself in a gloomy living room with a low ceiling.

An ashtray beside a crumpled sofa contained a small pile of cigarette papers and the remains of a freshly smoked joint. The sweet scent of marijuana was still in the air.

Carissa reddened and avoided his eyes as he waited for her to sit, then flapped her hand towards it. 'I don't often smoke, I—'

'I take it it's for personal use only?'

She nodded miserably.

'Then don't worry about it. Now, tea? Coffee?'

'Tea, please. I'm out of milk though.'

'D'you want some sugar in it then?'

'Yeah. Please.' She edged forward on the sofa. 'I'll show you where everything is.'

'That's okay. I'm house-trained.' He gave her a small smile, then glanced over to where Laura was settling into an armchair under the window and nodded before leaving the room.

Finding a chipped mug in a cupboard above a microwave and ferreting around the tiny galley kitchen until he found a cardboard box of generic brand teabags, he strained his ears to hear over the boiling kettle.

Laura's gentle voice carried over the rumbling water, then soft sobs accompanied her words, and his stomach flipped.

Exhaling, he poured the water over the teabag, added two sugars and mashed it a few times with a tannin-stained spoon.

When he walked back into the living room, Carissa's face was blotchy and she wiped at tears with a tissue from a freshly opened packet in her lap. After setting down the tea mug beside the ashtray, he wandered over to a low cabinet with a small collection of framed photographs along the top.

His breath caught in his throat when he recognised Katrina in three of them, her arms thrown around Carissa's shoulders as they laughed in various poses, one in a Maidstone bar he recognised from nights out with his girlfriend, Leanne. In one, they bookended a black shorthaired cat with enormous ears, the animal batting its paw at a fluffy goldfish that Katrina dangled from a piece of string.

'Is this your cat?' he asked, glancing over his shoulder.

'Yeah. Katrina found him at an animal shelter about a year ago and suggested I got him. My old cat died a while back.' Carissa sniffed. 'Watch out if he makes an appearance though. He doesn't like strangers. He'll have your arm off given half a chance.'

Gavin smiled, then wandered over and sat at the other end of the sofa. 'I'll bear that in mind, thanks.'

'Carissa, I'm sorry to do this after giving you bad

news, but we're trying to understand more about Katrina's movements these past few weeks,' said Laura. 'Would you mind if I ask you some questions?'

'Go on then.'

'How long had you known Katrina?'

'We met working at the supermarket. She's a bit older than me, obviously, but we just hit it off.' Carissa reached out and rummaged down the side of the sofa cushion, extracting a crumpled packet of cigarettes before lighting one with a shaking hand. She leaned back and blew smoke into the air before erupting in a fit of coughing.

'How long ago was that?'

'Eighteen months ago. I got laid off from a bakery in town but got lucky – my boss there knew a supervisor at the supermarket and introduced me.' She shrugged. 'It was either that or go on the dole. I ain't got a licence so I couldn't do delivery driving or anything like that.'

'We've been informed that Katrina lost her job at the supermarket in January when they put in more self-service tills – were you not affected by that?'

Carissa shook her head. 'I don't work on the tills. I sort out all the grocery orders that come in online, so my job's pretty safe at the moment.'

'How often did you two socialise?' said Laura. 'Seeing those photos, it looks like you had a lot of fun when you did.'

'Yeah, she's – was – awesome. Didn't judge me, or tell me I could do something better with myself. She was a good listener, too. I ain't got much money, nor did she so we used to look out for free stuff to go to – gigs in the park in the summer, things like that.'

'Did you notice if Katrina seemed nervous lately, or have something on her mind in recent weeks?'

'She was quieter than usual.' Carissa tapped the end of the cigarette amongst the ash, then took another drag. 'I asked her a few weeks ago if she was okay. She looked tired, too. I said to her she ought to quit one of the jobs she was doing. That's when she said it didn't matter because the part-time job she'd been doing had dried up.'

'The cleaning work?' Laura frowned. 'I thought she was still doing that.'

'Not that. The online admin stuff. She was working through one of them sites that do – what's it called? – virtual assistant work. That's it. She was doing bits and pieces for an estate agent in Portsmouth, just uploading new listings and stuff on the side, but then they found a way to do it in-house for cheaper.'

'How did she manage three jobs? She must've been exhausted.'

'She was, you're right there. I mean, the supermarket don't pay much but you get some benefits like discounts on your groceries and whatnot, and I know she was doing the cleaning sideline on a regular basis. I think she must've been doing the real estate stuff late at night.' Carissa took a last drag of the cigarette and stubbed it out while tendrils of smoke escaped her lips. 'She'd lost weight though. See that photograph on the left over there? I took that back in January in that park near the train station. By last month she must've dropped half a stone or more – her cheeks looked hollow, and I noticed she'd quit smoking too. But she'd still bag one of mine if I offered.'

'Did she get the cleaning work through an agency or something like that?'

'She never mentioned it. I thought she might've put a few cards up in shops or something. I know she wasn't keen on going to an agency for the extra work because they skim off some of your earnings to cover admin charges and stuff, don't they?'

Laura paused to update her notes before asking her next question. 'Did Katrina mention if she was having money troubles?'

'No. I asked her if everything was all right, and she kept insisting it was. Even though I could see it wasn't.'

'Was that unusual for her? You seem close in the photos.'

'Yeah, it was weird.' Carissa scrunched up the tissue and plucked another cigarette from the packet. 'That's why, when she didn't turn up at the pub on Friday night, I started worrying.'

'Pub?'

'I managed to convince her to let me treat her to dinner. She took some convincing.' Carissa sighed. 'Katrina was brilliant at helping others, but crap at letting me help her in return. My dad gave me some money last week for my birthday and I thought it'd be nice to have a night out. Proper food y'know? Not takeaways or whatever I throw together here. I didn't want to go on my own though – I split up with my boyfriend four months ago – so I thought it'd be nice to treat Katrina. Then she didn't turn up. I tried calling her…'

Laura leaned forward. 'What's her number, Carissa?'

Gavin wrote it down, underscoring the information, his

mind already turning to the work they'd have to do back at the incident room.

'Did Katrina seem scared or worried about someone when you last spoke with her?' he said.

'She didn't mention anything. I know she wasn't seeing anyone at the moment. She tried one of them dating apps but it didn't work out with the last bloke – he lived up in Newcastle, and she didn't want a long-distance relationship.' Carissa shrugged. 'She reckoned she couldn't afford to go on dates anyway. Said she had to save her money.'

'Was she saving for anything in particular?' asked Laura.

Carissa flicked the wheel of her lighter, sending a flame shooting upwards that illuminated her pale features. 'If she was, she didn't tell me.'

Five minutes later, Gavin stood on the pavement beside the car inhaling lungfuls of fresher air while Laura handed Carissa a business card and then jogged across the road to join him.

'What do you think, Gav?' She unlocked the car and rested her hand on the roof while a motorbike purred past, then opened the door. 'Katrina looked like the life of the party in those photos, but it sounds like she became a recluse in recent months.'

He got in beside her and fastened his seatbelt. 'Three jobs, but she lived in an empty flat and didn't go out. She was losing weight from not eating, and stopped socialising. She had to be scared of someone, right?'

TEN

The next morning, Barnes pulled the car into a busy retail car park on the fringes of the town centre while Kay scrolled back and forth through a myriad of emails on her phone.

She groaned as he braked to let a young mother cross a pedestrian crossing, glancing up and wondering how to respond to the latest missive from Northfleet HQ. 'They've turned down my request for more manpower on this one. Apparently there've been two stabbings in Gravesend over the weekend, potentially related to a stand-off between three rival drugs gangs, so that's taking priority.'

'Over a woman tortured to death?' Barnes shook his head, accelerating slowly away. He cursed under his breath as he crawled back and forth trying to find a space that wasn't assigned to disabled drivers or parents with children, finally emitting a strangled cheer when a sparkling sports car reversed out of one at speed, narrowly missing his front bumper.

'I'll let you off that, mate,' he murmured. 'Because I'm not driving around again.'

Kay chuckled. 'Sometimes I'm glad I work shifts and miss some of this mayhem.'

She peered up at the enormous warehouses that lined one side of the car park where a bright sign above each set of double doors depicted a mixture of household names that sold electronics, pet supplies and furniture.

At the far end was an independent shop, its large windows plastered with sale signs. An arrangement of cheap metal shelves had been dragged outside and now framed the open double doors, displaying a clutter of fake plants in pots, wicker storage boxes and metal pedal bins in various sizes and colours.

Bright, chirpy music accompanied her as she followed Barnes into the shop, her gaze scanning the aisles she passed. All around her, customers browsed, poked, sniffed and prodded the different displays that ranged from scented candles to fluffy bales of towels and cute knick-knacks that would surely gather dust once taken home.

'Help you?' called a bleach-blonde woman in her sixties who prowled the cashiers' area. 'We haven't reported any shop-lifters, have we?'

Kay bit back a snort.

'There goes our undercover efforts,' Barnes said under his breath, then opened his warrant card. 'DS Ian Barnes, and DI Kay Hunter. We're here to see Hayley Prendle.'

'She's out the back.' The woman pointed beyond the aisles. 'Go down there and look for the blue door. You'll have to knock – she locks it when she's working in there.'

Nodding her thanks, Kay walked briskly along the

aisle and found the door beside another with a sign that stated "Staff Only – storeroom" hanging from its handle.

It opened after she knocked and a petite woman with short auburn hair peered out. 'Are you the detectives?'

'We are,' said Kay, holding up her warrant card. 'Hayley Prendle, is it?'

'Yes. I saw you on the CCTV cameras.' The woman moved out of the way, swinging the door open and pointing at a pair of computer monitors on a cluttered desk. She pulled out a pair of fold-out metal garden chairs from beside a four-drawer filing cabinet and placed them beside the desk with a rueful smile. 'Best I can do, unfortunately.'

The door swung shut behind Barnes with an audible click, and Hayley rolled her eyes.

'It locks automatically, and I haven't worked out how to stop it. I've been trying to persuade head office to pay to get a locksmith out to look at it and the dodgy lock on the warehouse door, but the management team keep avoiding my emails.'

'I know the feeling.' Kay shot her a sympathetic smile as she tried to get comfortable on the hard seat. 'Thanks for seeing us this morning. I appreciate my phone call last night must've been a shock.'

'It was.' Hayley sank back into her own chair, which looked like it was being held together with sticky black electrical tape and not much more. It creaked ominously when she leaned forward to use her keyboard. 'I took the liberty of finding Katrina's job application for you when I got in. I don't know if it'll help, but I figured… oh, I don't know. I just wanted to do *something*.'

'We appreciate it, thank you.' Kay squinted at the screen. 'I understand she was working at a supermarket before coming here?'

'Yes, for about two years. Don't worry, I can print this out for you. Hang on.' Hayley pressed a series of buttons then returned to the original screen while a slim printer on top of the filing cabinet whirred to life. 'Before that, she was at a garden centre so working here came second nature I think. She certainly fitted in quickly.'

'Were you aware that she was doing cleaning work part-time?' Kay asked while the woman stapled the printed pages together then handed them to her. 'Thanks.'

'I wasn't, no.' She sat down and frowned. 'I wondered why she looked tired all the time.'

'How many hours did she work here?'

'Twenty hours a week spread between Monday to Friday, then every third Saturday and Sunday. Same as the rest of my staff.'

'Not full-time?'

Hayley shook her head. 'You won't find many full-time contracts in retail, Detective Hunter. Not unless someone's a manager, like me. We only have to pay the basic hourly rate that way. It helps us keep the overheads down, you see.'

'You mentioned that Katrina looked tired all the time – was that something recent, or…'

'Only in the past four weeks or so.' Hayley paused to lock her computer screen, then spun her chair around to face them. 'I did ask her if everything was all right – despite what it looks like, I do make sure my staff can come in here and speak to me whenever they want, even if

I can't literally keep the damn door open. She said she was fine, but there were a couple of times in the past week that she seemed distracted. You met Beverley out there – she's one of the supervisors. She told me last Thursday that Katrina was short-tempered with a customer that morning, and then she had to be told to put her mobile phone in her locker because she kept checking her messages instead of stocking the shelves.'

'Was that unusual for her?'

'Very.' Hayley dropped her hands to her lap, twisting a wedding band, her voice dropping to a murmur. 'And then you called and said she was murdered on Friday night.'

Barnes looked up from his notes. 'Did you ever see or hear anyone acting threateningly towards her at work?'

'No, but I'm in here a lot of the time.' She waved her hand at the paperwork and files littering the small wooden desk. 'You're welcome to interview the staff though – Beverley keeps an eye on things out there for me, as do the other two supervisors that work here. They might've spotted something.'

'Did Katrina ever report any customers acting threateningly towards her?'

'No. And I can assure you, if she had we would've taken it very seriously. The CCTV system isn't just there to put off shoplifters – it's there for our staff's safety too.'

Kay glanced down with a frown as her phone buzzed in her bag, then looked through the pages Hayley had printed off as she stood up. 'Thanks for your time this morning, and for this. If we want to take a look at your CCTV footage…'

'I can copy everything onto an external drive for you,'

said Hayley. 'It's only kept for eight weeks at a time as that's all our insurers require, but if you think it'll help.'

'It could.' Kay handed over her card. 'And I'll have uniformed officers arrange to interview your supervisors as soon as possible, if you could email me their contact details please?'

'I'll do it now.'

'Thanks. We'll be in touch.'

Hurrying from the shop, Kay followed Barnes back to the car as she pulled out her phone and saw the missed call number.

'Hang on, Ian. Andy Grey over at Northfleet was after me.' She pulled her seatbelt on while Barnes started the engine and tapped his fingers on the steering wheel. 'Andy? It's Kay Hunter.'

'How soon can you get yourself to Northfleet?' he said by way of greeting.

'Forty minutes perhaps. Why? Have you managed to get into Katrina's laptop already?'

'No, but there's something I need to show you, and we can only access it from here.' Andy paused, and she heard a shaking breath. 'I'll warn you now – it's not going to make easy viewing.'

ELEVEN

'Did he say what he'd found?'

Barnes swiped his security card over the access panel beside a set of smoked glass double doors and followed Kay across a tiled floor towards a set of lifts.

A cool air-conditioned breeze crept across her shoulders while they waited, sending an uninvited shiver down her spine, a chill seizing her as she recalled Andy's words.

'No, but it doesn't sound good. Especially if it's something they can only access from here.'

'Dark web stuff, you mean?' His eyes widened. 'How did he—'

'I don't know.' Kay moved when the lift doors opened to reveal a pair of high-ranking officers, giving them a curt nod as they passed without breaking their conversation, then stabbed the button for the digital forensic unit's floor. 'But he did say before hanging up that he hasn't managed to find anything on her laptop yet. She wiped the hard drive before taking it to the pawnbrokers, so he's having to do a deep dive on the system to see if there's anything lurking elsewhere that might help us.'

Barnes blew out his cheeks as the lift rose through the building. 'Whatever he's found, I'm glad it's us and not Gavin or Laura who's here. Not after having to witness the post mortem.'

They stepped out into a corridor lined with an industrial-looking carpet that deadened their footsteps but did little for the overall aesthetic of the place. Doors were spaced evenly down the right-hand side, the one that would offer office occupants a view across the busy dual carriageway if they had time to contemplate it, whilst the left-hand wall was dotted with various landscape photographs that looked as if they'd been bulk purchased from an online stationery store.

Kay led the way towards a door near the end with a frosted glass panel set into its heavy wooden surface above a security key panel.

She rapped her knuckles against the glass, and waited, her gaze finding the small camera above the door frame, where a lone red LED light blinked at her.

After a few moments, the door was wrenched open and a man about her height with close-cropped hair and wire-rimmed glasses beckoned them inside.

'Thanks for coming over,' he said. 'This isn't the sort of thing I'd want to load up to HOLMES2, even if I could. The less eyes on this, the better.'

Andy Grey walked briskly over to a large screen with an enormous computer tower beside it and gestured to the otherwise sparse room. 'Bring a chair. Any will do –

everyone else is in a health and safety training course this morning.'

'Get a lot of sharp objects in here, do you?' Barnes joked, wheeling over a chair with a wobbly caster.

'Another tick in the box for the HR department.' Andy managed a smile before his eyes clouded once more. He removed his glasses and frowned, turning to the screen. 'I've cued this up, and I'll start it in a moment but tell me as soon as you've seen enough, all right?'

'Have you watched it all?' Kay said, her mouth dry.

'Had to. Same with everything we see in here. It's the only way you get a full report for your investigations.' The digital forensic analyst grimaced. 'I had a feeling this one was going to be bad though, after hearing how you found her.'

Kay forced herself to look at the screen when he started the video, her fingers digging into the soft fabric of the chair's arms as an unsteady camera angle first showed the familiar plush rose-coloured carpet of the Brassicks' master bedroom, then straightened to show Katrina struggling under the grip of a masked figure dressed in black who wrestled her over to the double bed.

The woman's attacker wore a black balaclava that obscured his features, and a simple black jogging ensemble of sweatshirt and bottoms. No logos were visible on any of his clothing.

Katrina was begging for her life, her breath coming in gulps as she pleaded, first in English, and then in what Kay assumed was Czech. Her eyes widened as her attacker brandished a knife in front of her eyes, and then whoever was holding the phone and filming the attack stepped closer to the bed.

Neither the person filming or the attacker said anything or seemed to acknowledge Katrina's words, the woman's voice little more than a gasp as she struggled.

Then her attacker drew his knife across her abdomen, a deep cut that made Kay gasp.

Katrina's scream filled the sound-proofed office space, shrill against the plasterwork walls, at odds with the cheery photographs of Andy's family that surrounded his desk.

Bile rose in Kay's throat as she watched tears stream down Katrina's cheeks, the woman writhing in agony as her attacker reared back, straddled her, and then drove the knife into her thigh.

'Stop.' Kay held up her hand, turning away from the screen.

'Jesus.' Barnes spun his chair around after another second or two, then walked over to the window and ran his hand over his mouth.

Kay blinked, trying to lose some of the imagery replaying in her head. 'I don't know how you and your team do this every day, Andy.'

'Someone else resigned last week,' said the analyst. 'And I've got two part-time staff off with stress.'

'I'm not surprised.' After a few more seconds, Barnes wandered back to join them, and exhaled, pulling his reading glasses from his jacket pocket and peering at the text under the frozen video. 'Fucking hell. This was only posted six hours ago, and it's already had more than three hundred views.'

'Ah, I was going to bring that up.' Andy's fingers

swept across his keyboard, and Kay watched as a new data string appeared in the left of the screen. 'See here? This is the length of the whole video. Just over ten minutes long…'

'Ten minutes?' Kay swallowed, seeing that they'd only viewed the first minute and fifteen seconds. 'It seemed longer watching that part.'

'I know. But look.' Andy reached out and tapped the screen. 'The average viewing time is less than forty-five seconds.'

'So people saw more than enough and moved on,' said Barnes.

'That's not what I mean.' Andy closed the video and turned to them, his tone patient. 'The point is, this was loaded up to the dark web – the sort of place where people go to watch this sort of thing. They're looking for stuff like this, so I'd expect them to watch the whole video, not bail out after a few seconds. I'd expect the average duration to be higher, and for the number of views to be higher for a snuff video. Much higher. But there's code here to suggest it was shared. A link was generated shortly after the video was uploaded, probably with the purpose of sharing it via other means such as email.'

Kay frowned. 'What are you getting at?'

'I don't think this was shared online so that some twisted individuals could get their kicks. I think this was posted and then shared elsewhere as a warning.'

TWELVE

An audience of grim faces stared back at Kay when she stood in front of the whiteboard, ready to begin the late morning briefing.

The recent rain showers had turned to bright sunshine that filtered through the window blinds and sparkled across the desks, the effect at odds with the photographs from the crime scene that were pinned to the board.

Kay took a brief sip of water from her drink bottle, flipped the cap shut and cleared her throat.

'Right, let's start with the digital forensics update before we go any further,' she said. 'Andy Grey discovered that a video of Katrina's torture and death was uploaded to the dark web earlier today. That video file is now linked within our system but for anyone new to the team – that's off limits to you and anyone else not authorised by me or DS Barnes to view it. All I will say is that it's nasty, and the attack on Katrina was prolonged.'

A shocked silence met her words.

'Moving on, from the interviews with Katrina's friends we were given a mobile number that Andy is now working on to try to ascertain what Katrina's movements were leading up to her death. None of her friends saw her on Friday, and there's nothing on her social media to suggest where she went prior to turning up at the Brassicks' house to clean it before their guests arrived that evening. As soon as we've heard from him, I'll provide another update. In the meantime, her boss at the shop where she worked part-time confirmed that over the past four weeks Katrina looked exhausted, and one of her supervisors reprimanded her for using her mobile phone when she should have been working. Uniform are currently interviewing the other members of staff, but at the moment it appears that no one knew about the cleaning work she was doing on the side and there are no reports of customers threatening Katrina.' She put aside her notes and lifted her chin until she could see Aaron Stewart. 'What about CCTV from the house?'

'The Brassicks have four cameras set up, one on each side of the house,' he said, raising his voice to be heard. 'And all of them had their lenses and motion sensors spray-painted before Katrina was killed.'

Kay's sharp intake of breath was echoed by the officers around her. 'Shit. Didn't Stephen Brassick notice? I thought he had access to the camera feed on his laptop?'

'He does, and when I told him he was understandably shocked – he said the system should've sent him an alert immediately that any activity was detected by the motion sensors and given how sensitive they are, whoever did this–'

'Knew about them.' Kay sighed, brushing her fringe from her eyes. 'Christ. Any chance you could see movement on the footage prior to the cameras being disabled?'

'No, guv – they blindsided the cameras completely.' Aaron's lip curled. 'They probably checked out the layout of the house using online satellite imagery before turning up.'

'The house is in the middle of nowhere. How did they manage to see where the cameras were located? They wouldn't show up online, would they?'

Nadine raised her hand. 'Guv, if they didn't know exactly where those cameras were, all they'd have to do is move slowly enough that the sensors didn't trip.'

'Bloody hell.' Kay raised an eyebrow.

'My brother's in the Royal Marines,' the probationary constable explained, colour rising to her cheeks. 'He tells me stuff like that about their training. It's just a suggestion.'

'And it's a good one.' Kay turned back to the whiteboard and updated the notes. 'That could suggest our killer – or killers – have had some sort of military or other specialised training.'

'Or they've done this before and know what to look out for,' Barnes added. 'And they're patient.'

'Not to mention having bloody big balls to spend that much time approaching the house without knowing if the owners or someone else could turn up at any time.' Kay frowned as she turned to Gavin. 'I don't recall anything in the post mortem report suggesting this, but did Lucas mention whether Katrina's wounds suggested a military angle? I'm thinking special forces, that sort of thing.'

'No, guv, but I'll call him after this to run it by him.'

'Aaron, can you work with Debbie to go through the camera footage for the past four weeks? That's the timeframe Katrina's manager told us she'd seen her looking tired and stressed out about something so maybe the Brassicks' place was scoped out prior to Thursday night.'

'Will do, guv.'

'What about her ex-husband – has he got an alibi?'

Kyle Walker looked up from his notes. 'He was in Copenhagen on a work junket all last week and didn't get back until Saturday night. I've spoken to his manager, who corroborated the hotel checkout time and flight arrival.'

'Okay, thanks. Moving on – how did Katrina's killers get into the house? If she was afraid of someone, why would she let them in? Is there any evidence to suggest that they broke in while she was inside the house?'

'I've been going through the reports from Harriet's CSI team and there's nothing in these to point to a break-in,' said Laura.

'So potentially, she knew her attackers.' Kay lobbed her pen onto a nearby table. 'We need more information about Katrina's background – including everything we can dig up about her upbringing, what her parents did, and why they moved to the UK in the first place.'

'Do you think this might be payback for something her family did?' said Barnes. 'Or someone she knows?'

'I've no idea at the moment, but Nadine's suggestion

that Katrina's killers might've had military training opens a whole new angle doesn't it?' Kay ran her gaze across her team. 'And if it isn't someone ex-military from here, then we're going to have to look into whether a foreign entity is involved.'

THIRTEEN

Kay stabbed her fork into an unsuspecting fried prawn and checked her mobile phone with her other hand.

Scrolling through a swathe of new messages, she bit back a sigh as she saw the latest missive from Headquarters and then looked up at a polite cough.

'I take it you suggested meeting for dinner so we could discuss something other than life at the top?' Detective Chief Inspector Devon Sharp took a sip from the bottle of lager and shot her a smile. 'Or was it a ruse to get me to pay for all this food?'

'Sorry, guv.' Kay lowered her phone and pushed the remaining Thai curry around her plate for a few moments. 'This case...'

'Hmm. Lucas said it was a nasty one.'

'You've spoken to him?'

'In passing, earlier today. He was at Northfleet briefly for a meeting with one of the East Division teams. And while we're out, first names, remember?' His tone softened. 'After all, we've been through a lot together over the years.'

'That we have. How's Rebecca by the way?'

'At her weekly squash session. They've set up a six-week coaching programme for the ladies, which means she'll thrash me next time we're on a court together.'

'She reckons she beats you most times anyway.'

Sharp chuckled. 'I'll be having words with her about that.'

Kay paused to have a sip of wine, then lowered her fork and pushed away her plate. 'That's it, I'm stuffed.'

'Then talk. I'll finish the rice.'

After checking over her shoulder to make sure none of the tables behind her had filled with customers, she kept her voice low while she brought him up to date with the progress of the investigation. 'One of our new probationers has a brother in the Marines, and she came up with the suggestion that whoever did this might have military training.'

'On what basis?'

'That they disabled the cameras in such a way that they were never spotted approaching. PC Fenning reckons the only way they could have negotiated the motion sensors was to move very slowly.' Kay turned the stem of her wineglass between her fingers. 'Given that Stephen Brassick told us those cameras can be tripped by a fox mooching about in the garden, that's very slow.'

Sharp dabbed his mouth with his napkin and then leaned back in his chair, his eyes thoughtful. 'It's a valid point.'

She watched as the ex-Royal Military policeman's jaw clenched, his gaze drifting to the empty plates for a moment before he spoke again.

'Have you had a chance to look at local ex-military personnel with a criminal record?'

'We've been working on it all afternoon, but there's nothing that's come to light recently.' Kay exhaled. 'The other thing I'm wondering is, with the victim's heritage being Czech, whether there's a security angle there.'

Sharp's eyes widened. 'An attack by a foreign power? That's a leap.'

'It is, but it's something we're going to have to look at, if only to rule it out.' She cleared her throat. 'Which is what I wanted to talk to you about. I wondered if you've got any contacts you could make some discreet enquiries with. The last thing I want to do is have the media get wind of this.'

'God, no. We can't have that.'

'Do you know anyone who could help?'

'Not offhand, but I'll have a think about it. If I do find someone I'll let you know once we've either confirmed there is a link, or that there's nothing to suggest foreign involvement.' He grimaced. 'And it won't be by the usual means so best keep this between ourselves.'

Kay's heart quickened. 'You mean security services.'

'That's what you need, isn't it?'

'True.'

'It might take me a while, so keep going with your other angles until we can rule it out. I'm thinking you should take a closer look at the Brassicks as well.'

'Oh? Why? They're in New York at the moment, and have been for months.'

'Yes, but you mentioned that Stephen Brassick could monitor the cameras and reset the locks on the house remotely using his online security system.' Sharp leaned forward and rested his elbows on the table as he warmed to his subject. 'And if he can do that, then he could have also let someone into the house without Katrina's knowledge, couldn't he?'

Kay swallowed, her mouth suddenly dry. 'God, you're right. She could've been busy cleaning upstairs and never heard them come in.'

'Or they were already in the house when she arrived. Waiting for her.'

His gaze flickered to the right moments before Kay heard movement, and she glanced over her shoulder to see the waiter approaching.

'Everything all right here?' he asked, already reaching out for the empty plates. 'Would you like anything else?'

'We're good, thanks. Just the bill please,' said Kay. She waited until he retreated to the kitchen, and then turned back to Sharp. 'I'll have Laura do a deeper dive into the Brassicks' background and work history first thing tomorrow.'

'I would,' he said. 'And ask her to see if there's a military connection there, too. Given the amount of travel Stephen Brassick does for work, who knows who he might have crossed paths with?'

Kay pulled out her purse, her hand hovering over her credit card and looked up. 'Do you think Katrina was killed to send a message to the Brassicks, rather than this attack being directly linked to her?'

Her old mentor waggled his eyebrows. 'That, Detective Hunter, is something you're going to have to find out.'

FOURTEEN

When Kay turned her car into her driveway half an hour later, there was already a muddy four-wheel-drive parked in front of the garage.

Climbing out, she smiled as the local blackbird chirped from the shrubs in the small front garden. A soft pinkish glow still clung to the darkening horizon beyond the houses on the opposite side of the lane.

Someone somewhere was having a barbecue, and the smell of charcoal wafted on the breeze as she shoved her key in the front door.

An involuntary shiver crossed her shoulders at the memory of a case from a few years ago and then she slammed shut the door, forcing the thought aside.

Warmth enveloped her while she toed off her shoes and shrugged off her suit jacket, the aroma of something delicious coming from the kitchen offset by an acrid smell of—

'Shit, you're home already.'

Her partner, Adam Turner, peered around the kitchen door, a guilty look on his suntanned face.

Kay narrowed her eyes. 'What's going on?'

'I was hoping to have this cleared up before you got back.' He stepped aside to let her pass, then pointed at a box in the corner. 'The kids had an accident.'

Her gaze travelled from the mess on the kitchen tiles to four prickly creatures tumbling over each other in the box, which had been lined with fresh straw.

'I thought I'd let them have a run around in here while I cleaned out their bedding,' Adam said, plucking more pages from a depleted roll of kitchen paper and then swiping up the muck. 'I forgot how much mess they make at this age.'

'They're adorable.' Kay crouched beside the box, resisting the urge to reach out and touch the baby hedgehogs. 'Where did you find them?'

'One of the neighbours brought them round earlier this afternoon – there was a nest behind his shed and he'd been putting out food since April. There's a dead hedgehog just up the lane from here, so he kept an eye on them overnight to see if any parent returned but it looks as if this bunch are orphaned.' Adam straightened, grimacing. 'I'll pop this in the dustbin – back in a minute.'

Kay pointed at an empty wineglass on the central worktop. 'Fancy another, or are you out early in the morning?'

'I'll have another glass, thanks – there's a chardonnay open in the fridge.'

She poured two glasses, then padded through to the living room, the undertones of a favourite album of

Adam's playing in the background, a band they'd seen live several times.

Eyeing the paperwork strewn across the coffee table, she placed Adam's drink as far away from the documents as possible, then sank onto the sofa with a sigh and rubbed at tired eyes.

'I take it your rostered week off won't be happening, then?' Adam walked in, eased onto the sofa and clinked his glass against hers.

'No, not now.' Kay rolled her shoulders. 'I can't. Not with this one.'

'How was Devon?'

'Good. He sends his regards.' She angled her glass at the paperwork. 'What're you working on?'

'I've been asked to contribute an article to a journal later in the year, but I'm a bit rusty on the latest research developments.'

'Homework, then?'

He nodded. 'There's some good stuff happening out there at the moment, too. It'd be good to have it consolidated into one article. If I can get my thoughts together, that is. The journal's aimed at undergraduates, so I can't afford to blind them with science.'

Kay leaned over and kissed him. 'It's great you're getting more invitations to do this.'

'Well, hopefully this one might lead into some speaking events too.'

'Do you fancy teaching?' She sat upright. 'Rather than running the practice, I mean?'

'No, not to replace actually doing the work. But it's nice to pass on some of what I know, I suppose. Besides, I usually learn things from other speakers too.' He put down his glass, then leaned forward and began gathering the papers together into a neat pile. 'So, how was your day?'

'Frustrating.' She took another sip. 'Part of me feels like my brain's going to explode with the amount of information coming in, the other part of me is worrying that we're already four days into the investigation, and yet we know next to nothing about who killed our victim, or why.'

'Did you ask Sharp about getting some more bums on seats?'

'I did. He can't do anything though – too many other cases taking as much priority as this one, as usual.' She put down her glass, a bitter taste clouding her palate. 'I'll just have to manage with what I've got. Whoever murdered that woman is sadistic.'

Adam squeezed her hand. 'I know you can't tell me everything about what you do, but you know you can talk to me if it gets too much, don't you?'

'I do.' She forced a smile. 'And, thanks.'

He pulled her into a hug and kissed her hair. 'Be careful, Kay. That's all I ask. If this killer is as bad as some of the others you've put away, then don't do anything…'

'Stupid?' She pulled away and shot him a rueful look. 'I won't. I've learned the hard way in the past, haven't I?'

'I'm not so sure about the learning part.' He reached out and tucked a strand of hair behind her ear, a worried expression in his eyes. 'I know what you're like once you get your teeth into a case.'

FIFTEEN

'I can't believe I had to take a day off work just because you couldn't be bothered to do this over the weekend like we agreed.'

Alana Winkman stood with her hands on her hips and glared at her brother before turning her attention to the over-stuffed interior of the storage unit. 'And I can't believe how much *crap* Dad has in here. I thought when Mum died, he took everything to a charity shop.'

'Apparently not.' Richard Zilchrist shuffled from foot to foot. 'And I couldn't get here over the weekend, I told you that. Diane wanted to go and see her sister.'

Alana rolled her eyes. 'Whatever.'

'Where's Matt, anyway? I thought you said he was coming.'

'Someone went off sick so they asked him to work today.' She acknowledged his exasperated huff with a curt nod. 'Which is a pain in the arse because we could've really done with using his van. As it is, we're just going to have to make do with the two cars.'

Dust motes spiralled into the air as she put her weight against a large box and shoved it to one side in an attempt to make a gap at the front of the unit.

A mustiness clung to everything, the sharp undertone of mould coming from somewhere, while the sun's rays tried and failed to warm the cool air that emerged from the shadows.

Richard sneezed when he opened a box, sending a cloud of dust shooting upwards. 'Where the hell do we start with all of this? I mean, do you want any of it?'

'I don't know. We don't even know what's in here yet.' She blinked back tears, and sniffed. 'Why didn't he tell us about this when he was alive? We could've asked him what to do.'

'Hey, it'll be okay.' He put his arm around her shoulder and squeezed. 'We'll work it out. Besides, the solicitor said the owners of this place are giving us until the end of the month to clear it. What if we just chip away at it a bit at a time starting with today and then come back here at the weekend? We'll sort out what needs to go to the charity shop and throw everything else away. I honestly can't imagine there's anything in here we're going to want, do you?'

'I suppose not.' Alana sniffed again. 'Anyway, at least sorting this out will keep us busy while the solicitor's sorting out all the other finances.'

He groaned. 'Don't remind me. I had to hand over all of Dad's paperwork to them yesterday – I couldn't make head or tail of any of it.'

'Well, we're paying them enough so let them get on with it.' Alana leaned over and dragged a box towards her, cringing as a large spider shot past her canvas shoes and out of the unit in a hurry. 'God, I hope there aren't any rats in here.'

'I doubt it. I can't see any damp in here, and there aren't any rat droppings – I mean, just look at the dust. Anyway, this place wouldn't have many customers if everyone's stuff was getting chewed.'

She glanced over her shoulder towards the old shipping container at the entrance to the site that had been converted into a makeshift office. 'I don't think they have many customers anyway. How the hell did Dad find this place?'

'God knows. Some of this stuff has been here a long time. Look.' Richard held up a bundle of car magazines, the once glossy paper curling with age. 'These are from when he was renovating the Morris Minor.'

'He sold that three years ago, didn't he?' Her stomach flipped as she cast her eyes around the other boxes. 'How old are those at the back, then?'

'Only one way to find out.' Her brother stepped over to the left-hand side of the opening and found a light switch. Four bright fluorescent strip lights blinked to life above their heads. 'How about we work for a couple of hours, then find somewhere to have a bite to eat before coming back here?'

'Sounds good.' Alana rolled up her sleeves, took a deep breath at the thought of finding a spider's nest, and started rummaging through the boxes beside her.

After twenty minutes, there were six boxes that had been dragged out of the unit and now stood beside their parked cars for disposal at the nearby recycling centre. Two more boxes were destined for the charity shop after

Richard discovered some of their mother's clothing neatly packed inside, and an antique clock Alana remembered from their childhood was now sitting in the footwell of her car.

She wasn't sure what to do with it yet, but was reluctant to let it go.

An hour and a half had passed by the time Richard straightened, digging his knuckles into his back with a groan, and turned to her.

'Right, that's it – time out. I need coffee.'

She grinned, dragging a pair of moth-eaten sweatshirts from a box. 'Me too. God, what on earth did he keep these for? I'm sure I remember Mum telling him to throw them out years ago.'

'You know Dad, always reluctant to let go of something that was perfectly good for—'

'Gardening,' they said in unison, and then Alana laughed. 'I'm glad we're doing this together. It just feels... right, doesn't it?'

He smiled. 'I'm sorry we lost touch these past two years, Al. It's just with work and stuff, and then Damien's problems at school...'

'I know.' She held up her hand. 'There's no need to apologise. How's he doing anyway? Settling into the new place all right?'

'No problems so far, thank God.' He checked his watch, then squeezed past a pair of decrepit wooden chairs and eyed an old wardrobe beside a row of boxes that had been stacked along the back wall. 'Okay, one more box and then lunch. Sound good?'

'Works for me.' On cue, her stomach rumbled. 'There's

a place down the road that does an all-day breakfast. We can get coffee to bring back here, too.'

She heard a muffled response from her brother as she delved into another box, then turned at the sound of retching. 'Rich?'

He was pushing his way out from the back of the unit, shoving his weight against the chairs so hard that they bashed into a shelving unit, sending the contents flying across the floor.

Face grey, he put his hand to his mouth and pelted for the open door.

Moments later, she heard him vomit over the pockmarked concrete hardstanding, and rushed outside.

'Rich? Whatever's the matter? What's wrong?'

He shook his head in response, closed his eyes and leaned over, resting his hands on his knees.

Alana looked over her shoulder towards the gloomy unit, squinting against the bright sunlight. 'What happened?'

Her brother eased upright, then turned and spat on the ground. When he spoke, his voice shook. 'Call the police, Al.'

'Wha…?'

He rounded on her, eyes wild. 'The police. Call them. Now. And for Christ's sake, don't go back in there.'

SIXTEEN

Barnes wobbled on one foot and pulled the leg of the protective suit over his trouser leg, swearing under his breath as the hem caught on his big toe and nearly sent him careening into the young CSI technician hovering at his shoulder.

To her credit, she managed not to laugh, and instead reached out to steady him.

'Thanks,' he said gruffly. 'Where's Harriet?'

'Inside.' She jerked her gloved thumb over her shoulder as he straightened. 'It took us an age to work a path through all the boxes so she's only just had a chance to take a look at the body.'

'How bad is it?'

'I've seen worse.'

'That doesn't exactly fill me with hope.'

She grinned behind her mask, the movement crinkling the skin at the corner of her eyes. 'Will you be okay with the other leg?'

'What?'

In reply, she pointed at his suit and he looked down to see he was still half-in, half-out of it, and sighed.

'I can dress myself, you know.'

'Just checking, Sarge.'

She winked, then hurried away as Lucas Anderson walked towards them, his hand smoothing down a wayward mop of hair.

'Am I getting old, or are they getting cheekier?' Barnes demanded.

The pathologist gave him a weary smile. 'No comment. Are you here on your own?'

'Kay's gone straight to the incident room to organise things at that end.' He tugged the sleeves of the protective suit over his wrists, and pulled on gloves before jerking his chin towards the open door of the storage unit. 'Male or female?'

'Male, in his late twenties or early thirties, I'd say.' Lucas turned to face the unit. 'Hard to tell until I do the post mortem, but I'd suggest he's been in there about two months, give or take.'

'Dave Morrison said on the radio that the victim was found naked. That true?'

'Naked, and tortured before he was strangled.' Lucas raised an eyebrow. 'I hate to tell you this, Ian, but from what I could see while the body was still in situ, the knife marks to the victim's arms and hands look similar to those inflicted on Katrina Hovat. There's the same placement of wounds for example on the soft skin between the fingers.'

'Shit.' Barnes flexed his fingers, his skin already sweating under the protective nitrile material. 'You said the body's still in situ...'

'He was stuffed inside an old wardrobe that's been stored along the side wall of the unit.'

Barnes looked over as Dave Morrison broke away from a small group of younger officers and headed towards them.

'Morning, Sarge. The couple who discovered the body are a brother and sister who were clearing this place out. It belonged to their dad, a Mr Angus Zilchrist – he died two weeks ago.'

'Naturally, or—'

'Heart attack, at home.' Dave adjusted the volume on his radio as it crackled to life. 'Apparently, he was mowing the lawn when it happened. Just dropped dead on the spot.'

'Where are the brother and sister?'

'Nadine Fenning's arranged to drive them home. I took their statements before they left. They didn't even know about the unit until they spoke with their father's solicitor three days after he died.'

'Okay, so we need background checks on this Angus Zilchrist then. How—'

'Detective Barnes? We're ready for you.'

Barnes saw Harriet beckoning to him, her mask pulled down to her chin while she stood outside the unit.

'I'll give Kay a call once I'm back at the office to let her know when I'll be doing the PM,' said Lucas, turning away. 'It should be sometime tomorrow.'

'Thanks. Dave, I'll catch up with you before I leave here.' Barnes trudged over to where Harriet stood waiting. 'Morning. We must stop meeting like this.'

'No kidding.' She handed him a disposable mask. 'Don't worry – he doesn't smell too bad. I reckon if those two hadn't discovered him, we'd have a mummy on our hands. Lucas said that the environment in here is perfect.'

Barnes wrinkled his nose under the paper covering. 'He also mentioned he thought the victim had been here a few weeks at least.'

'Well, let's see if we find anything to help with that. Mind your step – I need you to follow this line of flags, okay?'

He followed her into the unit, careful not to brush against a box that had tumbled over, spilling its contents of rag-eared paperbacks over the concrete floor, and then stepped over a pile of old clothing that had been scattered around.

A few steps more, and they reached the wardrobe, its flimsy doors wide open.

At its base, the crumpled pale form of a naked man lay sprawled across the ground, his face contorted into a grimace of pain, teeth bared while his eyes—

Barnes gulped. 'Bloody hell. Narnia's gone downhill, hasn't it?'

A collective groan filtered amongst the gathered CSI technicians, and Harriet rolled her eyes. 'We've had quite enough of the jokes already, thank you, Detective Barnes. We think one of these boxes was holding the door shut. When Richard Zilchrist moved the box, the doors opened and the victim tumbled out.'

'Jesus, that must've given him one hell of a fright.' Despite his revulsion, he crouched beside the victim's body and craned his neck to see the different knife wounds that covered the man's legs and arms.

Some were no more than a small nick to the skin, but

as Lucas had said, these were in areas of delicate skin, places where even the tiniest of cuts would cause excruciating pain. Larger stab wounds were in the man's outer thighs, and Barnes's lip curled behind his mask as he realised at least one of them would have cut to the bone.

'Lucas checked his jaw, and there are three teeth missing that we could see,' Harriet said. 'Maybe more – when he gets him back to the morgue, he'll be able to confirm whether those were old extractions, or inflicted prior to death.'

'It does look similar to Katrina's injuries. It'll be interesting to hear whether he can compare the wounds to see if it's the same weapon used.' Barnes straightened, then eyed the concrete floor. 'I can't see any blood, so I'm guessing he was killed elsewhere, then dumped here. Anything in here to suggest *how* he was put in the wardrobe, if the brother and sister have alibis?'

Harriet led him back out to the door, out of the way of her technicians. 'Not yet. PC Morrison has already requested CCTV footage from the manager here, but the brother and sister moved the boxes to get to the wardrobe so we've probably lost a lot of evidence. We're processing everything to check for latent prints and taken swabs from them before they left so we can eliminate them if necessary, but don't hold your breath.'

After walking outside, Barnes pushed back his protective hood and removed his mask, unzipping the top of the protective suit. 'Okay, thanks, Harriet. I'll let you get on.'

Dispatching the suit into a nearby biohazard bin, he made his way over to where Dave Morrison leaned against the back of his patrol car, head bowed over his notebook. 'Who had keys to the storage unit?'

'There's a master key held by the office over there, and then the one Alana Winkman said she found at her dad's house while they were sorting through some paperwork they found stuffed in one of the kitchen drawers. When she asked the solicitor about it, he was the one who suggested it might belong to this storage unit – that was the first time either of Angus's children had heard about the place.' Dave tucked his notebook into his protective vest. 'Richard Zilchrist confirmed he didn't have a key, and corroborated Alana's version of events when I interviewed him separately.'

Barnes rubbed at his hastily shaven jaw and glared at the unit, his mind working over all the tasks he would have to set the team on his return to the incident room. 'Did you get the solicitor's name?'

'Mrs Winkman gave me this.' Dave grinned and handed over a dog-eared card. 'I thought you might want a word with him.'

SEVENTEEN

Kay placed the desk phone back in its cradle carefully, despite wanting to rip the cord out and fling the whole thing across the incident room in a tantrum.

Another murder victim, possibly linked to the torture and killing of Katrina Hovat, and yet still she couldn't rouse any more officers from her superiors at Headquarters.

Bad timing, they said.

Not enough trained officers available, they said.

And no, we can't afford any extra overtime.

She pushed back her chair and glared at the mounting paperwork in the in-tray on the corner of her desk, mindful of the other cases she was trying to manage, and bit back a loud sigh.

When she had first been given the promotion to detective inspector, she had known she would be exposed to more of the politics of policing, with expectations that every move she made would be analysed against a meagre budget that had other DIs in West Division hunting for scraps, and yet this…

'Guv, Barnes just pulled into the car park downstairs.' Gavin crossed to her desk and then frowned. 'Are you all right?'

'We're not going to get any extra help on this one, Gav. I've just had the final "piss off and get on with it" conversation with Northfleet.'

'Shit.' His frown deepened for a moment, and then his face brightened. 'I guess you'll be bribing us with even more pizza than normal then, guv?'

'Not everyone is as easily coerced as you when it comes to overtime, Piper.' Despite her frustration, Kay smiled, then gathered up her briefing notes. 'Okay, get everyone together so we're ready to start as soon as he's up here. Do you want to get a coffee for him? He's probably going to need it.'

Five minutes later, Barnes appeared. He walked over to where she stood beside the whiteboard and shrugged off his jacket, hanging it over the back of a junior constable's chair.

The gathered officers gradually fell silent, and Gavin handed him a steaming mug of caffeine.

'Are you okay to do this straight away?' Kay murmured as they faced the team. 'It's just that I wouldn't mind this lot hearing what's been going on this morning as soon as possible.'

'It's fine, guv, honestly.' He slurped the coffee, smacked his lips, then began.

'All right, so we've got a male victim possibly late twenties, early thirties, found stuffed into an old wardrobe in a storage unit out at Quarry Wood. The storage place is independently owned, and is managed during the day by a team of four staff on rotation. Uniform on scene are getting contact details for the staff members who aren't there today so they can be interviewed.' Barnes pulled out his reading glasses and handed his coffee mug to Kay with a grateful nod before taking out his notebook. 'The storage unit was first rented by Angus Zilchrist four years ago. He died recently, and his son and daughter were clearing it out this morning. They say they didn't know about the place until a few days ago.'

'Do either of them know the victim?' said Kay.

'Richard didn't get a clear look of him when he tumbled out the wardrobe – the poor bloke was too shocked. Alana didn't see the body at all. After the body fell out, they both had the sense to stay away from the unit while they waited for us. I thought we could get Simon over at the morgue to send us a photo of the victim's face after the post mortem's been done to rule out them knowing him though.'

Laura raised her pen in the air. 'Did Harriet find any ID?'

'He was butt naked,' said Barnes. 'So unless he's got his driving licence tucked up his—'

'Stop.' Kay held up her hand while a smattering of muffled giggles filled the room. 'I don't need that image in my head, thank you. What about Angus Zilchrist? What do we know about him so far?'

'He was from Peckham,' said Barnes, eyeing his notes. 'He took early retirement and moved down here with his wife, Louise, to a house in Downswood. She died a while back. From what we've learned so far, Angus had the only key to the unit apart from the master key held by the owners. We're waiting for the manager at the storage unit to sort out CCTV footage, but they only keep it for four weeks unless there's a break-in or a complaint, and Lucas reckons that body could've been there longer.'

'Thanks.' Kay handed back his coffee then turned to the whiteboard and updated the notes. 'Okay, so let's make a start on today's tasks. On top of what you're already doing in relation to Katrina's murder, I need the following from you. Laura, Gavin – get yourselves over to Angus Zilchrist's solicitor's office after this and find out how much he can tell you about his client's legal dealings and whether there are any other properties like this storage unit that we need to be aware of. Ian, I'd like to read the statement Dave Morrison's taken from the manager at the unit this morning, then we'll decide whether we want to speak to him again, or interview the owner.'

'Right, guv.'

'Who last visited the place?'

Barnes checked his notes. 'Angus is the last person to sign in, in April over the Easter weekend.'

'All right, thanks.' Kay turned to the team. 'Kyle, Nadine – as we get more information coming in about Angus Zilchrist's background, I'd like you both to cross-reference it against what we know about Katrina Hovat to see if their paths ever crossed. If Lucas's post mortem points to the same killer, then we need to start thinking about connections.'

'It might be worth cross-referencing Angus and the victim – once we find out who he is – with the Brassicks, too,' Gavin said. 'I mean, just because they're over in New York doesn't rule them out from being involved, does it?'

Kay eyed the growing number of notes and threads she'd drawn on the whiteboard, then exhaled.

'You're not wrong there, Gav.'

EIGHTEEN

Laura buttoned her jacket and read the brass plaque fixed to a freshly painted stone column, the four-storey Georgian building casting shadows across the paved pedestrian thoroughfare.

A sudden waft of diesel exhaust fumes consumed her as an older model delivery van rumbled past, its progress slowed by the number of mothers with pushchairs that seemed to crowd the street at this time of day, the cafés doing a busy trade during the lead-up to the lunchtime rush.

Pressing the entry button below a panel listing three different businesses, she introduced herself to the receptionist and heard a metallic *click* as the door lock released.

'Blimey, he's doing all right for himself if he can afford the rent here.' Gavin ran his fingers through his spiky hair in the reflection of the brass, then waved her forward. 'You can lead this one, if you like.'

'Ooh, ta.' She grinned, then pushed against a heavy

oak-panelled door to find herself in a plain-looking entrance hall.

A wide staircase took up the left-hand wall, with two doors leading off from the right and plastic-mounted signs on the plasterwork beside them displaying the business names.

'Lee Mesurier has his office on the second floor,' said Laura, leading the way up the first flight of stairs. 'Actually, I think he has *all* of the second floor. He's one of three partners in this firm.'

'Do they only do wills?'

'Probate and family law. Mesurier's website bio says he specialises in wills and trusts.'

They reached the top of the stairs and she passed through a glass-panelled door with a long stainless steel handle down one side polished within an inch of its life.

'Pity the person who has to do that every time someone leaves,' Gavin murmured.

Laura nudged his arm and strode over to the reception desk, a large mahogany edifice that wrapped itself around a tiny woman in her early twenties who eyed them suspiciously.

'Are you the detectives?' she said, sliding across a visitors book and an expensive-looking pen.

'We are. DC Laura Hanway, and my colleague, DC Gavin Piper.' She scrawled her signature on the page and slid the book across to Gavin, watching while he did the same. 'We're here to see Lee Mesurier.'

The woman glanced at their signatures with disdain as she took back the book, as if affronted that they'd ruined her perfect stream of client interactions, then rose from her chair. 'Follow me. I'll let him know you're here.'

A thickly-carpeted corridor led from the reception area to several rooms with closed doors, murmured voices filtering through as Laura passed. She took in the various paintings that lined the cream-coloured walls, then paused as the receptionist opened one of the doors and ushered them inside.

'Wait here. He won't be long.'

With that, the door closed behind them, and Gavin raised an eyebrow.

'Guess she doesn't want us cluttering up the reception area, then.'

Laura made her way over to one of six leather chairs set around a mahogany table and sank into it. 'I suppose it wouldn't look too good with two police officers hanging around if a potential client walked in.'

'Do we stand out that much?' Gavin wandered over to one of the two enormous multi-paned sash windows that overlooked the square. 'What do you think, then? Do you reckon Mesurier was Zilchrist's regular solicitor, or just the one who did his will?'

Laura wrinkled her nose. 'This place feels expensive, doesn't it? Too much for a teacher's pension perhaps.'

Gavin turned away from the window at the sound of movement outside the door. 'Guess we're about to find out.'

The door opened, and a man in his late fifties burst in, a shock of white hair creating a halo effect around his face while he balanced four different coloured manila folders in his arms, a yellow legal pad sliding about on top of them.

'Morning, morning,' he said, hurrying towards the table and dropping the lot before it tumbled from his grasp. He stuck out a hand to Gavin first. 'Lee Mesurier.'

'I hope we haven't caught you at a bad time, Mr Mesurier,' said Laura.

'Every time is a bad time.' He guffawed, then retraced his steps and closed the door. 'I was understandably shocked when I heard from Richard earlier today.'

'Richard Zilchrist spoke to you?' Laura said. 'When?'

The solicitor nodded, the movement sending his hair into another frenzy. 'Oh yes. This morning. While they were at the unit. I think he was waiting for your lot to turn up.'

He sat down in the chair at the far end of the table, pulling the folders towards him. 'Right, now I only have twenty minutes or so until my next client's due here, so let's make this quick, shall we?'

Laura waited until Gavin joined her, then turned back to Mesurier. 'How long had you acted as Angus Zilchrist's solicitor?'

'About six years. He and his wife were using someone in Peckham – where they used to live – until then, but I suppose they felt engaging someone local was more convenient so when they decided that their wills needed updating, they came to me.'

'How did they find you?'

'Beg pardon?'

'How did they hear about your services?'

'Well, I suppose either a website search or a recommendation.' Mesurier's brow furrowed and he dived into the first folder, a dull red one faded with age. 'Hmm.

There's nothing on their new client form that says that though, so I can't be sure.'

'Apart from their wills, did you do any other work for the Zilchrists?'

Mesurier gave a low chuckle. 'Now, detective, you know I can't divulge details about the sort of work I do for my clients.'

'What about generally? Was it all family law related, or were there any business interests…?'

'Just the will. The Zilchrists led quite a simple, quiet life as far as I know.'

'How did you know about the storage unit that Angus rented?'

'He'd mentioned it a while back, after Louise passed away.' Mesurier's eyes saddened. 'He missed her dreadfully but I think he realised he needed to have a clearout of the house to restore some sort of order to his life. He just couldn't bear to part with everything. Until Alana told me about the key, I'd assumed he'd got rid of everything ages ago.'

'When did you last see Angus?'

Mesurier slid the newest folder towards him, a bright blue one this time, thin with sparse contents. 'Let me see. Ah, the end of April. He dropped off an envelope to be kept with his will. I assumed it was instructions to set out his wishes upon his death. Some people like to do that, to address the finer details that we don't necessarily include in the will itself.'

'And what were Angus's wishes?' Laura scooted forward in her seat. 'His will was read out a while back wasn't it?'

'I can't divulge the exact details,' said the solicitor, but then rubbed his chin. 'However, I have to admit I was shocked, and so were Alana and Richard when I opened it and read it out to them.'

'Did he end up leaving all his money to charity?' said Gavin.

'No,' said Mesurier. 'That's the thing. He had no money. Well, almost no money.'

Laura frowned. 'Didn't he own the house he was living in?'

'He'd done one of those equity release deals,' said Mesurier.

'So what about Alana and Richard's inheritance?'

'That's what I'm alluding to.' Mesurier closed the folder and gathered up his legal pad. 'There *was* no inheritance really. All I can deduce is that Angus Zilchrist was in debt for a considerable amount of money. Apart from the equity release – which, if he'd thought to ask me I'd have strongly objected to – he also remortgaged the property with his bank. Both loans leave his heirs with very little once everything else is paid out.'

Laura battened down her frustration. 'Did Angus own or lease any other properties apart from the storage unit?'

'There's no paperwork, and no one has contacted Alana or Richard to demand any rental payments. Unless he was instructing another firm, I can't help you, I'm afraid.' Mesurier checked his watch pointedly. 'I really must get back to my office. My client is due in five minutes.'

Laura pushed back her chair and handed over a

business card, her thoughts spinning as they were shown out to reception and then left the building.

Once outside, she turned to Gavin to see the same perplexed expression on his face.

'So, what do you reckon?' she said.

He peered up at the second-floor windows to see a blind twitch back into place. 'I think we're going to spend the rest of the day phoning around solicitors to find out if Angus Zilchrist was a client. I don't get the feeling he was being entirely honest with Mesurier, or with his kids.'

Laura groaned. 'In that case, I'm going to need more coffee.'

NINETEEN

When Richard Zilchrist opened the door to his modest semi-detached home on the fringes of Harrietsham, Kay noticed the worry lines etched into his face.

His hand trembled as he gestured towards the living room, his movements tense. He paced the oak-effect laminate floor while she and Barnes eased themselves into armchairs facing a large television screen, then collapsed onto the sofa beside them and steepled his fingers under his nose.

'I can't get that man's face out of my mind,' he murmured, closing his eyes for a moment. 'Do you know how he died?'

'It's very early days, Mr Zilchrist,' said Kay. 'Is there anyone here with you?'

'Alana's staying with us while we clear out the unit. She'll be down in a sec.' He blinked, then sniffed. 'The kids are at school, and my wife's at work – she's on shift at the hospital.'

'Have you spoken with her?'

'Yes. Briefly. She can't leave though – they're understaffed.' He leaned back as Alana Winkman appeared in the doorway. 'Sis, this is DI Kay Hunter.'

Kay nodded to the woman as she perched on the sofa arm. 'I know this has all been a shock for you both, but we need to ask some questions to help with our investigation.'

Alana wiped a stray tear from her cheek. 'Do you think our dad killed him?'

'Do you think he did?'

'Dad wouldn't harm a fly. That's why I can't… I just can't…' She broke off, sniffed, then dabbed at her eyes with her sweatshirt sleeve, leaving telltale streaks of mascara across the grey cotton. 'No, I don't think he killed him.'

Kay turned her attention to Richard. 'Did you recognise the dead man?'

'Never seen him before in my life.' The man's voice was gruff, and he cleared his throat. 'Like I said, I'll never forget his face now, but I didn't recognise him.'

'Had either of you been to that unit prior to today?'

The brother and sister shook their heads in unison.

'Okay. And you're sure your dad never mentioned having a storage unit?'

'I don't recall him telling us,' said Alana. 'I knew he left it for a year after Mum died to start sorting through her things, and he was still able to get up in the loft back then.'

'He must've just thrown out what he didn't want and stored the rest at the unit rather than trying to sell it or put it back up in the loft,' Richard said. 'I mean, we're currently clearing out Dad's place to put it on the market, and I've been up in the loft – it's empty.'

Kay paused, knowing her next question would hit a nerve. 'I have to ask both of you this, and I realise it's a difficult subject, but I understand there are two loans on the house that have to be paid out from the sale. Were you aware that your dad was in debt to anyone?'

'We didn't have a clue. I mean, I knew Dad liked a flutter on the horses, but this...' Richard broke off, his voice etched with frustration.

'I think his gambling got worse after Mum died,' Alana said. 'She always managed to keep his spending in check I think, sort of like giving him a weekly budget.'

Kay flicked back through her notes. 'When did your mum pass away?'

'Five years ago,' Richard said. 'She had a stroke that August, and never came out of hospital. She died two weeks later.'

'I'm sorry to hear that. How did your dad seem to be coping this past year? Did he seem stressed or worried about anything?'

Alana clasped her hands in her lap. 'Not that I noticed. I used to try to get over to see him every six weeks or so, depending on work and stuff, and he never mentioned anything to me.'

'Me neither, and I used to see him every week.' Richard sighed. 'But then, I never asked either. I just assumed everything was okay. He *looked* okay, the last time I saw him. That's why having him die suddenly like that was such a shock. He'd lost a bit of weight, and seemed to have cut down on the drink – even though he wasn't a big drinker, he said he'd stopped going down the pub so often.'

'Which pub was that?' Kay asked, then wrote down the name of the public house. It was one she was familiar with, but closer to Maidstone town centre than her local one. 'If I needed to, who would I speak to about your dad's health? Do you know who his GP was?'

'I don't, but I've got his address book.' Richard heaved himself off the sofa and walked over to a bookshelf, pulling out a slim black book before flicking through the pages. 'I only kept it so I could let his friends know about the funeral arrangements and things. Here you go. Doctor Gus Marlett, and I've got a phone number for his surgery.'

'Thanks. Out of interest, did your father have a mobile phone contract?'

'Yes. I've just been onto the provider to try and cancel it, but they're being slow.' Alana rolled her eyes. 'They'll probably bill us until they've closed it too.'

'Do you think we could have access to his phone records, if you have his login details that is?'

'Sure, I suppose so.' Alana looked to her brother, then back. 'But why?'

Kay gave a slight smile. 'It's standard procedure in cases such as this.'

'Would we be right in presuming that your father's house is on the market at this time?' said Barnes.

'It is, and the bank obviously have first dibs on that,' said Richard bitterly. 'Then that damn credit agency are next.'

'Any chance the landline is still connected?'

'Don't tell me – you want the records for that too.'

'Please.'

'They're in a file in the spare room. I brought

everything over from Dad's while the estate agent is showing people through. Hang on.'

Ten minutes later, Kay and Barnes walked back to their car, arms laden with files full of bank, credit card and phone statements.

'I get the impression they're starting to wonder what their dad was up to as well,' said Barnes as he stacked the boxes in the back of the car, then draped his jacket over the top of them and rolled up his sleeves.

Kay got in, then started the car and pulled a face. 'I'm worried they're not going to like the answer.'

TWENTY

By the time Kay gathered her team for the final time that day, the distinct aroma of pepperoni and grilled cheese filled the incident room.

She had tasked Debbie with phoning through the order to the local pizza place an hour ago, scheduling the delivery so that as many officers as possible were present, many of whom had spent the day conducting house-to-house enquiries and taking witness statements from Angus Zilchrist's neighbours and those whose names appeared in his address book.

The group now gathered around the tables on each side of the whiteboard, their normal banter silenced by the need for sustenance.

Plastic blinds covered the windows, blocking out the twilight enveloping the town, and the sound of traffic outside had lost its steady daytime roar.

Kay signed off the last document in a folder Debbie had left on her desk, slapped it shut and shoved it into the top tray, then wandered over to join the team.

'Anything left for me?'

'There's a pile of pineapple Laura's been knocking off her pizza you could have, guv,' said Kyle. 'I told her to stick to the meat feast one next time.'

'But I don't like the chicken on that one,' Laura pouted amid the laughter from her colleagues. 'Guv, here you go.'

She thrust a paper plate with two slices on it at Kay, then lightly punched Kyle on the arm and wandered over to a seat facing the whiteboard.

Taking a moment to savour the fast food, swearing to go for a longer run that weekend if she got the chance, Kay moved amongst her team, enquiring about their families, and making sure they were adequately fuelled up ready for the meeting.

She couldn't afford for them to lose focus, despite the late hour.

Moving towards the whiteboard, she waited while they took their places.

Barnes leaned against one of the desks and sipped at a can of soft drink while Gavin murmured in his ear, her two colleagues watching for her signal to begin, and gradually the conversation amongst her other officers fell silent.

'Okay,' she said, checking the agenda that Debbie had printed out from the HOLMES2 database. 'We've had a busy day, you're all keen to get home, so let's crack on. There won't be a briefing first thing tomorrow because Barnes and I have to attend the post mortem of the victim found in the storage unit, but make sure you're available for a meeting at two o'clock. There's a lot of information to cross-reference, and I don't want you chasing a lead that isn't relevant, understood?'

A smattering of agreement flittered through the assembled group.

'Gavin, Laura – if you'd like to start us off?'

Laura looked over her shoulder to her colleague, then at a nod from him wiped her fingers on a napkin and opened her notebook. 'Right, so we've spent the afternoon phoning around local solicitors to find out if any of them acted on behalf of Angus Zilchrist at any time in the past six years – obviously under current law, they can't keep personal documents for any longer than that. Only one local firm had any information, and that was to confirm that they'd acted for Angus and his wife when they decided they wanted lasting power of attorney paperwork put in place in the event of illness.'

'I also spoke to the solicitor in Peckham who did the conveyancing for their house sale a while back,' Gavin added. 'He hasn't got the paperwork anymore but remembered them because they got their previous wills done by the same firm. He confirmed that once the house sale went through, that firm didn't do any more work for the Zilchrists.'

'What about background checks on the current solicitor, Mesurier?'

'He's clean, as far as we can tell,' said Laura. 'No connections on record with any known criminals, and nor has anyone else in that firm.'

'Okay, that's good work, thanks both of you.' Kay turned her attention to Barnes, who was halfway through another pizza slice. 'Got a minute to tell us about the GP?'

'Mm-hm.' He swallowed. 'Gus Marlett is one of four GPs at the practice, and last saw Angus for a routine check-up six months ago. He said that he got the impression that Angus was worried about something but despite Marlett's assurances of confidentiality, Angus didn't want to talk about it.'

'Typical bloke,' tutted Debbie.

One of the male uniformed sergeants tossed a scrunched-up napkin at her, and Kay smiled.

'Did he mention whether Angus had any health issues leading up to his heart attack?' she said.

'His blood pressure was higher than normal,' said Barnes. 'And Marlett said he'd lost weight too. He asked him about his diet, but Angus told him he was fine – he was just trying to get healthy.'

'The weight loss is something Alana and Richard mentioned, and yet no one's suggested that Angus had taken up a regular exercise routine, which makes me wonder if it was caused by stress. Especially given Marlett's report about his blood pressure being high.' Kay updated the whiteboard notes, then took another bite of pizza and mulled over the new information. 'Has anyone got anything yet to suggest Angus knew Katrina?'

The team fell silent, a few officers throwing hopeful glances at their colleagues before turning their attention back to Kay.

'I'll take that as a no, then. So, what do we think?' She paced the carpet, waving her pizza slice at the whiteboard as she spoke. 'Did Angus Zilchrist owe someone a hell of a lot of money, which is why he took out an equity release on his home as well as remortgaging with his bank? Who killed the man who was found at his storage unit? And why leave the body there?'

'Speaking to his neighbours this afternoon, Angus wasn't viewed as someone who was violent or caused trouble,' said Dave Morrison.

'The landlord at his old local pub said the same, although one of the regulars said he'd got a bit morose in later weeks,' Nadine added, the young probationer's voice just audible from the back of the group.

'Did that regular say anything else about Angus's mood before he died, or whether he seemed worried about something?' Kay said. 'And speak up, I don't bite and I need to make sure everyone can hear what you say – it's important.'

'Yes, guv.' The constable cleared her throat and stood a little straighter. 'Kyle and I spoke to four regulars who were at the bar, all pensioners well into their seventies – I got the impression they liked to spend their afternoons there watching the horse-racing. All of them said that Angus used to be the first to shout them a beer if he saw them, but since about March or April, he'd seemed more reticent – and less generous.'

Kay's gaze flickered to Barnes, then back to Nadine. 'Did you say horse-racing?'

'Yes, guv. They weren't betting or anything, nothing like that. There's a betting shop just around the corner from the pub.'

'Gav, can you and Laura go and speak to the manager of that betting shop first thing tomorrow to see if Angus was a regular? Alana and Richard have told us that they reckon their dad whittled away his savings and the loans on the house on gambling since their mum died, so Angus must've had a regular haunt locally. Richard mentioned before we left that his dad wasn't keen on using computers and had an ancient mobile phone, so I don't think he'd have used online apps to gamble.'

'Will do, guv.'

'Where are we with regard to Katrina?'

Dave Morrison dusted crumbs from his trousers and stood. 'Guv, we've finished interviewing the other members of staff at the shop where she worked, and some of them have stated she seemed very on edge in the two weeks leading up to her death. She wouldn't talk about it, though – I got the impression that none of them are close. One of the other supervisors mentioned that Katrina was jumpy if she was interrupted while doing something – she accidentally broke a vase the other week because a member of staff tapped her on the arm to ask her something. Sean here spoke to a few more of her friends.'

'I managed to catch up with two other women who knew her from her days working at the care home,' said the young constable. 'One of them, Sally, last saw Katrina three weeks ago – they caught up for coffee at one of the cafés just off Jubilee Square. Sally told me that she phoned Katrina to organise it, because she felt she owed her lunch for helping her move house a couple of months ago. She said she'd never seen her look so thin, and she only picked at her food.'

'Did this Sally ask her what was on her mind?'

'Yes, guv, but Katrina told her it was nothing to worry about, and then changed the subject.'

'Thanks, all of you.' Kay glared at her shoes for a moment. 'So we have two murders but no suspect. We have a man so scared that his health deteriorates such that he has a heart attack out of the blue – possibly caused by finding that man's body in his storage unit. Or, Angus killed that man and put him in the unit. But we still can't connect them all to each other... Gavin, what's the latest with the Brassicks – anything there?'

'Not yet, guv, but we're still digging. Laura and I plan to re-interview their neighbours tomorrow morning based on this new angle of the investigation and then we've got an appointment with Stephen Brassick's direct manager in the afternoon.'

'In person, or video conference?'

'We're meeting him at Headquarters, guv. I spoke to someone there to organise an interview room rather than us going to their London offices, and Duncan – that's Stephen's manager – has an appointment with a client in Rochester earlier in the day, so it works out well for him too.'

'Given that I'd like to hear how all those interviews pan out, let's delay tomorrow's briefing until five o'clock then,' said Kay, then eyed the crumbs on her plate with a sigh. 'And hopefully by then, we'll start getting some bloody answers.'

TWENTY-ONE

The next morning Kay eyed the health and safety posters on the locker room wall and took a couple of deep breaths before opening the door and following Barnes along a brightly lit corridor.

A pungent stench of antiseptic floor cleaner assaulted her nostrils, the bitter lemon aroma doing little to disguise the waft of decay that swept over her when her colleague led the way into the mortuary's examination room.

Stainless steel equipment and tables glistened under the harsh lights, casting dull reflections across the rows of box-like doors that lined one wall.

She shivered in the air-conditioned space, goosebumps prickling her forearms, then adjusted her mask over her mouth and nose, the coarse material rubbing against her skin.

The sound of running water caught her attention and she looked over to the sinks to see Lucas Anderson giving his hands and arms a thorough scrubbing while he peered over his glasses at them.

'Nice and early, that's what I like to see,' he said. 'I take it the traffic wasn't too bad?'

'Thank goodness.' Barnes pulled up his mask and walked over to a table at the far end where the victim's body was laid out ready. The material creased as the detective wrinkled his nose. 'Are you okay if I take a photo of his face before you start? I'll have a word with someone in IT to tidy it up so we can use it for ID purposes.'

'Be my guest.' Lucas dried his hands and nodded his thanks to Simon as the assistant handed gloves to him before returning his attention to a laptop, the steady *tap-tap* of keys filling the room.

'What about Angus Zilchrist?' said Kay. 'Have you had a chance to review the post mortem report for him?'

'I have, and I have to concur with the original findings. The man might've lost weight but according to the pathologist who conducted the PM, his arteries were a mess, and he was carrying a lot of excess fat around his liver and kidneys. Add stress to that, and it's a recipe for disaster.' Lucas tugged on protective gloves, giving them a satisfying twang against his wrists. 'I spoke to my colleague by phone this morning but he confirms there was no indication of foul play. Nothing turned up on the blood tests or anything like that. If it weren't for the stress, your Mr Zilchrist might've lived for another ten years before experiencing any serious symptoms.'

Simon pushed his laptop away and wheeled a trolley over to the examination table, the stainless steel surgical instruments rattling within their different compartments.

'Right, shall we begin?' Lucas clapped his gloved hands together and beckoned Kay to follow him.

Tucking his phone in his back trouser pocket, Barnes adjusted his protective gown and stepped aside as they approached.

'From what I can tell from the exterior examination I've done this morning, your man here is about twenty to thirty years old,' Lucas said, prising open the victim's jaw. 'His teeth aren't yet showing the wear I'd expect to see from someone who's older although there's a telltale crisscross pattern to his back molars that suggests he was grinding his teeth on a regular basis, not just in his last days. The extractions are older, and don't relate to his death.'

Kay crossed her arms and leaned closer to look. 'If someone was worried or stressed, they'd do that wouldn't they?'

'Stress, pain, an old habit…' Lucas shrugged, closing the man's mouth. 'Hard to say. Simon's also taken fingerprints and emailed those across to Gavin in case he's in your system.'

'Thanks.'

The pathologist glanced over his shoulder. 'Simon, I'm ready to make a start, if you'd like to give me a hand?'

Kay moved over to where Barnes stood beside the victim's feet while the post mortem progressed, her gaze flitting to the floor when Lucas's saw started its screaming, unable to watch the more gruesome ways much-needed answers were gleaned.

'Coffee after this?' Barnes murmured.

'A strong one, yes.' She blinked, then looked up at a muttered expletive from Lucas. 'Something wrong?'

'Your victim's missing a kidney.'

'What?' She walked over to where Lucas and Simon peered into the victim's abdominal area, the ribs peeled apart so the two men could access the internal organs. 'When?'

'A while back, looking at these old scars.' Lucas ran a gloved finger across a tiny gap. 'This is the other one, nice and healthy by the look of it. But the other one isn't here, look.'

'Damaged, do you think?'

'Or donated.' His eyes sparkled behind his protective goggles. 'Which means—'

'He'll be on a donor register.' Kay's heart lurched. 'Oh god, that'll be massive won't it? We still need a name to narrow it down. I haven't got enough manpower to go through it name by name in the hope we find him.'

'We could start with local donors, guv,' said Barnes gently. 'Split up the list between all of us and work through it in between everything else.'

Kay's mask lifted from her face as she exhaled. 'It's a long shot, but…'

'It's all we've got, so far.' Barnes gave a slight nod towards Lucas. 'Unless you've got any other surprises for us.'

'I'm sorry, but I'm going to have to disappoint you there, Detective Barnes. Your victim died from multiple cuts to his skin over a period of several hours I'd say.' The pathologist moved aside while Simon began clearing away their surgical tools and sterilising the equipment. He paused by the man's head, and gestured to the abrasions and welts across the victim's arms. 'He put up a fight to start with, too – there are defensive wounds to his knuckles, so I'm positing that he was tied. You can see the marks here, in the soft skin around his triceps. They even sliced at his genitals before finishing him off with that deep cut down there, just across the femoral artery.'

'Is it the same killer as the one who murdered Katrina Hovat?' said Kay.

Lucas sucked his teeth. 'You know I'm uncomfortable with putting anything like that in a report, Detective Hunter. Very risky.'

'Personal opinion, then? Off the record.'

His warm brown eyes darkened. 'Given the careful placement of these cuts, the way the blade has pierced the skin… Yes, I think it's the same killer. Possibly the same weapon, too, but again that's not going in any report.'

'Shit.' Barnes shook his head. 'What happened in the past four months that triggered these murders, I wonder?'

'We need more answers,' said Kay, 'and soon. Because if this bloke isn't connected to Katrina Hovat then we've got a killer who's gone untraced until now, and one who's indiscriminate in how he chooses his victims.'

TWENTY-TWO

Gavin straightened his jacket, made sure his phone was switched to silent, then pulled the ornate brass chain beside the heavy wooden front door of the converted barn.

Laura stood beside him, the faint trace of her perfume mixing with the bouquet rising from several pots of flowers that lined the landscaped gravel path leading to the front step.

Bells chimed within the depths of the property, and he loosened his grip on the chain.

The sound of bees filled the air as the tiny creatures dived in and out of the lavender planted in clumps behind the pots, and he ran his finger under his collar, hoping the owner of the place would invite them in so he could get away from the sun's baking rays.

Laura shaded her eyes with her hand and stared back along the driveway towards the lane. 'I bet it's like this on Saturday, too. It's going to be a perfect weekend to go to the beach.'

'I don't think you and I will be seeing a weekend for a while yet,' he murmured, then straightened his shoulders as the door opened and a white-haired man in his seventies stared out at them. 'Conrad Lamberton?'

'Who are you?' The man's eyebrows furrowed together, his hand resting on the door. 'What do you want?'

'I'm DC Gavin Piper, this is DC Laura Hanway,' he said, holding out his warrant card. 'We're following up enquiries relating to the murder of a woman that occurred at a neighbouring property along this lane on Friday.'

Lamberton's eyes softened. 'Terrible business. You'd better come in.'

'Thanks.'

They followed the man into a large atrium with windows in the roof that sent pockets of light across the grey stone tiled floor. Ferns in tall planters were artistically placed against the matching walls.

A welcome coolness wrapped itself around Gavin as they entered an open-plan living space that incorporated an enormous living and dining area with a winding metal staircase at the far end that led up to an open landing. Several closed doors lined the walkway, and he guessed that the bedrooms and bathroom lay beyond.

An empty hearth took up most of the living room wall below the landing while floor-to-ceiling windows faced the driveway, a smoky effect applied to the glass to allow for privacy.

Lamberton saw him looking and shot him a rueful smile. 'The windows are triple-glazed for security reasons, in case you're wondering.'

'It's a beautiful home you have here.'

The man acknowledged the comment with a nod, then gestured to a set of three sofas surrounding the hearth. 'Sit. You do know I've already provided the police with my statement? Two uniformed officers were here late on Friday.'

'As I said, these are just some follow-up questions based on new information coming to light.' Gavin unbuttoned his jacket and sank into the plush cushions. 'Do you know Penelope and Stephen Brassick?'

'Only in passing.' Lamberton shrugged. 'If you're talking to everyone along here, you'll have seen how far apart the houses are from each other. It's why we like living here, the privacy it allows us.'

'Your partner…'

The man smiled. 'Jacob is on a video call with his publisher at the moment but if you want to have a word with him too, I can get him to call you. He'll be at least another hour or so.'

'What does he do?' said Laura.

'He's an art historian these days. Retired five years after me, lasted a year without working and then got bored.' Lamberton gave a shy smile. 'I told him years ago he'd be good at it – he always loved history and we spend hours in galleries wherever we travel. He's a natural. He gets enquiries from all around the world, and now he's writing a book.'

'Are you retired as well?' Gavin asked.

'Over ten years ago, and not missing a day of corporate life. I used to be the operations director for one of the financial institutions in the City.' He shuddered theatrically. 'No, I don't miss it a bit.'

'Back to the Brassicks – when did you see them last?'

'They were on their way to the airport, I'm guessing. I know Stephen works in America from time to time. I was out at the end of the driveway pruning back some of the lower tree branches next to the gate when the taxi went by to pick them up. About fifteen minutes later, it came back the other way with them both on the back seat.'

'What about speaking with them?'

Lamberton shook his head. 'Like I said, we don't tend to socialise with our neighbours. I don't even know what Brassick does for a living, just that he travels a lot for business.'

'Where were you on Friday night, say from about six o'clock onwards?'

'In here, reading.' The man gestured to two large armchairs over by the windows. 'We both were, actually. Opened a lovely bottle of Pinot Noir to celebrate Jacob's book deal, and then cooked dinner at about eight o'clock.'

'Which chair is yours?'

'Pardon?'

Gavin pointed at the two armchairs beside the windows. 'Which one is yours?'

'The one on the right.'

Gavin walked over and sat in the armchair. 'You can see the end of the driveway from here. Did you see any cars passing while you were sitting here on Friday?'

'No, we normally keep the gates closed so they block our view. You only got up the driveway this morning because I'm waiting for a delivery.'

Gavin gave the other armchair a cursory glance, then returned to the sofa, and leaned forward. 'You've got quite a bit of land to the back of the house – did you see anyone hanging around acting suspiciously on Friday, or any other day in the past few weeks?'

'I didn't, no.' Lamberton looked from him to Laura, then back. 'Hang on, are you saying whoever murdered that woman came through our garden to get to the Brassicks'?'

'We don't know that for sure at the moment,' said Gavin. 'But would you mind if we took a look outside, just to check for anything that might help us?'

'Come on, then.' Lamberton got to his feet with a low grunt and headed towards an open door at the far end of the room that led into a tidy modern kitchen, talking over his shoulder as they followed. 'Mind you, they'd have a job sneaking around without us noticing – we had security cameras put in when we moved here five years ago, and none of those have gone off in a couple of weeks. That last time was only a hedgehog, anyway. They hibernate under the garden shed during the winter.'

Gavin froze. 'When did you last check the cameras?'

'Jacob usually has a quick look through the footage every couple of weeks, just because he wants to find out if the local foxes have had any cubs yet.'

'Would you mind showing me where the cameras are before we take a look around the garden?'

Lamberton shrugged, pulled open the back door and ushered them outside. Leading the way along a paved path, he paused under a ventilation duct and pointed to a black camera fitted to a bracket underneath. 'There you go. Oh.'

Gavin's gaze followed the man's, his heart sinking.

'Christ,' said Laura. 'It's been sprayed with paint, just like at the Brassicks'.'

TWENTY-THREE

An hour later, Laura steered the pool car into a space beside a liveried mini-van and peered across the car park towards the four-storey building that housed Kent Police Headquarters.

The drive to Northfleet from Conrad Lamberton's house had passed by in a blur, with Gavin on the phone to the incident room while she navigated her way through congested traffic along the M2.

The old Watling Street route was thick with articulated trucks bearing foreign licence plates and early-season tourists adding to an already overburdened road.

Exasperated at the time, aware that they were meeting Stephen Brassick's boss in under fifteen minutes, she peered at her reflection in the rear-view mirror and ran her fingers through her hair before gently slapping her cheeks to add a bit of colour.

'Will do, guv,' Gavin said to Kay by way of farewell, and lowered his phone. 'She wants us straight back to the incident room after this. They're getting Harriet to send a team over to Lamberton's place to see if they can find any trace evidence.'

'They'll be lucky after all this time.'

After locking the car, they hurried across to the concrete paved pathway leading into the building, took the stairs up to the second floor and entered an open-plan space that hummed with quiet activity.

A walkway had been created between the entrance and the first row of desks, double-width to allow several people at once to pass by on their way to different departments within the building.

Laura's eyes widened at the sheer number of staff filling the room. There wasn't a single empty chair available, and every one of them had their head bowed over a computer screen, the sound of fingers tapping on keyboards only broken by the musical ringing of phones.

'Come on, down here,' said Gavin.

'Where were you based when you were here?' she said, lowering her voice so as not to disturb anyone.

'On the other side of the building. That's where they've got one of the major ops rooms.' He held open a door at the end of the room for her. 'I'd show you around, but we're going to be late if I do.'

'Next time, then.' To her surprise, the door opened into another corridor that twisted around the building until opening out into a smaller reception area.

A woman sat at a desk covered in documentation and brightly coloured sticky notes, a highlighter pen in her hand while she listened intently to a man who hovered at her side, his brow furrowed.

'Guv,' said Gavin.

Detective Inspector Devon Sharp looked up, his cool grey eyes softening at the sight of them. 'Good to see you both. What brings you up here from Maidstone, then?'

'We're interviewing Stephen Brassick's boss,' said Laura, shaking his hand. She eyed the clock on the wall behind the desk. 'And we're just in time.'

'We might have had a breakthrough at one of the neighbouring properties,' Gavin explained. 'Harriet's on her way over there at the moment.'

'What about the second murder?' Sharp said. 'Anything to connect the two of them yet, or too early to say?'

'Too early, guv.' Laura heard the frustration in her voice, and gave an apologetic shrug. 'But we'll get there.'

Sharp smiled. 'I'm sure you will. Right, best let you get on. Sarah here will show you where to find your visitor.'

The woman was already pushing back her chair, and to Laura's surprise she towered over Sharp. 'This way.'

Laura glanced down to see if the woman was tottering on heels, but was disappointed. She bit back a sigh, rueing the extra height she wished she had sometimes, especially when dealing with the more unruly suspects − or overbearing colleagues.

Sarah handed her a file as she led them farther along the corridor. 'That's the background checks from your team at Maidstone that were emailed across. Duncan Nithercott doesn't appear to have any infringements or encounters with the police to worry about, but I'll let you be the judge of that.'

She flashed a smile at them, then paused beside a

closed door, lowering her voice. 'This is you. If you could show him the way downstairs once you're finished, and make sure he signs out, that'd be great. I have a feeling Sharp's going to have me fixing spreadsheets for the rest of the afternoon the rate we're going.'

'Thanks.' Laura opened the file after the woman walked away and turned so Gavin could read over her shoulder while she flicked through the contents.

'Squeaky clean,' he said as she closed the file.

She could hear the disappointment in his voice. 'It's like Kay says though, Gav. We need to talk to everyone, even if it just means crossing them off our list.'

'I know.' He winked, then opened the door.

Duncan Nithercott looked up from a half-finished cup of water and frowned as they entered. 'About time.'

'Apologies,' said Laura, refusing to rise to the snideness in his voice. 'We're in the middle of a murder investigation, and other matters overtook us this afternoon. Can I get you a coffee or anything before we start?'

He bristled at her tone, but then shook his head. 'No, that's fine. Sorry. It's been a stressful few days with work, and my client meeting overran. I thought I was going to be late here.'

'Understood. We'll try not to keep you too long. We're going to make this interview formal, Mr Nithercott so I'll be recording it,' Gavin explained while Laura took the seat beside him. 'I'll start the machine, read to you your formal rights as a witness to our investigation, and then get some basic details from you before we ask some questions about your employee Stephen Brassick. Sound good?'

'All right.' Nithercott pushed the water away and

clasped his hands on his desk while he listened to the formalities.

'Can you confirm for me what your role is at the investment company?' Gavin said.

'I oversee all our in-house actuaries, and actively work with new clients to establish those fledgling relationships,' Nithercott replied. 'Stephen is one of our more driven employees, which is why we like to have him on the ground in New York and Zurich as much as possible. He's a safe pair of hands.'

'How long has he been working for you?'

'Eleven years.' The man shot them a smug look. 'We poached him from one of our competitors. I don't think they've ever forgiven us.'

'Do you socialise with him at all?' said Laura.

'No, not really. The odd occasion organised through the company, but that's it.' Nithercott chuckled. 'Mind you, Jackie – that's my wife – gets on well with Stephen's wife, Penelope, whenever we do see them at events. Probably a good thing they don't see each other more often, given the way they go on about antiques and shoes. I'd be broke, and I'm sure Stephen would be too.'

Laura gave a small smile at the man's attempt at humour, then glanced down at her notes. 'Any problems with Stephen or his work in the past?'

'None. He's an exemplary employee.'

'Does your company have any military connections?' said Gavin.

Nithercott's eyebrows shot upwards. 'Military connections?'

'Security companies, private contractors, anything like that.'

'No. Why?'

'Do you know if Stephen's work has brought him into contact with anyone who has a military background?' Laura pressed.

'None at all, and I'd know because I oversee all Stephen's clients. We review them on a quarterly basis together, and plan who he should meet with to extend our reach at the same time.' He leaned back in his chair. 'What's going on?'

'Just routine questions,' said Laura. 'All part of our ongoing investigation.'

'Right.' Nithercott settled once more, although he didn't look convinced. 'Well, I can tell you that most of our work comes from banks and other financial institutions, private equity firms, that sort of thing. We branched out from the insurance sector about twelve years ago, which is why we brought Stephen on board. His experience in the banking sector prior to that was essential in our growth strategies at the time.'

'What does your wife do?' Gavin said.

'She's actively involved with a couple of local charities here in Kent, fundraising and that sort of thing,' said Nithercott. He waved his hand dismissively. 'No need for her to work, not with the hours I keep. It might seem old-fashioned but she enjoys being a homemaker, and it means while she's organising the day-to-day things we can relax at weekends.'

'I didn't realise you were local,' said Laura innocently, moving her hand to cover the man's address in the file open before her. 'Are you close to the Brassicks?'

'No, we're this side of the county – I prefer to be closer to the City to be honest. Our place is on the outskirts of Eynsford.'

'Have you experienced any break-ins or suspicious activity in the past twelve months at your home?'

'None at all – and I can assure you, after what's happened to Stephen and Penelope, I ordered the security company to come back and check all the systems yesterday.' Nithercott shivered. 'I couldn't bear to think of something happening to Jackie.'

'Thanks, Mr Nithercott, I think that's all for today.' Gavin confirmed the time for the end of the interview, then ended the recording. 'We'll show you out.'

Once downstairs, Laura waited while Gavin saw that the visitor's pass was returned and Nithercott was signed out, and scrolled through her emails on her phone.

She looked up at the sound of heels clacking across the tiled floor to see a woman in her forties approaching, her tailored suit a bright contrast to the shades of grey and black and pressed uniforms around her.

Nithercott's eyebrows shot up in surprise. 'Jackie?'

'Duncan, darling – have they finally let you go?' The woman clasped her husband's arms and leaned in while he kissed her cheek. 'I thought I'd never see you again.'

'How did you get here?' He craned his neck to look out the floor-to-ceiling windows. 'Did you drive over?'

'I got bored, darling. Thought I'd see if you'd buy me lunch.'

'Detectives Piper, Hanway, this is my wife Jackie.'

Nithercott turned back to them, slipped his arm through hers, then eyed the bulging handbag slung over her shoulder. 'And I suspect she's done some more damage to my platinum card account by the look of it.'

The woman laughed, flicking her hair over her shoulder. 'Well, if you will leave me alone for hours, what's a girl to do, hmm? Besides, there's a summer sale on at Bluewater.'

Nithercott groaned, before his wife turned to Gavin.

'So, have you caught the wretches who murdered that woman? Dreadful business.' She shuddered. 'Makes me glad that Duncan doesn't travel as much as he used to anymore. The thought of someone wandering around loose while I'm at home alone – it doesn't bear thinking about.'

'It's still an active investigation,' Gavin murmured, then breathed a sigh of relief as Nithercott made his excuses and led his wife away.

Laura sighed as she watched them walk towards their car, then turned to see Gavin grinning at her. 'What?'

'I saw the way you were eyeing that handbag, Hanway. How much?'

'Put it this way, Gav. I wouldn't make my rent payments for the next three months if I bought one of those.'

TWENTY-FOUR

Barnes thumbed a text to his other half, Pia, then glanced towards the whiteboard as flashes of lightning scorched across the sky beyond the incident room windows.

An underlying sense of urgency filled the space as his colleagues dragged chairs across to where Kay waited, a fatigue setting in to the way they walked.

The usual banter had reduced to a tired murmur, the oppressive atmosphere echoed by a rumble of thunder that shook the window panes and made heads turn.

Laura and Gavin were nowhere to be seen, a phone call five minutes ago confirming that they were stuck in traffic just north of the town and hoping to make it in before the meeting ended.

Barnes looked over his shoulder as Kay shoved the door open with her foot, her arms laden with folders and a sheaf of papers.

'Here's the deal,' she said as she strode across to stand in front of the team and passed over the freshly printed agendas. 'Debbie's at an appointment, so no one had better breathe a word that I just nicked a ream of paper and a toner cartridge from the other team's stationery cupboard, or else there'll be hell to pay knowing the way she runs the admin in this place.'

Her comments drew a few smirks while the briefing notes were handed out, and then the murmurs fell silent.

Barnes ran his gaze down the page in his hand, bit back a groan at the number of outstanding actions, and loosened his tie.

It was going to be a long meeting.

'Okay, so first of all, the post mortem on our second murder victim confirms he died from a fatal stab wound to the femoral artery,' Kay said, her voice carrying across to where he sat. 'Strictly off the record, and not to be repeated outside of this briefing, Lucas feels that we *might* be looking at the same killer given the placement of the different knife cuts to the man's limbs and torso. Like Katrina, he was likely tortured before that final cut. Whoever did this knows what they're doing. Both victims underwent a horrendous and protracted attack before being killed.'

She let her words sink in for a moment. 'I spoke to DI Sharp earlier this afternoon, and his enquiries into any military angle with regard to the Brassicks has turned up nothing. Following Gavin and Laura's visit to Conrad Lamberton's house just up the road from the Brassicks', Harriet's team concluded their search just before this storm blew in, and unfortunately they've confirmed any trace evidence has been lost due to the weather on Friday. No latent prints were found on any of the security cameras around the property either.'

Barnes removed his reading glasses and lowered his head, pinching his nose. 'We're buggered.'

'There's a slim chance we might get some information from the neighbouring landowner,' Kay said. 'Harriet's manager on scene, Patrick, found possible signs of entry into the garden. There's a barbed wire fence next to a small stream separating the property from the farmland beyond that's been cut – and recently, he says, given the way none of the metal has rusted yet. The ground on either side is very stony and given the recent rainfall, there are no footprints but I've tasked a uniform patrol to speak to the landowner this evening to see if they have any security footage.'

'As long as their cameras haven't been sprayed as well,' Dave Morrison grumbled under his breath.

'Quite.' Kay picked out a red pin from the collection on the tray beside the whiteboard and jabbed it onto the aerial photograph of the countryside surrounding the Brassicks' house. 'But until we hear otherwise, this farmhouse remains on our list of actions. Has anyone found anything on local CCTV showing any suspicious vehicles or people on Friday afternoon?'

Aaron Stewart looked up from his notes. 'Nothing to suggest anything linked to Katrina's murder, guv. All the vehicles on camera have been traced to local residents, and none of those have criminal records.'

'Christ.' Kay sighed. 'Well, I guess that would've been too easy. I—'

She broke off at the sound of a loud mobile phone, and Barnes looked across the heads of the gathered officers to see Nadine leap up and scurry towards her desk, her phone to her ear. When he glanced at Kay, she raised an eyebrow, but said nothing for a moment.

He watched Nadine while the young probationary constable flopped into the chair at her desk, phone tucked under her chin while she listened to the caller and took notes, her free hand motioning whoever she was listening to that they should hurry up.

As soon as the call ended, she launched herself at her keyboard, fingers flying while she stared at the screen, ignoring the murmured comments from her colleagues.

The door opened, and Gavin and Laura entered the room, and Barnes noticed the confusion sweep across their faces as they saw everyone watching Nadine expectantly. He beckoned them over.

'Just in time,' he murmured.

'What's going on?' Laura whispered as Gavin perched on the desk beside him. 'What've we missed?'

'Nothing yet.'

Then he saw Nadine sit back in her chair.

She blinked at the screen before rushing back over to the waiting officers. 'Sorry, guv.'

'No problem,' said Kay. 'What's the emergency?'

'That was Simon over at the morgue. I was running the details about our second victim through the system this afternoon, and got stuck when I was looking at the fingerprints. One of them had smudged a little bit when it was taken so I asked him to redo it.' Nadine paused, then frowned. 'I take it that was okay, guv?'

'Absolutely fine.' Kay pointed at the phone in the constable's hand. 'What've you got?'

'I think we've found him, guv. Our second victim.'

An explosion of excited voices cut across the incident room, and Barnes felt a shiver across his shoulders.

'Everyone, pipe down.' Kay glared at them, then turned back to Nadine. 'How?'

'Once I had the full set of prints I could put them through the system again. I got a name – Preston Winford. Simon's had a word with a colleague of his at the hospital who accessed the donor register for us, and he just confirmed that Preston donated a kidney to his brother when he was nineteen.'

There was a shocked silence, and then Barnes grinned, clapping his hands together. 'That's a bloody fantastic result, Nadine. Well done.'

'It is, and great work,' Kay added as the constable retook her seat, blushing under the attention from her colleagues. 'Right, well – thank goodness. An excellent way to end the day.'

Barnes watched while she flipped through the pages of the agenda, then put it aside.

'This breakthrough gives us some new angles to check out,' she said. 'First of all, I want a full background check on what Preston Winford has been up to since he was nineteen and had that kidney removed. Make it a priority to check social media first, and find out who his family is and how I can contact them.' Kay paused, grimacing. 'I need to let them know what's happened before the media get wind of anything. And speaking of media, if *anybody* leaks this, I'll string you up myself. Understood?'

A sombre flurry of agreement carried over to where Barnes sat.

'Next we'll need to find out whether Preston is

connected to Katrina in any way, and if and how he's connected to Angus Zilchrist. I don't think it was bad luck that saw him shoved in that wardrobe in Angus's storage unit. It feels too personal, a move like that. Finally – find out if Preston ever came into contact with the Brassicks. He was killed before Katrina, so maybe he led the killer to her, even by accident.'

She finished updating the bullet points on the whiteboard then turned to them once more. 'Anything else?'

'I'll look into whether Preston ever had any military training or came into contact with anyone who did,' Gavin said. 'Just to rule that out. Mind you, we were talking about that in the car on the way over here, and I think any experienced burglar would know to use the same tactics. There's enough information about how to use stealth tactics online these days after all.'

'True,' said Kay, drawing a question mark next to the original note. 'And we haven't found anything yet to suggest that there is a military angle to this.'

'I can stay tonight to make a start on the background checks about him,' said Nadine. She shrugged. 'After all, it's me who's created all this extra work.'

'It's good extra work, so don't let me hear an apology from you,' Kay replied. 'If you're going to do that then I don't want to see you before ten o'clock tomorrow. There's no overtime available, and I don't want you working while you're exhausted – you'll be no good to me like that.'

'I can stay too, guv,' said Kyle. 'What with the social

media angle, there'll be a lot to get through if we're going to make any progress on this.'

Barnes smiled at the constable, then winked at Kay, proud that she commanded such respect amongst her team, even from the newest recruits.

'Me too.' Sean Gastrell stuck his hand up from his position at the back of the room. 'I was only going to go down the pub to watch the football after work. My team will probably lose anyway.'

'Best I stay as well then, guv,' said Aaron Stewart, and grinned. 'Who knows what these youngsters will get up to on their own otherwise?'

TWENTY-FIVE

Kay fought back the urge to gag, then flicked another wet wipe from the packet that lay on the tiled floor of the kitchen.

Four tiny squirming hoglets tumbled over each other in the tray beside her while Adam gently placed them one by one onto an old set of kitchen scales and wrote down each animal's weight, apparently oblivious to the streak of shit one of them had left across the towel lining their temporary enclosure.

Kay wiped the offender's backside, then rocked back on her heels and covered her nose with the crook of her arm. 'Oh my God. What on earth have this lot been eating?'

Her other half grinned. 'A healthy blend of protein, carbohydrates and other essential vitamins and minerals.'

She eyed the open packets of food beside two metal bowls. 'How much money are these companies making on so-called hedgehog food anyway? Surely this is just kitten food.'

'Just be glad they're not still on liquid feed.' He shot her an evil smile. 'I've seen projectile poo with that stuff.'

Kay placed the hoglet in amongst its siblings, then glanced over her shoulder as the doorbell rang. 'That'll be the takeaway.'

'Okay, you get that, I'll finish here.'

After dashing across to the kitchen sink and scrubbing her hands, Kay hurried to the front door and wrenched it open, just as the delivery driver was lowering his phone.

'Just texted to see if anyone was in,' he said, handing over the food.

'Sorry, we're dealing with hungry hedgehogs at the moment.'

His jaw dropped, and then he tried to peer around her. 'Really? My sister reckons she wants one as a pet. There're loads of people on social media with them.'

'Here's a hint,' said Kay, taking the paper carry bag from him and handing him a cash tip. 'Tell her not to. They crap everywhere, and she'll never get the stains out, trust me.'

Biting back a smile at the look of horror on his face, she shut the door and wandered back to the kitchen, the aromatic smell of freshly cooked Chinese food failing to mask the stench from the animals.

Adam had already opened the kitchen windows, and looked up from replacing the soiled bedding in the hedgehogs' tray with fresh. 'Don't worry, the smell will fade.'

Pulling plates from a cupboard next to the microwave, Kay rolled her eyes. 'Until they have another feed. Let's eat this in the other room – it's still a bit… ripe in here.'

A few minutes later they were sitting side by side on the sofa, their plates loaded with food and a glass of wine each on the coffee table in front of them.

Kay groaned at the first bite. 'God I was ready for this.'

'Same. I've been so busy with paperwork and feeding that lot all day I haven't had time to eat.' Adam scooped up a forkful of noodles, then reached out for his glass and took a sip. 'Do you want to watch a film after this?'

'I can't, sorry – I brought home some of the budgeting paperwork to go through. I'll never get a chance to do it at work with this investigation taking up all my time.'

He lowered his glass and eyed her warily. 'Don't let them burn you out.'

'I won't. Trust me, half an hour or so and it'll all be done. It's just that if I don't, I'll miss the deadline. I want to check my emails too – there's so much information coming in on these two murders I'm scared I'll miss something important.'

'Good job you enjoy what you do, right?' He smiled, and turned back to his food.

'Who's looking after the practice while you're babysitting the kids, then?'

'Scott. He and Claire have it all under control – thankfully it's been a quiet week. There haven't been too many emergencies, only standard check-ups and vaccinations to do. He knows he can call me though if something crops up.' Adam put his empty plate on the table and leaned back, suppressing a belch. 'I've got to go over to a farm at Hawkhurst first thing tomorrow to check over a horse before it's sold but that won't take long. The hoglets will be fine while I'm gone.' He stood up as she pushed her knife and fork to one side. 'Give me your plate, I'll sort out the washing up while you're working.'

'Thanks. Won't be long, promise.'

He grinned. 'I'll bring you a top-up in a bit.'

Kay took a moment to savour another sip of wine, then turned her attention to the courier bag at her feet. Rummaging inside, she pulled out a red folder full of spreadsheets and handwritten notes, her heart sinking as she pored through the numbers.

No wonder she rarely saw Sharp in Maidstone these days. It was bad enough being a detective inspector, let alone having a higher rank with more paperwork than hands-on investigating.

She opened her laptop and clicked the email application open, her gaze falling on the latest updates from her team. As tempting as it was to lose herself in the murder enquiries, she scrolled instead to the instructions from Headquarters and went back to the spreadsheets, determined to complete her task within the hour.

Twenty minutes later, her phone vibrated on the coffee table, jerking her thoughts from the complicated formula she was trying to emulate, and she gave a wry smile at the name on the screen.

'Guv, I was just thinking about you,' she said.

'And no doubt swearing under your breath.' Sharp chuckled. 'I just saw the email from Headquarters. Are you still in the office?'

'At home. If I can work out how to write this sodding formula, I'll have my figures over to you tonight.'

'What are you stuck on?'

They spent the next couple of minutes resolving the issue, and Kay breathed a sigh of relief as she emailed the finished files to him.

'Thank God for that,' she sighed, and reached for her wine. 'Thanks, guv.'

'Any time. I hear you've got a name for the body found in the storage unit.'

'Preston Winford.' She scanned her emails until she saw one from Aaron Stewart, and paraphrased his update. 'Latest in from the team is that Preston was twenty-four at the time of his death, and working part-time as a delivery driver. We'll interview his manager tomorrow morning – so far, all this information has been gleaned from social media. We've traced his parents too, so I'll take Barnes with me to speak to them tomorrow before we contact the press, and Aaron's put together a list of acquaintances we'll interview over the course of the next two days.'

'Good, okay. Sounds like a plan. I take it there's no more news about Katrina's murder?'

'I've got two officers going to speak to a landowner close to the Brassicks' house tomorrow morning. Looks like whoever killed her crossed through a neighbour's property to get to their place. Whether or not we find anything though…'

'Hmm. I don't like this one bit, Kay.'

'Me neither. Both murders show a vindictive edge to them, rather than violence for the sake of violence. Their injuries were calculated to induce as much pain as possible without killing them outright, until whoever did this was ready.'

'Has anyone been released from prison lately who matches the profile?'

'Not that Laura could find, and she was bloody thorough. She even went through records for Essex and Sussex.'

'All right. Sorry, I've got to go – I've got a couple more phone calls to make tonight. Shout if you need me, and say "hi" to Adam.'

'Will do. Thanks.'

Ending the call, she shoved her laptop and papers back in the bag then wandered out to the kitchen with her empty glass.

Adam was sitting at the central worktop, his head bowed over a veterinary journal. He looked up when she entered, and smiled. 'All done?'

'All done.' She crossed to the refrigerator and retrieved the wine, pouring them each another glass before joining him, and plucked a leftover prawn cracker from the bag next to his elbow. 'Sharp sends his regards.'

'I thought that might've been him.'

Kay nibbled on the cracker. 'We ought to organise a barbecue soon. It's been ages since we got everyone together.'

'Let's do it once your workload calms down a bit,' he said, pulling her into a hug. 'Otherwise I know what'll happen – you'll all sit around talking about this case instead of relaxing.'

'True.'

On cue, her mobile phone rang. She kissed Adam, then pulled away to answer it.

'Hunter.'

'Guv? It's Sean Gastrell.'

'Are you still at the station?'

'We're just finishing for the night, guv, but Aaron said I ought to give you a call. I found out something about Preston Winford that you should know straight away.'

'Oh, what?'

'I ran his name through a credit check to see what his spending habits were like in case there were any new leads there about how he spent his time and all that,' said the young constable. 'It turns out, he owes over twelve thousand pounds across four credit cards. He wasn't keeping up with the repayments either, looking at these records. He was up to his eyeballs in debt.'

Kay froze on the spot, her heart hammering.

'Just like Katrina,' she murmured, 'and Angus Zilchrist.'

TWENTY-SIX

Alec Mingrove gripped the back of the seat as the bus eased to a standstill, then held his breath until he had walked past the old man with an overpowering stink of body odour to reach the door.

Stepping onto the pavement, he eyed the clouds snatching away the last of the evening light as the bus pulled away from the kerb, and offered a silent prayer that it wouldn't rain before he reached the restaurant.

Three weeks ago he had finally sold his car, although the man who turned up at his flat had smelled the desperation emanating from him and knocked two thousand off the asking price after taking it for a short test drive.

Alec hadn't had the energy to argue with him, or the time to wait for a better offer.

He had handed over the money as soon as it landed in his bank account, too. For a moment, he had been tempted to use it to run, to get away, to hide.

And then he remembered that others had tried to get away too, and failed.

Fighting down the nausea, he walked briskly towards the town centre, cursing the fact he didn't know the right bus routes and was now fifteen minutes away from the restaurant.

His shoes were already pinching his toes, the fashionable pointed toes more suited to social gatherings or sedentary office work than for covering any distance.

The irony wasn't lost on him either.

Two hundred quid for a pair of shoes was nothing to him a year ago, and now he was taking the bus.

As he passed through the shadow of the multi-storey car park, his stomach twisted at the thought of adding more to his credit card tonight.

But he didn't have a choice.

Ed had phoned two days ago with instructions to meet, and the chance to be introduced to his friend's business partner was too good an opportunity to turn down.

Especially when tonight might lead to a permanent job offer with a regular income, which he desperately needed if he was going to get out of the mess he was in.

Being a contractor and living on the government's idea of a minimum basic wage, Alec was struggling. Until four months ago, he had frittered away his salary on material things like the car, expensive watches, clothes, holidays – all paid for on plastic.

All to try and impress co-workers in a job he was suddenly made redundant from.

All because his employer elected to move its headquarters from Aylesford to The Hague because export laws were making it too hard to deal with its European customer base.

The rest of winter had been spent lowering the thermostat every week to save money until there was no point in lowering it any further. The flat was freezing cold through to the end of April and he had spent his evenings hugging a hot water bottle to keep warm while eating food that used to sustain him during his student days.

And still the debts piled up: the mortgage, the mobile phone contract that he couldn't cancel because he needed to look for work, those damn credit card bills.

The offer of a cash loan at the end of March had seemed like a godsend.

Until four weeks ago and the sudden request that the loan be paid back immediately – with interest.

And still the endless churn of job applications, interviews, and the knowledge that he couldn't ask for a pay rise or a permanent contract at the company where he worked because that's how people didn't come back the following week.

There was always someone else who would work for less rather than not work at all.

He bit his lip, blinking back the urge to cry with frustration.

'Alec!'

'Fuck,' he mumbled, then turned with a smile plastered to his face. 'Ed, mate – thought you'd already be at the restaurant.'

His friend gestured to the gorgeous woman beside him. 'Someone couldn't decide what to wear, so we're running a bit late.'

'Not fair, and not true,' she said, laughing. 'The cat decided to throw up on the carpet just as we were leaving.'

'Hi, Lisa.' Alec bent down and gave her a swift peck on the cheek. 'And, nice.'

'I know, right? Good job he's cute.'

Ed looked him up and down. 'I *thought* it was you that I saw getting off the bus next to the supermarket when we drove past. What's going on? Where's your car?'

Alec's smile faltered a little as they set off along the street, turning at a junction before entering the pedestrianised section. 'The bastard clutch gave out earlier this morning and the garage had to order in a replacement because they don't stock it. I'll get it back sometime this week.'

'So you had to use a bus? Bloody hell.' Ed's nose wrinkled.

'I know, right?' He clapped a hand on his friend's shoulder as they turned towards a narrow alleyway. 'I don't think I've had to do that since we left school. Remember that time you got us kicked off the school bus for a whole term?'

Lisa's eyes widened. 'He never told me about that.'

'Hasn't he? Maybe you should ask him.' Alec waggled his eyebrows. 'Or I could tell you about the time he…'

'It's nothing.' Ed grinned and slipped his arm around his wife. 'All that happened was…'

Alec let their voices drift around him as they walked ahead, a sickness clawing at his stomach while his gaze swept the faces behind the windows of a bar overlooking the cobblestoned courtyard.

Nobody was watching him.

Nobody cared.

'Alec?'

His gaze snapped to the front door of the restaurant. Ed's hand was on the brass handle, the glass sparkling under carefully placed lighting that illuminated the logo above their heads.

Forcing a smile, he hurried over. 'Sorry, miles away there.'

'Angela's already here.' Ed jerked his chin towards a brunette in a tailored dress who was standing at the bar beyond the glass. 'Just be yourself, and you'll be fine. This is only a formality, trust me.'

'Thanks.' Alec went to reach out for his friend's arm, then paused awkwardly. 'This means a lot.'

Ed winked. 'Thank me when you sign the contract. And buy me a bottle of that vintage Krug we used to drink. Haven't had any for a while, have we?'

'Okay, you're on.' Alec nodded. 'Let's do this.'

Following Ed into the restaurant, he hung back a little while the formal introductions were made, then held out his hand to Angela.

'Pleased to meet you,' he said. 'Thanks for letting me take up your time this evening.'

She smiled, her grip firm. 'No problem. Ed's told me a lot about you, and I'd like to hear what you think you can bring to our new business.'

A waiter walked over, murmured that their table was ready, and led the way to an alcove tucked away at the rear of the restaurant.

'I thought we'd keep away from the crowd,' Angela explained. 'Easier not to have to worry about confidentiality that way. I'd like to hear more about your experience, Alec, particularly in light of two clients we're hoping to gain next week.'

'No problem.' Alec sat between her and Ed, and nodded his thanks to the waiter as he was passed a leather-bound menu.

Running his gaze down the list of entrées and main courses, he felt his eyes stinging at the prices.

He couldn't afford any of it.

Not now.

Bitterness enveloped him.

What the hell was Ed thinking, suggesting they meet here?

'What will sir have?' The waiter hovered at his elbow. 'I can recommend the steak tartare to begin with…'

'Actually, I'm not that hungry. Could I have the soup of the day please, and the tuna salad starter as a main course?'

'On a diet, Alec?' Lisa smiled. 'It's not like you to worry about what you eat.'

He patted his stomach dramatically and forced a laugh. 'Late nights, junk food, it all catches up eventually. I figured I'd behave myself for a while, so I can treat myself properly in a few months.'

'Well, I have to say that's admirable.' Angela raised an eyebrow. 'Right, well I've got to have the gravlax – it's absolutely divine here, and I'll have the veal escalopes after that please.'

'Thank you, madam.' The waiter plucked the menus from their hands. 'And what about wine?'

Alec looked at the untouched water in his glass. 'I'm fine, th—'

'We'd best have a bottle of the vintage Châteauneuf du Pape,' said Angela, smiling expansively. 'After all, we've got plenty to talk about, haven't we?'

———

Two hours later, Alec's hand shook as he typed his card pin code into the machine the waiter held out, and wished he hadn't acquiesced to Angela's insistence that they have a second bottle of the most expensive wine on the menu.

He hadn't even had more than a couple of sips from the first, refusing the waiter's attempts to top up his glass and ignoring the quizzical glances Lisa had shot his way from time to time.

Picking at his food, he had focused instead on answering Angela's questions with the right balance of aplomb and humbleness, raised a few polite laughs and expanded upon some of his past work where appropriate.

As coats were fetched and chairs were pushed back, Ed's business partner had thrust out her hand once more, her eyes sparkling.

'I'm really glad we had a chance to meet like this,' she said. 'I find it's much easier to get the measure of someone outside of an office environment, and Ed was right about you. I think you'll be a perfect match for us.'

With that, she'd nodded to Ed, air-kissed Lisa and breezed out the door without a backward glance.

Alec's relief at the job offer was short-lived when he saw the bill.

Ed grinned, then raised an eyebrow. 'Best we split this one, don't you think?'

'Sounds good,' Alec replied, hoping the relief in his voice wasn't too obvious.

'Look on the bright side, mate. It'll help butter her up ready for when I suggest to her that you start straight away when I catch up with her for coffee in the morning.'

Cool air slapped Alec's cheeks when they left the restaurant, and he looked up as a few spots of rain began to fall.

Despite the feeling that summer had finished before it had even begun, he hoped tonight was a sign that he could finally try and put the past few months behind him.

Perhaps he could ask Ed and Angela for an advance on his salary to clear his debts sooner once he had a chance to impress them.

Perhaps in another year's time he would look back at this time as something of a test that he had passed.

Character building, his dad used to say.

As they approached the multi-storey car park Lisa elbowed him in the ribs.

'Congratulations on the new job.'

'Thank you – and thanks for coming tonight, too.'

'I wasn't going to miss that meal for the world,' she said, smiling. 'Not with the waiting list they've got for the next two months. Oh, bugger. Hang on.'

She paused and delved into her handbag as her mobile phone began to ring, and he heard Ed curse under his breath as she spoke in a hurried voice.

'Shit, that's our babysitter by the sounds of it.' He

grimaced as the rain started to fall in earnest. 'I was going to offer you a lift home, but…'

'Don't worry, I'll—'

'Ed, love.' Lisa ended the call and turned towards the car park entrance. 'Hayley's got a temperature and just threw up. I told the babysitter we'd be home as soon as poss—'

'Go.' Alec squeezed her arm, kissed her cheek and then turned to Ed. 'I'll call you tomorrow, but thanks. I owe you.'

'You do. But no need to thank me. I knew you'd be perfect. Oh, hey – taxi!' Ed waved over a passing car and peered through the open window as it drew to a standstill, before pointing Alec's way. 'He needs to get to the far end of Tovil, that all right?'

'Hop in.'

'Talk tomorrow,' said Ed, slapping Alec's shoulder as he hurried back to Lisa.

'Okay.'

Alec waited until they'd disappeared into the car park, then turned to the waiting taxi driver and hoisted his suit jacket over his head to offset the rain now pouring down his neck. 'It's okay, I'll walk thanks.'

'Mate, it's pissing down. You sure?'

'Yeah, thanks.'

The driver rolled his eyes, then pulled away from the kerb, the car's brake lights flashing at the T-junction before disappearing into the night.

Alec shivered, then stomped away, keen to put some distance between himself and the car park before Ed saw him.

Hunkering under the jacket, he cursed under his breath that no one else at the dinner had thought to ask if he could afford to eat there. They had simply assumed he could.

'And you didn't have the balls to tell them otherwise, you tosser,' he fumed under his breath.

A bus splashed past him as he reached the next junction heading out of town, the wheels dislodging most of the water from a puddle at the kerb and soaking his trouser legs before it pulled into a stop a few hundred metres from him.

A woman stepped off, hoisted an umbrella and dashed towards the open gate of a nearby house, the faint tap-tap of her heels reaching him. The doors to the bus remained open for a few seconds, and he realised the driver was probably waiting for him to jump on.

Alec slowed his pace, his neck flushing with the embarrassment that he couldn't even afford the ride home.

The driver took the hint, and pulled out into the road, leaving him to shake the suit jacket to lose some of the water pooling in the folds before setting off once more.

At least there were tea bags at home. No milk, but anything hot to drink right now would temper the chill that was soaking through to his bones.

He exhaled, berating himself for the stupor that enveloped him. After all, by the end of the week he would have a new job to look forward to after tonight's informal interview and, even if Ed wasn't able to convince his business partner to employ him as an associate straight away, there were at least some career prospects.

And once he cleared his debts, he could start saving – properly, like Ed and Lisa had, rather than buying all those material things that had left him with nothing to show for the past ten years of his working life.

Squaring his shoulders, a renewed bounce in his step, he paused at the kerb to let a car pass before crossing the road, then watched as it crawled to a standstill next to the kerb and a man emerged from the driver's side.

Alec slowed, then saw the man crouch beside the front wheel, a loud curse reaching him before the figure stood and kicked the offending tyre.

'Got a puncture?' he called out as he drew nearer.

The man glanced over his shoulder and gave a slight shrug. 'Might be. It was pulling to the right suddenly.'

Crouching, Alec peered through the gloom, then frowned. 'Looks all right to me. What—'

He cried out as a thick arm encircled his throat then dragged him upwards, the man's hand wrapping around his arm.

Then the back window lowered, and he staggered backwards before the man's grip on his arm tightened.

'Hello, Alec.'

A voice carried from the back seat of the car, sending a chill crawling down his spine.

He swallowed, his mouth remaining dry as his guts threatened to turn to liquid. 'I was going to call you when I got home, I promise. I was—'

'Get in, Alec. Time to have a little talk about that debt you owe me.'

TWENTY-SEVEN

An air of desperation clung to the incident room when Kay walked through the door the next morning.

She swept her eyes over the officers, all of whom wore harassed expressions while they fielded phone call after phone call, trying to cope with the barrage of information from both the new crime scene and their existing investigations.

Despite the early hour, a subtle taint of body odour wafted across to where she paused at her desk, the gentle hum of the air-conditioning vent above her doing little to dispense it within the enclosed space.

The voices around her distilled to a faint white noise while she scanned through the latest emails and then worked her way through half a dozen voicemail messages that had been left on her desk phone.

After jotting down the more important ones, she deleted the rest and stretched her arms above her head, feeling her upper vertebrae creak in protest.

'Guv, Preston Winford's parents are downstairs,' Gavin

said, walking over and handing her a freshly printed case summary before tailing her across to the whiteboard. 'Do you want me to interview them, or...'

'You lead it, but I wouldn't mind sitting in.' Kay scanned the bullet points and notes on the page, then bit her lip.

There was so much to do, so many leads that had been cross-referenced and processed, and yet a week later they were no wiser to who had savagely murdered Katrina Hovat – or why.

She blew her fringe from her eyes and glared at the looping handwriting covering the board. 'Preston has to be the key to this, doesn't he? Date-wise, we don't have any victims displaying these sorts of injuries in other cases until he was murdered and dumped in Angus's storage shed.'

'None that we've found yet,' Gavin said. 'But we still haven't been able to link him to Angus or Katrina. Laura and the two probationers have been through all their social media accounts again in the past twenty-four hours, and we've got nowhere.'

She heard the despondency in his voice, and tried to inject some enthusiasm into her own despite the growing sense that the case was running away from her. 'Well, we *do* know that the victims were in debt. Maybe it's time to ask for some specialist help.'

Her colleague frowned. 'What sort of help?'

She glanced over his shoulder, and beckoned to Debbie West. 'Can you get onto Headquarters and ask if Amanda Miller is still available? She helped us on that case with the mummified body a few years ago.'

'Will do, guv.'

Gavin watched the uniformed officer return to her desk, then turned to Kay. 'The forensic accountant?'

'That's the one. I'm hoping she might spot something in amongst their bank statements that we've missed, or at least provide us with some background information as to where else they might've borrowed money from.'

His mouth tightened. 'Loan sharks, you mean.'

'Maybe, yes. Amanda's team must've crossed paths with illegal lenders before now. Let's see if she's got any insights into that side of organised crime that might help us.' She paused and checked her watch. 'Right, let's go and speak with Mr and Mrs Winford. Perhaps they can shed some light on what their son was up to before his death.'

———

Marion and Colin Winford were sitting side-by-side at a table in interview room three when Kay followed Gavin into the meeting, the couple holding hands while Preston's mother dabbed at her eyes with a scrunched-up tissue.

Colin Winford rose to his feet as the door closed and thrust out a paw of a hand to Gavin, the man's build suggesting he might have played rugby in his younger days.

'Are you the detective who's going to catch the fucker who killed my son?' he demanded.

'Colin, *language*.' His wife's eyes widened as colour shot to her cheeks. 'I'm so sorry, we…'

'It's all right, don't apologise – I've heard worse,' Gavin said stoically, 'and yes, I am. One of them, anyway.

This is Detective Inspector Kay Hunter, who's leading the investigation.'

'Mr Winford, Mrs Winford, I'm so sorry for your loss.' Kay motioned to the chairs around the table. 'Shall we sit down, Mr Winford, and I'll answer any questions you've got as best I can at the present time?'

'Okay,' he said gruffly. He squeezed his wife's hand, then sighed. 'Sorry for the language. It's just that... Preston was... was...'

He broke down then, huge wracking sobs that shook his enormous frame while his wife wrapped her arm around him, her own tears leaving wet streaks across the pale coloured jacket he wore.

Gavin reached out for a box of tissues beside the recording equipment and slid them across to the couple, giving them a few moments to compose themselves.

'Preston wouldn't hurt anyone,' Marion said eventually, her face blotchy with tears. 'He never even got in with the wrong crowd at school.'

'We just can't understand why anyone would hurt him,' Colin added, and sniffed.

'Well, hopefully we can get some answers for you, and arrest whoever was responsible for his death,' said Gavin. 'Do you mind if we ask a few questions about Preston, to help us get a better idea of him as a person?'

'Sure.' Colin wiped at his eyes with his jacket sleeve, and straightened his shoulders. 'Anything you need from us, just ask.'

'Thank you.' Gavin paused, opening his file to scan his notes, and Kay glanced across.

It was a good way to let Preston's parents have a few

more moments to gather their thoughts, and pride swelled in her chest at the way her colleague had matured as an investigator in their time together.

It meant she could listen and observe the interview, gauging the couple's answers and try to detect any undercurrent of stress.

Often, it was something that was left unsaid that could provide the slightest breakthrough they so desperately needed.

'When was the last time you saw Preston?' Gavin began.

'Early April,' said Colin. 'We live in Suffolk these days, so with him being busy with work and me not liking motorway driving so much we probably only saw him half a dozen times a year.'

'We spoke on the phone every few weeks though,' Marion added. 'And email.'

'But nothing since early April?'

Both parents shook their heads.

'No.' Colin gave a sad shrug. 'I just assumed he was busy with work. I emailed him a couple of weeks ago but I didn't worry. Sometimes it was like that – we'd go a few weeks without talking to each other, and then have a big catch-up when he came up for air.'

'Could you confirm what he did for work?' said Gavin.

'He was working as a delivery driver, but only as a contractor.'

'Did he mention any issues at work?'

'He was frustrated they weren't offering pay rises or extra hours this year,' said Colin, a frown forming. 'That's the third bloody year in a row. He mentioned back in April that he was starting to look for another job, but it's difficult, isn't it? Employers know people are desperate so they're only offering a pittance.'

'What about hobbies?' Gavin said. 'What did Preston like to do in his spare time?'

'He always enjoyed sport.' Marion's brow furrowed. 'He used to be into cycling until last year, then sold the bike he had. I noticed he'd lost a bit of weight too. When I asked if he was okay, he said he'd dropped his gym membership to save money. He said he wasn't eating as much as he used to because he didn't want to put on weight if he wasn't exercising as much. I did wonder if he was taking it too far though. He always ate enough for two when he visited us.'

'I asked him in April what he was up to lately, and he was… cagey,' Colin said. 'Instead of telling us about the latest series he'd been streaming, or what holiday he'd booked for the summer, he just shrugged it off. Come to think of it, he changed the subject when Marion asked him too.'

'Was that unusual?'

'Yes. Preston was always the chatty one, lively as anything, always on the go.'

Gavin sifted through the paperwork in the file, then paused. 'Were you aware that Preston had a considerable amount of debt?'

Marion stiffened. 'He never said anything to us. And if he did, we would've helped him out where we could. Why?'

'As part of our enquiries into his death, we've been made aware that he owes twelve thousand six hundred pounds to four different credit card companies.' Gavin looked to each of the Winfords in turn. 'And he hasn't made the minimum payments to two of those since January.'

'Twelve thousand...' Colin's eyes widened. 'He never said anything...'

'Did he talk with you about money at all?' said Kay. 'Or did you notice anything else about his spending habits that seemed out of character for him?'

'No. We didn't have much when he was growing up but we made sure he always understood about budgeting and that sort of thing. What on earth was he spending all that money on?'

'We're in the process of obtaining statements from the credit card companies,' Gavin explained, 'but that can take a while. It may be that the debts were incurred a while ago, and Preston had been paying them back for some time. Years, even. And he never said anything to you?'

Colin shook his head. 'I mean, I know he was bitching about the lack of pay rises at work, but he was earning a decent amount, Detective Piper. I wouldn't say he was struggling, you know? At least, he never gave us the impression that there was a problem.'

Kay watched while Gavin extracted two photographs from the file, and held her breath.

'I'd like to show you these,' he said to the Winfords. 'They've been tidied up but I need to advise that they are of two deceased people who we think might be connected to Preston in some way. Would you mind taking a look?'

Marion paled, but then set her jaw and nodded.

'Okay,' said Colin.

They leaned closer when Gavin slid the photographs across, their eyes sweeping the images of Katrina and Angus.

'Have you seen either of these people before?' Kay asked.

'No, who are they?' said Marion, confused. 'Were they killed by the same person who murdered my son?'

'We don't know yet.' Kay pursed her lips for a moment. 'We couldn't find any connection between your son and these two people through their social media. Did Preston ever mention the names Katrina Hovat or Angus Zilchrist to you?'

'No, I'm sorry,' said Colin. 'I don't recognise either of those names.'

'Me neither,' his wife added.

Kay leaned back in her seat, fighting back the wave of disappointment that swept over her.

They were no closer to finding out what had happened to the three victims, or why.

And she was running out of time to prevent their killer from striking again.

TWENTY-EIGHT

Gavin removed his sunglasses and stared up at the signage protruding from the façade above a converted shipping container.

A cluster of green and gold streamers floated from a sandwich board outside the door that was covered in chalked writing screaming the latest deals for temporary storage space.

When he opened the door into the office, he was struck by how much was squashed into the tiny room. A counter made from cheap Formica formed a T-shape to his left, the surface strewn with cardboard, crumbs and strips of leftover packing tape, while to his right were two plastic chairs and a stainless steel tree displaying various brochures about the services offered by the storage company.

The smell of cardboard and glue clung to the walls.

A man was wrangling a tea chest-sized box at the back of the office, his face rueful when he saw Gavin.

'Back again?'

'Just some follow-up questions, if that's okay.' Gavin held out his warrant card. 'Are you William Clyborne?'

'Will, yeah. Hang on.' A few more flaps of the cardboard ensued, and then the man expertly whipped a tape dispenser around the folds and shoved it to one side. 'The phone can go to voicemail for now – d'you want to have a seat?'

'Thanks.'

Will wiped his hands down the front of his jeans and sank into the chair beside the brochures. 'First time I've had a chance to sit down all morning.'

'Busy?' Gavin failed to keep the surprise from his voice.

'Uh-huh. More than usual. I guess some people can't stay away from a murder scene, right?' Will snorted. 'Ghouls, the lot of them. Most have only come in to gawp, pick up a brochure or some packing tape and then bugger off. We'll probably never see them again.'

'Anyone asking questions?'

That caused a splutter of laughter. '*Everyone* asks questions. Fishing, you know? One bloke even said it'd make a great story for his true crime podcast.'

'Fucking hell.' Gavin shook his head. 'Sorry.'

'No, you're all right. I thought the same thing. Right, what did you want to know?' The man jerked his thumb over his shoulder. 'I've got eight more of those to put together for a legit customer who's going to be here at one.'

'Angus Zilchrist, the bloke who rented the unit – did you ever see him with this man?' Gavin handed over the photograph of Preston Winford. 'We're trying to find out if they knew each other.'

Will held the photograph between finger and thumb, running his other hand across his jaw. 'Can't say for sure. He looks sort of familiar, but I see so many people come through here. Is this the dead bloke? The one who was found here?'

'Yes.'

'Christ.'

'We haven't spotted them together on the security footage you gave us earlier this week yet,' said Gavin, taking back the photograph. 'If someone accesses their unit here and they've got someone with them, would both parties have to sign in, or just the person who rents the unit?'

'Just the person paying the rent.' Will scratched his jaw once more, then glanced over Gavin's shoulder and pointed out the window. 'Brian Melgren runs the classic car restoration place over the road – it might be worth your while having a word with him. He's got cameras all over that forecourt and you never know, you might get lucky.'

Gavin grinned. 'I will, thanks. Keep your fingers crossed for me.'

———

Covering the distance between the storage facility and the car restoration business in long strides, Gavin followed the sound of hammering into a wide two-bay garage and across to a service pit.

Above it, raised on a hydraulic ramp was a late 1960s

MG, the British racing green paintwork showing signs of rust around the front wheel arches.

Another loud *whack* from the hammer resonated off the walls, and then there was movement from under the car and a man in his fifties peered up at him.

'Help you?'

'Brian Melgren? DC Gavin Piper, Kent Police. I wondered if I could have a quick word?'

Melgren sighed, reached up and placed the hammer beside Gavin's feet and then walked up the steps set into the service pit, wiping his hands down a pair of oil-streaked grey overalls. 'I spoke to your lot earlier in the week. This about that body you found?'

'It is.'

'I said to the copper that came over here that I didn't see anything.' He squinted against the bright sunlight that pierced the dark interior through the front roll-up doors. 'Can't from here, look.'

Gavin turned to see what Melgren meant.

Sure enough, even though the double metal gates to the storage facility were wide open, only the corner of the office was visible from where they stood, and none of the units could be seen.

Turning back to the man, Gavin pulled out his notebook. 'I was wondering about your CCTV cameras actually. Do any of them face those gates, or the road outside?'

Melgren sniffed, contemplating the question. 'Might do, I suppose. Want to take a look?'

'I wouldn't mind.'

'The office is this way.'

Gavin followed him past the raised MG, and eyed an Aston Martin DB5 that gleamed beside it. 'Do you have anyone else here working with you?'

'A couple of part-time enthusiasts. James only works on Saturdays, and I contract out any of the electrical stuff to a chap who comes in on Tuesdays if I need him. The rest of the time, I'm on my own.' Melgren pushed open the door to a shoebox-like office at the back of the garage and sank into a barely-stuffed swivel chair. He pointed to another behind the door. 'Sit yourself down. Takes a while for the laptop to start up.'

'Thanks. How long have you been here?'

'About fifteen years. I used to do this out of my garage at home to start off with, but then word got around and I got busier so I quit my job and did this instead.' Melgren drummed his fingers on an open A4-sized diary while the computer operating system went through its start-up procedures. 'Time's gone quick, though. I keep saying I'll do this for another few years then sell the business, but I never do.'

'There're some gorgeous cars outside.'

'Hence the cameras. Most are brought inside at night but it's busier out there today because I've got customers coming later to pick up the Aston Martin and the Ford GT. Ah, here you go. What did you want to see?'

'Can I take a look at the angles first?'

'Sure.' Melgren moused over to an on-screen menu and clicked. 'I've got six cameras in total – two inside, and four on the outside covering each corner of the building.'

'That's impressive.'

'There was a special deal on the price when I bought

the system. You'll probably want the two front ones, right?'

'Probably. What's out the back?'

'Just the bins for this place and the paint shop next door. There's a concrete wall behind those, and that separates us from the courier depot on the other side.'

'Okay. Do the cameras move?'

Melgren shook his head. 'They're both at fixed angles. Mostly to cover any cars that are parked out there, but also to watch the front doors. Those are alarmed, but with the value of some of the cars that come through here, I can't risk not having a back-up. This is the one that catches a little of the storage unit place across the road.'

Gavin scooted his chair closer and peered at the screen.

The camera angle was perfect, giving him a clear view of the road approaching the storage company beyond Melgren's forecourt.

'How long do you keep the footage for?'

'Forever, I suppose. It saves everything online.'

Reaching into his jacket pocket for a business card, Gavin tried to keep the excitement from his voice. 'Could you send me a link to download everything from this camera, say between November and last week?'

'If it'll help, yes.'

'Oh, it'll help, Mr Melgren.' Gavin smiled. 'It'll help a lot.'

TWENTY-NINE

'Amanda, thanks for seeing me at such short notice.'

Kay shook hands with the shorter woman, the financial investigator shifting a leather briefing wallet tucked under her other arm.

'You're lucky. I just finished wrapping up another investigation this morning so I'm free for a few hours until Sharp or one of the others needs me.' The woman checked her watch. 'It's getting on in the day, but do you want to grab a coffee?'

'Sounds good.'

In her late fifties, Amanda Miller exuded confidence, her brunette hair swept up into a fashionable chignon that accentuated high cheekbones and her navy suit complementing her slim frame. Her greetings to colleagues they passed on their way to the canteen were returned with warm smiles.

Kay bit back a sigh, ruing the creases in her jacket from the drive over from Maidstone and the dark circles under her eyes from lack of sleep.

'How're things over here?' she asked, eyeing the cereal bars in the vending machine before selecting two.

'I think the best way to describe it is "steadily busy". Organised crime is growing, despite our efforts, but at least that means the top brass saw fit to give me a slightly bigger budget to recruit three more bums on seats.' Amanda poured coffee from a large urn and passed a cup to Kay. 'What about you?'

'It never stops.' She gave a tired laugh, helping herself to milk and sugar. 'I mean, I wouldn't have it any other way, but…'

'A moment to come up for air would be good occasionally, wouldn't it?' Amanda's eyes softened. 'And how are you, Kay? Losing a team member is difficult in any circumstances, but especially when you've worked so hard to create such a tight-knit bunch of investigators. I remember what it was like when I was working in Maidstone with you.'

Kay swallowed, her eyes stinging at the kind words. 'Thanks. Um, yeah – it's been hard. The officer who was with him is back at work now though.'

'That's good to hear.' Amanda pointed her coffee mug towards a table at the back of the canteen. 'Shall we sit over there? Might as well hide down here while it's quiet.'

Grateful for the change in subject matter, Kay settled into a chair beside her and opened her briefcase, fanning out the paperwork. 'I'm hoping you can help us with this one. We've had two murders. One victim was killed some weeks ago and his body only discovered on Tuesday, and the other was a woman who was killed last Friday night. Both exhibited the same wounds, leading us and our pathologist to believe they were tortured before being stabbed to death.'

Amanda nodded, her mouth tight. 'I heard about it on the news, obviously. You mentioned on the phone that there was a third victim though?'

'The chap renting the storage unit where the older body was found, yes. Angus Zilchrist. The PM report says he died of natural causes – a heart attack – but we're working on the hypothesis that that might've been caused by finding out that this chap was stuffed into a wardrobe inside the storage unit he was renting.'

'Okay. Why do you need me?'

'These are our findings so far having gone through the financial statements we've obtained from the victims' banks, credit card lenders, that sort of thing. Each of them was in debt, and struggling to pay the bills. But although they were earning money, or in Angus's case had access to a pension, they weren't keeping up with the repayments. I think the money was going elsewhere.'

Amanda blew out her cheeks. 'Loan sharks.'

'Exactly.' Kay gestured to the sample statements she had laid out. 'But we can't prove it from these, and I don't know what I need to do to confirm the theory – or anything to tell me that I'm wrong and I need to be looking for a different motive.'

Reaching out for her coffee, Amanda took a sip, her eyes never leaving the documents strewn in front of them. 'Is there nothing else connecting these three people?'

'Not that we've found yet. The team have scoured social media and interviewed friends and family. There aren't any connections at all.'

'And yet they must've all come into contact with the loan shark at some point in the past few months, and at a similar location.'

'We've used CCTV to trace the movements of Katrina Hovat from her two jobs – the legit ones anyway – and we've seen no evidence to suggest she was being threatened prior to being killed. Her flat... there was nothing there.' Kay shivered at the memory. 'She was working all hours, and yet only just getting by. The team didn't find any threatening notes when they searched the place. I'm going to check with Andy about her laptop after we've finished here, but it's not looking hopeful.'

Amanda collated the papers together and slid them back. 'Okay, so let's discuss first steps. I can give you fourteen hours of my team's time before we'll have to escalate this and get clearance for more. Does that work for you?'

Kay blinked. 'It'll have to. I haven't got any more budget on this one.'

'Jesus.' The older woman shook her head. 'Right, well – it is what it is. I'll assign two people to the searches because that's going to eat up most of the time, but you need answers as soon as possible. We'll run a search through the ELMER database to see if there are any Suspicious Activity Reports specifically for the Maidstone area, and with the emphasis on the sort of transactions being made by your victims. We'll obviously include their details so we get an alert if their names crop up. Those SARs will include every company involved in the financial industry.'

'But we don't think they were worried about a

legitimate company, Amanda – I'm thinking drug gangs with a sideline in lending and intimidation.'

'I know,' said the financial investigator, her eyes sparkling. 'But that money had to come *in* to your victims' lives somehow, didn't it?'

Kay sat back in her chair, realisation dawning. 'So if you can find out how the money was received—'

'Yes. With any luck, we can find out who or where it was received *from*.'

THIRTY

Early the next morning, Kay eyed the swirling mist that hugged the River Medway, then shielded her eyes and peered towards the jagged skyline beyond as sunlight crested the town's apartment buildings and offices.

The noise of commuter traffic carried on the air around her, at odds with the duck quacks and excited chatter from house martins that swooped over the surface of the water, scooping up midges mid-flight.

A dank smell of rotting vegetation clung to the reeds and long grass that grew beside the paved River Walk, the water lapping against the bank as a team of divers worked their way along the watercourse, their neoprene suits glistening.

She loosened her grip on her car keys, made sure they were securely tucked into her blazer pocket, and made her way over to where Kyle Walker stood beside a stretch of crime scene tape that had been knotted between two saplings, effectively blocking the path.

'Morning, guv.' He handed a clipboard over to her and

paused while she signed her name. 'Sorry to wake you early.'

'Not a problem. What time did you get here?'

His mouth quirked. 'Just after six. It still felt like the middle of the night though.'

'I'll bet.' She nodded towards another strip of tape a few metres inside the outer cordon. 'What's the story, then? You said on the phone that someone saw a body in the river.'

'Yes, one of the contractors working here at the market site. He'd wandered over to the far edge of the car park next to the riverbank there to have a cigarette, and saw what he thought was a man's leg sticking out from behind one of the wooden pilings. Turns out, he was right – the body got caught on the remains of an old jetty.' Kyle smirked. 'I don't think he'll be having any more sneaky smoke breaks for a while.'

'Who's down there with the dive team?'

'Simon Winter arrived ten minutes ago with the van. Lucas has been and gone. Patrick's leading the forensic side of things – Harriet's at the scene of a stabbing in Ashford from last night.' He ran his gaze down the list. 'DS Barnes has clocked out but said he'll be back soon, and Aaron Stewart's running the scene as acting SIO. Dave Morrison's started the house-to-house enquiries along this stretch.' He jerked his chin towards a group of stylish flats to their right, the balconies overlooking the river. 'There are security cameras along the walkways between the blocks so they're going to speak to the management team to see if we can take a look at the footage as well as interviewing residents.'

Kay felt some of the tension leave her shoulders while she listened to him, relieved that her team had acted so swiftly, especially as many of them had completed overnight shifts prior to the emergency call-out or, like Kyle, had worked late into the previous day's shift.

'That's good work, Kyle – thanks.' She handed back his pen then glanced over her shoulder as a familiar voice called her name. 'Morning, Ian.'

Barnes handed her a takeout coffee, steam rising from the little hole cut into the plastic lid. 'That's four bodies now if we include Angus Zilchrist, guv.'

'That we know of. Thanks.' She cradled the cardboard cup between her hands and squinted towards the bridge spanning the river farther downstream. 'I can see at least one telephoto lens, so turn your back. I don't want the bastards lip-reading this conversation.'

'Patrick's okayed the path between the two cordons, so you're fine to walk along there if you want to check what's happening,' Kyle said, standing to one side and eyeing the coffee with envy.

'I'll see you back at the station when you're done here. I wouldn't mind another update.'

'Guv.'

Falling into step beside Barnes, Kay blew across the hole in the coffee cup and took a tentative sip before wincing as the scalding liquid caught her tongue. 'I take it you've been down there. What are we dealing with?'

'Male, late twenties or early thirties.' Barnes removed the lid from his own drink before pausing underneath a young silver birch. The cordon tape fluttered in the breeze, the end tied to the tree trunk flapping against the bark with a low rustle. 'Suit trousers, good shoes. No shirt or ID yet though. That's why they're working their way across the river and then downstream, in case anything caught in the silt.'

Kay's gaze wandered beyond where the divers worked and found the Archbishop's Palace on the opposite bank. Two uniformed officers guarded the signposted river walk, turning away any cyclists or joggers to stop them from photographing the crime scene.

She looked up, taking in the multi-storey car park that overshadowed the concrete apron where the market was held at the weekend. 'Anyone checking in there yet?'

'On the list, guv.' Barnes gulped his coffee before sighing at the sound of a car horn. 'We've closed it until we've had a chance to have a look, hence the noise you can hear.'

'Where's the bloke who found the body?'

'Being interviewed at the station.' He pulled out his phone as it vibrated in his pocket, rolled his eyes, then put it away again. 'And that was Laura – apparently Sharp's just phoned to say he's on his way in. Headquarters want an urgent update from us and our thoughts about whether this is related to the other bodies.'

Kay peered at him over her cup. 'I got the impression you thought it was.'

'I took a look at the body while Lucas was giving him the once-over. Our victim's got the same sort of cut marks on his torso and arms.' He paused, his face troubled. 'A lot of blood around his groin, too.'

'And you said there was no ID?'

He stuck his thumb over his shoulder. 'Not unless the divers find something.'

'Maybe it's a robbery gone wrong then, rather than something to do with the other deaths.'

Even Kay could hear the uncertainty in her voice.

They both looked down as Barnes's phone vibrated again, and he groaned when he looked at the screen before turning it to face Kay.

Laura had sent a screenshot of a well-known social media site, a photograph of the crime scene accompanied by the words "Man's body dragged from river".

'Looks like they beat us to the press release, guv,' he said.

Kay wandered over to a drain, tipped the remains of her coffee down it, then tossed the empty cup into a nearby recycling bin used by market traders.

'Best get back to the station, then. We're in for a busy morning.'

THIRTY-ONE

Kay bit back a yawn as she walked towards the whiteboard, her eyelids crusty with lack of sleep.

She still wore the sturdy walking boots she had worn down to the river, the soles on them more comfortable than the heeled shoes she had thrown under her desk upon arriving in the incident room.

The room was quieter than the previous day, with many of her team still at the new crime scene or out following up leads and taking statements.

Debbie West gave her a wan smile as she walked over with the daily briefing agenda and a pile of folders. 'I need your signature on a few things before you disappear, guv. That includes this weekend's rosters and the reports from Harriet Baker about the Brassicks' house. Do you want me to phone them to let them know they can have the place back now we've finished with it?'

'Please. Were there any new updates from Harriet apart from what we already know?'

'No, and Aaron said there wasn't any security footage at that farm either. The one we thought the suspects might've cut through to get in and out of the Brassicks' place.'

'Bugger.' Kay took the pile of folders from her and started flicking through the contents, adding her signature with a flourish where Debbie had placed sticky arrows. 'Who's rostered off today?'

'Nadine, Dave and one of my admins. Nadine and Dave are back in on Sunday. I spoke to Ian before you got here, and he's planning on working straight through the weekend. Gavin and Laura are in tomorrow, but rostered off for Sunday at the moment.' She shrugged. 'None of them want to take a break while there's a killer loose out there.'

Kay closed the last folder. 'Okay, thanks Debbie. Get everyone over here and we'll make a start.'

Five minutes later, the team were gathered around her, their conversations falling silent when she cleared her throat.

'We'll make a start with you, Gavin – how did you get on at the storage unit yesterday?'

'Will Clyborne couldn't help, but he pointed me in the direction of a bloke called Brian Melgren, who owns the classic car restoration business over the road.' Gavin took a sip of his energy drink before continuing. 'Luckily for us, he has two cameras facing the storage unit place and he backs up the footage online – he's never had to delete any of it yet due to a shortage of data space, and he's emailed me a link to all the footage for the two cameras from late last year through to the end of last week. I figured we could go through that to see if Preston Winford ever went to the storage units with Angus, or if he turned up there with anyone else. Will Clyborne said only the person renting the unit has to sign in, so Angus could've turned up with anyone and we wouldn't know about it yet.'

'That's great, thanks Gavin.' Kay updated the whiteboard, then called over her shoulder. 'I'm going to need some help going through all that footage, you lot. Who's got some time to help him?'

'I can,' said Laura. 'I was going to work the weekend anyway while the phones are quiet.'

'Same here,' Barnes said. He looked over his shoulder towards a desk where Kyle and Aaron sat. 'What about you two? Any plans this weekend?'

Both men shook their heads.

'I'm still working on following up the leads from Katrina's murder,' said Kyle, 'so I could take a look at some of the footage in between that.'

'Good, okay – Ian, I'll let you coordinate the work.' Kay re-capped her pen. 'I spoke to Andy Grey while I was at Northfleet yesterday – he's managed to retrieve some files from Katrina's laptop computer but so far it's just things like old payslips from her job at the shop that she'd downloaded, old resumés, and things like that. He'll keep digging, but it doesn't look like he's going to find anything to move along our investigation. We've also finally been granted access to Preston Winford's phone records, so I'd like someone to cross-check those against Angus Zilchrist's mobile number to check if those two were ever in contact with each other.'

Sean Gaskell raised his hand. 'Guv, I can take that on. I can work the weekend too if it helps.'

'There's little by way of overtime available, but I'll try to squeeze a few hours out of the budget for you all,' Kay said, smiling. 'Thanks.'

'No worries.' The probationary constable shrugged. 'I just want to help, guv.'

Kay flipped the page of the briefing agenda, ran through the administrative updates for the team, and then placed it to one side. 'Finally, I caught up with Amanda Miller yesterday at Northfleet. She and her forensic accounting team can give us a few hours to go through the bank statements and other financial records we've obtained so far for Katrina, Preston and Angus. They've also got their own database of information that they can cross-reference, as well as having in-depth knowledge about a lot of the organised crime gangs that are currently under active investigation by Headquarters. As soon as she's got anything to tell us, I'll make sure you're updated. My feeling is that—'

She broke off as Laura's mobile phone trilled, and gave her a slight nod as she pushed back her chair and scurried to the back of the room. 'Okay, while Laura's dealing with that, what I was going to say was that the debt angle is worth pursuing until we have evidence to the contrary. What I can't see yet from the information we've got so far is how those three were targeted by the person – or persons – that murdered them, or why the killings have suddenly started now. What's happened that's triggered them?'

'Guv?' Laura hovered at the fringes of the group.

'What've you got?'

'That was the media team on the phone. Someone's just phoned them to say he thinks he knows the bloke who was pulled out of the river this morning.'

THIRTY-TWO

Laura stood outside the garden gate of a smart pale brick end of terrace house on the fringes of Wateringbury and flicked her phone to silent.

Beyond the gate, a pebble path led to a uPVC front door with frosted glass panes set into the top of it. On either side of the door, large blue painted pots contained bright red geraniums, the scent carrying across to where she waited for Gavin.

Eventually, he finished his call and walked over. 'Sorry – had to take that. Leanne's sister's getting married in March and the pair of them are flapping about where to hold the hen party.'

She chuckled. 'What was she doing, asking you to do a check on the venue?'

'No,' he rolled his eyes. 'Asking how much she could spend if they held it in Ibiza or somewhere like that.'

'Ouch. And there's us with no overtime, too.'

'Thankfully she's had a few extra shifts since the new

year.' His smile faded. 'Although some of those were difficult. Search and rescue doesn't always end well.'

Laura gave his arm a soft punch. 'Come on.'

She walked to the front door and rang the bell, stepping back as the sound of a lock turning reached her ears.

A man in his early thirties opened the door, his face pale and his eyes red-rimmed. 'It's him, isn't it? It's Alec.'

Laura held up her warrant card and introduced herself and Gavin. 'And are you Edwin Moore?'

'Call me Ed.' He stepped to one side. 'Everyone else does.'

Showing them through to a tidy living room, he twisted his hands together. 'Do you want a drink?'

'We're fine, thanks.' Laura glanced over her shoulder as a woman appeared in the doorway hugging a soft cardigan around her shoulders. 'Hello.'

'Hi.'

'This is Lisa, my wife.' Ed wrapped his arm around her shoulder and gave it a squeeze before sinking onto the sofa beside her. 'Please, have a seat.'

Laura shot a grateful look at Gavin as he pulled out his notebook, then turned her attention back to Ed.

'Can you tell me what makes you think the body pulled from the river this morning is your friend Alec?'

The man swallowed, and looked down at his hands. 'I saw a social media post this morning saying there'd been a body pulled out the Medway. I've been trying since late last night to get in touch with him. We had dinner in town – a business meeting, really. I started an accountancy practice last year with someone I used to work with in the

City, and I managed to convince her to take on Alec. Last night was just an informal way for them to meet – the job's his. Angela – my business partner – wanted to meet him to gauge his personality, to see if he'd fit in.'

'What time did you leave the restaurant?'

'About half nine,' said Lisa. 'I remember, because we got a phone call from our babysitter just after that to say our daughter wasn't well.'

'And Ed, you said you tried to phone Alec last night. Why was that?'

'After the babysitter left, I had a phone call from Angela telling me to get Alec on board straight away. She was worried someone else might get him otherwise.' His mouth quirked. 'She doesn't hang around once she's made up her mind about something. As soon as I finished talking to her, I phoned Alec but it went straight to voicemail.'

'What time was that?'

'Hang on.' Ed shuffled in his seat, then pulled out his mobile phone from his trouser pocket and swiped the screen. 'That was at ten seventeen. I tried again at ten thirty-two. Then again at half seven this morning.'

Laura saw his hand trembling as he lowered the phone. 'Is that unusual for him?'

'Very. Alec doesn't let his phone out of his sight at the moment in case it's a job offer. He's been desperate to leave the place he's at because it's shit pay.'

'Okay. Could you describe Alec for me?'

'Um, about my height. Brown eyes, light brown hair. He's got a small scar on his chin – he got that falling off a swing when we were six years old. Oh, and he's got one of those Celtic armband tattoos on his left arm.'

'Do you have a photo of him?'

'Yeah.' More swiping and scrolling ensued, and then Ed turned his phone screen around to face her. 'Lisa took this one of us back in February at a mate's house. We'd gone round to watch the footy while the girls were chinwagging.'

Laura groaned inwardly, trying to keep her face passive. 'Thank you.'

She gave Gavin a slight nod.

He shifted in his seat, and leaned forward. 'Ed, Lisa, in the strictest confidence we're very sorry to tell you that based on what you've told us, and this photograph, that the man retrieved from the river this morning is Alec.'

A sob burst from Lisa, and Ed's face crumpled as he wiped at his eyes.

'There'll need to be a formal identification, and we have to insist you don't tell anyone else until that's been done,' Laura said, her voice soft. 'Do you know if Alec has any family, or—'

Ed sniffed. 'His dad died a few years back, and his mum's not well.'

'Can you let me have Alec's mum's contact details so we can go and see her?'

'Sure.'

'When you're ready, we have a few more questions we'd like to ask, all right?'

The man nodded. 'Could you excuse me a moment?'

'Of course.' Laura noticed he left his phone behind as he left the room, and exhaled.

'Ed's known Alec since kindergarten,' said Lisa, her

voice wobbling. 'They're like brothers. Inseparable. I don't know how he's going to cope—'

'I can send you a list of local specially trained counsellors,' said Laura. 'If, that is, you don't feel that you want to talk to your GP.'

'We'd be lucky to get an appointment these days.' Lisa sniffed. 'Jesus, poor Alec.'

Ed came back in, a balled-up tissue in his fist, his face blotchy. 'What happened? Do you know? He wasn't drunk – he hardly touched his drink last night.'

'At the present time we can't give too many details, not until there's been an official examination,' said Gavin. 'But Alec was attacked. We think he either fell in, or was put in the river following the attack.'

'Oh God.' Lisa raised her hand to her mouth. 'Was he mugged?'

'That's part of our ongoing investigation.'

'Ed, when you're ready, can you tell me what Alec was like when you saw him last night?' Laura asked. 'Did he seem worried about anything?'

The man rested his elbows on his knees and stared at the carpet. 'Not worried, no. More like… *withdrawn*. I mean, he put on a good show for Angela, but there were a couple of times when I looked up and thought he seemed distracted. I know he hates the place he works at, but here we were telling him he's going to have a new start with a better salary, and… I don't know. Something was worrying him, yes.'

'Was Alec having money problems, perhaps struggling to get by financially?'

'Yeah, I think so. I mean, he got the bus into town

yesterday. He said that his car's in the garage, but a year or so ago he would've just got a taxi or a ride share, y'know?'

'He looked thin, too,' said Lisa. 'I wondered if he wasn't eating properly. I noticed he was really careful about what he picked off the menu too. The cheapest options.'

Ed groaned, and closed his eyes. 'And then bloody Angela left without offering to chip in for the bill so me and Alec had to pay. Jesus, I didn't think…'

'How did he get home afterwards?' said Laura.

'We couldn't offer him a lift – we're in the opposite direction anyway but as we were walking back to the car with Alec, that's when our babysitter phoned to say Hayley had been sick.' Lisa wiped at fresh tears. 'If we'd taken him home first, none of this would've happened…'

'There was a taxi,' Ed said. 'I flagged it down, and asked the driver to take Alec to Tovil. Then I dashed off with Lisa. We got back to find that Hayley had picked up a bug from school and was starting to run a temperature.'

Laura looked up from her notes. 'Did you see Alec get in the taxi?'

'Yes. Well, I saw him talking to the driver so he must've got in.' He frowned. 'At least, I *think* he did.'

THIRTY-THREE

'Two trips to the morgue in one week,' said Barnes, turning into the crowded car park for Darent Valley Hospital. 'Lucas is going to have to start handing out loyalty card points at this rate.'

Kay shook her head, although a smile crept onto her lips at her colleague's words.

He always managed to lighten a sombre occasion, and seemed to know exactly when she was in danger of wallowing in her own dark thoughts.

'There's a space down there, next to the crimson four-by-four,' she said, checking her watch. 'Visiting hours. We're lucky to find one. Let me out here, I'll get a ticket.'

Jogging across to an old coin-fed meter, Kay shovelled the last of her loose change into it and hurried back to the car as Barnes shrugged his jacket off and put it on the back seat.

'Ready?' he said.

'This *is* going to be just like Preston and Katrina, isn't

it?' She followed him across to the large glass doors of the hospital, keeping her voice low. 'Exactly the same.'

'Now, now,' said Barnes, wagging his finger at her while they climbed the two flights of stairs to the next floor. 'Lucas will say you're jumping to conclusions.'

'But I'm right, aren't I?'

He sighed. 'Probably. I think so, yes. Too much of a coincidence, isn't it?'

Kay slowed her step at the sound of voices coming through the door to the mortuary's reception area, spying a consultant speaking to Simon in hushed tones. She pulled Barnes to one side to wait beneath a poster warning of the consequences of anyone threatening the staff, her shoulders stiffening at the thought that such a message was even necessary.

'I'm worried we've had no progress on Katrina's murder, Ian. There's nothing in the witness statements or house-to-house enquiries, nothing in her social media... If she was killed because she owed money, then how the hell did she find out about the people she borrowed from? Kyle and Nadine went through all the legitimate lending companies earlier this week – none of them have any record of dealing with her.'

'Hopefully Amanda will find something, guv. After all, that database of hers focuses solely on the financial side of things whereas we just don't get that sort of information coming in on a regular basis.' His face turned glum. 'Not until it's too late and we're investigating a death, anyway.'

'Detectives?'

They turned at Simon's voice to see the morgue assistant beckoning to them.

'We're ready for you now if you'd like to get ready.'

Kay shot him a grateful smile as she signed in. 'How many more have you got today?'

'Yours is the last, thank goodness.' He gestured to the paperwork covering his desk. 'This takes as much time as the examination these days.'

'Then we won't keep you waiting long.'

'I have a feeling he's probably already made a start before you got here.' Simon grinned. 'He's got drinks and dinner at his golf club tonight, so I don't think he's planning on hanging around.'

She and Barnes went their separate ways to get changed into protective coveralls and, ten minutes later, walked into the examination room to see Lucas brandishing a saw once more, the shrill sound reverberating off the stainless steel surfaces.

Kay gritted her teeth, the door swinging shut behind her, and a groan emanating from her colleague.

'If I'd just stopped to re-tie my shoelaces…'

She said nothing but agreed with the sentiment. The almost ritual taking apart of a human body was something she would never get used to, despite her acceptance that the process yielded the answers she so desperately sought.

The saw fell silent after another couple of minutes, and Lucas looked over his shoulder, a kindly look in his eyes above the protective surgical mask he wore.

'Come on, you two, the worst part's over.'

'How is the golf coming along?' Barnes asked innocently as he wandered over to the table, edging towards the victim's feet rather than the splayed open abdomen or skull.

'Cheeky bugger. Simon, have you been spreading rumours again?'

'I may have suggested you have dinner plans tonight, hence the urgency with this one.'

'Good grief. The first early finish I have in nearly three months, and this is what I get.' Lucas tutted, turning away with the saw and returning with a wicked-looking scalpel. 'Right, shall we?'

'Is it the same MO as Katrina and Preston?' Kay blurted, then held up her hands. 'Sorry, I know you haven't finished, but…'

'Then I'll put you out of your misery. Yes, I believe it is.' The pathologist made a precise incision, and then stepped back. 'The only difference I've found so far is this contusion to the base of the skull – and you'll see that unlike the other two, a fatal puncture wound wasn't used to finish him off.'

'Was he alive when he went in the water?' Barnes said, unable to keep the surprise from his voice.

'Yes.' Simon looked up from another examination table off to the side where various organs had been laid out. 'Plenty of water in his lungs to suggest that was the case.'

Kay frowned. 'Well, that's different. I wonder if his killer was interrupted so they had to improvise?'

'It could be the case that your victim passed out from shock before the killer could carry out the final cut. If they were unable to revive him, then shoving him in the river – if the attack took place near it – would make sense.' Lucas placed his gloved hand on Alec's pale shoulder. 'The poor lad wouldn't have been able to do anything once he was in the water. If he came to under the surface of the water, his first instinct would've been to inhale.'

'Thereby drowning himself if he didn't have the strength to resurface or keep afloat,' said Barnes.

'We're going to have to make sure our search continues along the river walk further back from where he was found,' said Kay. 'Laura's spoken to some friends of his, and they've told us Alec had a flat near the river in Tovil.'

Her colleague pulled out his phone, ignoring the glare Lucas aimed his way. 'I'll get onto Debbie now and ask her to relay that to the teams at the crime scene before we lose any evidence. Hell of a risk dumping him there though, guv. I mean, it's not like his body was going to get washed out to sea, was it? Too many obstacles along the way, not to mention the lock at Allington.'

Kay's heart skipped a beat as she took in Alec's injuries. 'Unless of course his killers *wanted* him to be found.'

'Baiting us you mean, guv?'

'Not us.' She turned away from the examination table and peered up at the X-rays displayed on the light box beside Simon's laptop. 'What if they're using the news about his death to scare everyone else, just like they used that video of Katrina?'

THIRTY-FOUR

Kay rubbed at tired eyes, then attacked her keyboard once more, her fingers stabbing at the plastic letters with a renewed viciousness.

Commuter traffic pouring out of London had exacerbated her return to the police station in Maidstone, with Barnes swearing at every panel van that cut them up on the way back from Gravesend.

A weary group of uniformed officers huddled in one corner of the incident room, the hems of their trousers blotched with mud and bits of undergrowth from the search along the Medway, their efforts thwarted by the effects of the weather and time.

No wallet or phone had been found belonging to Alec Mingrove amongst the reeds and weeds lining the river path, any traces of blood had been washed away by Wednesday night's rainfall, and if it hadn't been for Edwin Moore's hunch that something had happened to his friend, they would be at a loss to identify his body.

Kay hit "send" on the last email for the day, and opened up an online map.

Zooming in to the area where Alec had been found, she worked her way upstream towards Tovil, switching to the satellite view in an attempt to work out where he had been attacked.

She glanced up as Laura walked past. 'How are they getting on with the search at Alec's flat?'

'We got the spare key from his mum half an hour ago, guv. Uniform report there's no sign of a struggle there, or anywhere in the building. They've bagged his laptop though.' Laura jerked her chin towards the map. 'And they're organising a search of the landscaped area between the apartment block and the river, just in case.'

'Thanks.' She turned back to her screen. 'I can't help feeling that whoever murdered him attacked him closer to the town centre though. I mean, we'll have to corroborate the river flow and everything, but there're just too many obstacles between that jetty by the car park and his flat. I don't think it's possible for him to have travelled that far downstream.'

Pushing back her chair, she cricked her neck and then leaned over to lock her screen. 'Come on, it's time for the briefing. Let's see what else we've got.'

The team quickly congregated around the desks nearest the whiteboard, the atmosphere muted.

'I know it's been a frustrating week since Katrina Hovat was found murdered,' Kay began. 'But you know as well as I do that sometimes we have a fight on our hands to catch a killer. That doesn't mean we give up.'

As one, the officers in front of her straightened, two biting back yawns and lowering their phones to listen.

'Laura, can you give us an update following your interview with Edwin and Lisa Moore?'

The younger detective moved to the side of the whiteboard and faced her colleagues. 'Okay, so both of them had an alibi in their babysitter, who confirmed the time they got home on Wednesday night. Their daughter, Hayley, is still off sick from school too. Ed told us that Alec said to them that his car was being fixed, so he took a bus into town to meet them that night. They had dinner with Ed's business partner, Angela Boxcombe, who left the restaurant before them after the meal. I spoke with her earlier this afternoon, and she was shocked to hear about Alec's murder, but also provided an alibi as her husband was at home when she arrived back just after ten o'clock.'

Kay watched while the rest of the team bowed their heads to their notebooks, the soft *tap tap* of Debbie's fingers flying over her laptop keyboard the only noise while Laura paused for a sip of water.

'After the meal, Ed, Lisa and Alec left together,' she continued. 'Ed had parked his car at the multi-storey next to the supermarket, but when their babysitter phoned to say their daughter was sick, it scotched any plans to give Alec a lift home. Lisa said later that normally he'd drive home anyway, or get a ride share when they'd been out together in the past. By then, it was raining and when Ed spotted a taxi going past, he flagged it down for Alec. That was the last time he saw him.'

Kay let her colleague's words sink in for a moment, keen to reiterate the need for her team to maintain their focus. After a moment, she thanked Laura and turned to Gavin.

'Did you manage to locate the garage that has Alec's car?'

'No, guv,' he said. 'But that's because there was nothing wrong with his car.'

'What do you mean?'

'He sold it three weeks ago.'

A shocked silence filled the room.

'I didn't have any luck phoning around the local garages so before wasting any more time, I thought I'd run a DVLA search,' Gavin explained. 'He sold it to a bloke in Sevenoaks. When I spoke to him, he reckoned he got it for a steal. He said Alec didn't put up much of a fight when it came to negotiating the price, and seemed to be glad to get rid of it.'

'He needed the money,' Kay murmured.

'There was hardly anything in his flat either, guv,' said Laura. 'Like Katrina, he'd been selling stuff off. In a hurry, too, by the look of it – uniform said there were still dust marks where the TV used to be. Maybe he realised the car sale wasn't enough to cover the debt.'

'I'd be in a hurry too, if I'd seen that video,' said Barnes.

Kay turned her attention back to Gavin. 'Where did the taxi drop off Alec?'

'It didn't. Ed remembered the name of the company on the side of it, so I gave them a call and they managed to trace the driver. When I spoke to him, he said he tried to persuade Alec to get in, but he wouldn't – it was absolutely pissing it down by then. His words, guv,' Gavin added with slight smile.

'So he walked home. What about CCTV footage along that stretch of road?'

'It's been requested, guv. I've been promised it by five so I was going to make a start tomorrow morning.'

'I'll give you a hand,' said Laura. 'There's fuck all on the telly anyway.'

Laughter broke the tension in the room, and Kay grinned. 'I'll be in from eight so if I can clear some of the paperwork, I'll help too.'

'Guv, I don't get it,' said Barnes once the laughter had subsided. 'Alec had known Ed since kindergarten. They obviously trusted one another – and he was about to land a new job that was going to turn his life around. So why was he lying to his friends?'

Kay tapped the end of the pen against her lips, staring at the whiteboard. Eventually, she turned to her colleague.

'Because he was scared, Ian,' she said. 'Because he was shit scared.'

THIRTY-FIVE

Sophie Anderley stumbled out of the doorway of the off licence and clutched her bag to her chest.

Eyes darting left and right, she scurried past the darkened doorways and alley entrances, the stench of stale urine and worse assaulting her senses.

A light wind caught her dark lank hair, and she scratched at a patch of inflamed skin behind her ear.

That set off a burning sensation across her scalp, the eczema crawling over her pale flesh.

She sniffed, blinking back tears.

All she wanted was a cheap bottle of wine. It had been ages since she had treated herself to anything, and tonight she needed something to help her sleep.

Especially after seeing the news about the man's body in the river.

That could've been me.

'All right, love? Fancy a shag?'

She stumbled, rearing away from the figure who

lurched through the open doors of a dirt-streaked pub, and snarled at him. 'Fuck off.'

Raucous laughter met her words, the man reeling as his arm snaked around an equally inebriated friend before both disappeared back inside.

Her hands trembled, guilt seeping into her veins, and she increased her pace, dodging between two women in their forties who looked askance at her before one of them laughed, the other muttering something under her breath.

She sniffed, her eyes stinging.

She shouldn't have spent the money, not really.

Not when she still owed them.

Sophie glanced down at her faded jeans and the black sweatshirt that had frayed cuffs and a hole in one of the sleeves, then swallowed.

It could be worse, she reminded herself, squaring her shoulders.

Thanks to her sister, who thought Sophie had been seven years late in leaving the husband who'd abused her for eight years, she had a roof over her head.

Now she just had to find a job.

It wasn't perfect, but she was determined to turn her life around.

'I'll show him,' she murmured. 'I'll show them all.'

Turning onto the Tonbridge Road, she waited at a pedestrian crossing while traffic swooshed past, her gaze drawn to the river and the swirling eddies that tumbled downstream.

It was flowing fast after the recent rain, and she shivered at the thought of entering its murky waters.

Tearing her eyes away at the sound of the *zap* from the

pedestrian crossing, she increased her pace as the road began to incline.

A kebab shop on the corner ahead of her was doing a brisk trade, its bright neon lights advertising pizza and chips and anything else a less discerning passer-by might need.

Sophie's stomach rumbled, and she turned away as she passed, holding her breath so as not to inhale the heady aroma of spices and fat cooking on the grills.

Her sister could barely afford to pay her own bills, let alone provide food for two, so Sophie had insisted she pay her own way.

If that meant skipping meals two or three times a week, so be it.

She frowned as she turned into the narrow winding street where her sister lived, trying to recall if there were any rice cakes left in the cupboard, and hoping the tub of hummus in the refrigerator wasn't mouldy yet.

That was the only problem with the cheaper shelves in the supermarket – you either risked the "use-by" date, or took your chances and got a bad case of food poisoning.

She clutched the bag closer to her chest. If her sister was in, she'd share it.

And then hand over all the money in her purse for the next two weeks' rent, because that was the rule she had set herself when she had moved in.

Charmaine had argued of course, rolling her eyes at her insistence that she wanted to retain a modicum of independence in the circumstances.

But now...

Sophie bit her lip.

If only she had taken the time to *think* before accepting that woman's offer. After all, it was a little strange, the way she had approached Sophie a few hundred metres from the women's refuge centre.

But she had been desperate, and the woman had been kind, and… and…

She growled under her breath.

'Something's got to give,' she muttered. 'I *will* find something next week. Anything.'

As the last of the sunlight faded, she tilted her head to take in the soft twilight hues that hugged the sky, and took a deep breath.

She was doing better than she was this time last year, at least.

And things would change for her, she was sure of it.

After all, everybody deserved a lucky break once in their lives, didn't they?

She didn't hear the car behind her as it sidled up against the kerb and kept pace with her a moment until she registered its movement out of the corner of her eye.

Leaping back, startled, she took in the shiny silver paintwork and the shadowed rear windows, then frowned as it braked and the back door opened.

A thick-set man in his forties glared through the windscreen, then jerked his head towards the rear of the car.

Sophie's feet dragged on the pavement as she moved, her heart dropping to her stomach when a familiar face peered out at her.

'Rosalind? What are you doing here?' Sophie glanced left and right, but all of the neighbours' curtains were closed, and no one else was walking along the street. 'My next payment isn't due until July.'

The woman smiled, exposing grave-like teeth that glimmered in the twilight. 'Change of plans, Soph. I'm sorry, but we're going to need the full amount plus interest next week.'

'You're joking.' Her jaw dropping, Sophie stared at Rosalind. 'You told me I had six months to pay you back.'

'Well, like I said – change of plans.' The woman contemplated a perfect set of fingernails, then looked up. 'It's just business, I'm sure you understand.'

Sophie bit her lip. 'I don't know if I can get it all to you next week. The end of the month, maybe. I could… I could find some cash work, perhaps, or…'

'Not good enough, I'm afraid. I told you at the start this might happen, and you assured me then that you'd comply if the debt had to be called in early. After all it's been, what…?'

The driver glanced over his shoulder. 'Four months.'

'Four months,' Rosalind agreed. 'Four months, and you've had ample time to find something to do with your time, surely?'

'It's difficult. I've got a resumé that's got hardly anything on it because my ex wouldn't let me work, and I can't get interviews for office roles. The supermarkets have more applications than they've got jobs for, and—'

Rosalind flapped her hand impatiently. 'I don't need to hear your excuses, Sophie. Like I said, four months. And here's you, buying yourself treats. What *were* you thinking?'

'I told you, I'll pay you back.'

'Promises, promises, Sophie, and yet here we are.' Rosalind's gaze fell to the bag. 'After all, if you can afford to treat yourself to a bottle of wine, you can afford to pay us back, right?'

A tear flopped over her cheek, and she wiped it away angrily. 'I keep my promises. Always have.'

'Good. You've got a week.'

'But that's impossible. I—'

'A week. I'll expect full payment by next Friday.' Rosalind narrowed her eyes. 'After all, you'll know what will happen to you if you don't.'

'Okay. I'll have to—'

Rosalind waved her hand as if deflecting a bad smell. 'I don't need to know *how*, only that you *will*.'

Sophie bit back a sob, then nodded. 'I promise.'

'Good.' Rosalind smiled. 'And remember – it's our little secret, right?'

THIRTY-SIX

The next morning, groggy with sleep, Kay padded downstairs and into the kitchen, her hand automatically finding the switch on the kettle.

Upstairs, the sound of the shower running carried over the noise from the hoglets in their enclosure as they tumbled over each other, snuffling around for food.

Placing her suit jacket over the back of one of the bar stools tucked under the central worktop, she reached up and opened one of the windows above the sink to freshen the air, the stink from the hoglets' urine putrid after the room had been closed up all night.

Bright sunshine streaked through the glass, the local blackbird chirruping from the neighbour's garden. A fine dew coated the lawn, and she realised they would have to mow it soon, or else Adam would suggest he bring home another goat.

'Over my dead body,' she murmured, smiling.

Yawning, she made coffee for two, and added a spoonful of sugar to Adam's.

Then her phone vibrated on the worktop with a new message, the reality of work intruding on her thoughts.

'No rest for the wicked,' said Adam, walking into the kitchen and towelling his hair. 'Which one's mine?'

'Red mug.'

'Ta.' He pointed it towards her. 'Is that Ian?'

'Yes. He's picking me up in half an hour.'

'Got time to help me feed the kids first?'

'Okay. Let me go and put on my face, and I'll be ready.'

He wrapped his arm around her as she went to walk past, and kissed her. 'There's nothing wrong with your face.'

'The others might not appreciate this vampire skin first thing in the morning.' She grinned. 'But, thanks.'

'Let them know you want all the outdoor jobs for the next month so you can work on your tan,' he called after her. 'You're spending too much time stuck in the office.'

'Tell me about it,' she muttered, taking the stairs two at a time.

Ten minutes later, ruing the dark circles under her eyes that only so much make-up could conceal, she walked back into the kitchen to find Adam kneeling on the floor beside the hoglets.

Before she could wander over, her phone trilled, and she widened her eyes at the caller's name displayed on the screen.

'Amanda? What are you doing working on a Saturday?'

'Would you believe me if I told you it's because I love

my job so much, I can't stay away?' replied the financial analyst wryly.

'No,' said Kay, laughing. 'Seriously, everything okay?'

'Everything's fine. It's just that we had a major breakthrough on one of the organised crime cases I'm seconded to late yesterday, and I wanted to brief you on what my team's found in relation to yours before Monday. After that, I'm afraid you're not going to get any more help from my team for at least six weeks. As it is, I've got a meeting with the Assistant Chief Constable later today. She didn't want to wait.'

Kay closed her eyes, biting back her frustration at the continued lack of resources that hampered every investigation. 'No problem. Do you want to email me what you've got? I'd love to chat, but I'm being picked up in about fifteen minutes and I've got a briefing first thing this morning.'

'Actually, I'm running some errands in Maidstone before I head over to Gravesend, so I was going to suggest I pop in. Say, about nine o'clock – will that work for you?'

'That'd be great, thanks. See you then.'

Ending the call, Kay dropped the phone into her bag and crossed to where Adam was cradling one of the hoglets, a plastic dropper in his hand.

'Okay, what do I need to do?' she said, crouching down beside him.

'The droppers are just there – I've already filled them with the feed formula, so pick up a hoglet and off you go. Just be gentle how much you give them though – we don't want them to choke.' Adam nodded to a separate blanket-filled box where two more hoglets were curled in the corner. 'Those two have already been fed, and there are three to go.'

'How many times did you get up in the night to do this?'

'Four.' He gave a tired smile. 'They'll be off the liquid soon though. This is just a boost while they're adjusting to solid food. Once they're onto solids full-time we can try to get them into one of the rescue centres until they're ready to go back into the wild. It's this bit when they're so young that's critical, and there just aren't enough volunteers around here to cope.'

Kay rubbed her thumb across the tiny hoglet's back as it sucked on the dropper's teat with enthusiasm. 'Well, thank goodness you could take them in. At least they're easier to look after than—'

A sudden jet of warm liquid gushed across her lap, and she froze in horror as the hoglet emitted a tiny fart, the stench already overwhelming her.

Kay looked down at the brown streaks that now criss-crossed her suit trousers, bile rising in her throat while Adam spluttered with laughter.

Then a car horn honked outside.

'Oh shit.' She closed her eyes. 'I'm never going to hear the end of this.'

THIRTY-SEVEN

'So, the hedgehog shat all over her then?'

Gavin handed Barnes a copy of the briefing agenda, the heightened noise in the room from the other team members carrying across to their desks.

'Yep.' Barnes grinned, gathering his dog-eared notebook and a pen. 'I reckon the dry cleaners will ban her from ever using them again once they're done with those trousers.'

A wedge of paperwork batted him between the shoulder blades, and he spun his chair around to see Kay glaring at him, her eyes sparkling despite her efforts to look cross.

'Next time, I'll make you take them in,' she said. 'Enough gossiping, you two. Come on.'

Gavin shot Barnes a sideways glance as she stomped away. 'Reckon she'll ever let Adam bring something home again?'

Barnes chuckled. 'You underestimate how much of a

softie she is, despite the steely exterior. You wait – next time he has something small and fluffy needing some TLC, she'll be the first to be helping out. Remember the kittens?'

After they found seats near the front of the assembled officers, he flipped through his notebook and cricked his neck.

Kay didn't waste time, and launched into the briefing the moment the last uniformed sergeant hurried over.

'Right, Gavin – what's happening with CCTV regarding Alec Mingrove's last movements?'

'It was sent over as promised late yesterday, guv,' replied the detective constable. 'I've made a start on it this morning – thankfully they provided the spliced footage for me so I don't have to do that. So far, I haven't seen anything that gives me cause for concern close to town so I'm wondering if he was snatched nearer home. I'll keep you updated on that though. If I run out of camera angles then I'll start house-to-house enquiries from the last location he was seen at.'

'Sounds good, thanks. Anything yet to suggest he might have walked along the river path?'

'Not yet.' Gavin grimaced. 'Hopefully he didn't, because there are very few cameras along there. By the way, did you see Edwin Moore was quoted in that online news article this morning?'

Kay's eyebrows shot upwards. 'No. What did he have to say for himself?'

'Thankfully he didn't elaborate on anything we spoke to him about, by the look of it. It's a bit short on content, to be honest.' Gavin pulled out his mobile phone and scrolled through the news app until he found the piece. 'Here you go. He says "I'd known Alec since we were at school together. I can't believe he's gone. Not like this. He had everything to live for – he was starting a new job next week. He was my best mate, I don't know what we'll do without him." The article ends with the phone number our media team provided in case anyone's got any further information.'

Barnes turned in his seat as the door to the incident room opened, and Amanda Miller walked in, a determined expression on her face.

Kay greeted her with a warm smile, then introduced her to the team. 'Some of you will have worked with Amanda a few years ago, but for those who haven't, Amanda leads our forensic accounting investigation team over at Headquarters. Her team's been taking a look at each of the first three victims' finances – including Angus Zilchrist's – to see if there's a connection between them, and to try to find out where that connection leads.'

'Thanks.' Amanda opened her briefcase and handed a series of folders to her. 'This will all be emailed across and added to HOLMES2 later this morning, but I thought you might like hard copies too.'

Turning to a fresh page in his notebook, Barnes realised he was holding his breath as he waited for Amanda to continue. The woman had been integral to the success of the previous investigation they'd worked on together, so surely she would help provide the breakthrough they so desperately needed now?

'I'll skim the boring bits – you can read those in your own time,' said Amanda with a grin before facing the whiteboard and sketching a diagram of her findings while she spoke. 'The introduction to the report for each victim just sets out the parameters for our searches as discussed with Detective Hunter earlier this week, and then you've got a couple of pages about how we went about conducting those searches. I'm sure you all just want to hear about the results though.'

A smattering of agreement flittered amongst the officers before the forensic accountant continued.

'The first part of our investigation was to ascertain which of the legitimate lenders the three victims had accounts with, and then tot up the overall debt exposure. That includes for some of the newer types of lenders, mostly associated with online shopping, home equity dealers, that sort of thing. Happily I can confirm none of those appear to be guilty of anything except perhaps some shady practices in relation to background checks on existing debt before encouraging people to take out a loan with them. We've passed on the details of two of those to the financial ombudsman.'

She paused, and gave Laura a grateful smile as the detective constable passed her a glass of water. 'Thanks. Okay, so once we'd exhausted all the legitimate lenders, we were left with an anomaly that appeared on each of the victims' profiles we'd created. Every one of them, without exception, had paid in large sums of cash between last July and January – but they'd split the payment between several accounts, such as credit cards, home lenders, etc so it didn't raise a flag. Most banks these days limit cash deposits to one thousand pounds at any one time in accordance with anti-money laundering regulations.'

'Someone told them to do that,' Amanda said, turning to Kay. 'Whoever loaned them the money told them not to draw attention to themselves. I wouldn't normally stick my neck out and say that, but the pattern's too obvious between the three victims to ignore it. Like I said, the payments are split between regular accounts, but they all land on the same day in each instance. They start off with a larger amount, say four to five thousand pounds, then there are one or two smaller amounts after that – no more than nine hundred pounds. Some of those smaller cash amounts weren't necessarily paid into any accounts but we could see from our analysis that maybe a couple of times a month, each victim used their debit card less, suggesting—'

'They had spare cash to spend on necessities instead,' Barnes said.

'Yes.'

He crossed his arms and looked at the arrows criss-crossing the whiteboard between the four victims' photographs. 'Someone knew these people were desperate. Someone who was able to lend a few thousand pounds at a time…'

'And we can't find out how because they were paid the loans in cash.' Kay pinched the bridge of her nose and closed her eyes for a moment. 'We're buggered, aren't we?'

'We tried a few different angles to see if we could find anything else, but I'm afraid that's the crux of it,' said

Amanda. 'I'm sorry – I realise it's not the outcome you were hoping for.'

'Thanks anyway.' Kay sighed. 'I realise how much effort it took to pull all this together in the time we have.'

'Like I said, I'll email everything over to you later this morning,' Amanda said, collecting her things and turning for the door. 'And call me if you have any other questions.'

A stunned silence hung over the team after the door closed behind her, and Barnes caught Kay's anxious look as she scanned the haphazard notes now covering the whiteboard.

'What are you thinking, guv?'

'Whoever's doing this is escalating, aren't they?' she said. 'Preston's body was hidden so that Angus would find it, and yet both Katrina and Alec – working on the basis that we'll find the same sort of cash loans amongst his financial statements when we get them – were displayed publicly. It's as if whoever killed them wanted to advertise the fact rather than target just one person.'

'It's ballsy,' said Barnes. 'They seem to be incredibly confident that they're not going to get caught.'

'Are they, though?' Kay paced the carpet. 'Or is it a sign of desperation? I mean, we haven't had anything like this before, have we?'

'We haven't had the same method of killing, I mean with the torture with the cuts,' said Gavin. 'Not since I've been here.'

'Did anything come up on the records?'

'Nothing, guv. That was one of the first tasks I ran through HOLMES2 when Katrina was found.'

'What worries me is why those debts are being called in now.' Kay rapped her knuckles against the board then turned back to face her team. 'What's changed in the past three months that means whoever loaned this money needs it back in such a hurry that they're willing to kill some of their clients to make the others pay?'

THIRTY-EIGHT

Gavin cracked the ring pull on the can of energy drink, the soft *pop* and fizz of air wafting a sweet aroma across his keyboard.

Laura wrinkled her nose as he gulped. 'God, you can smell the sugar in that from here. Why don't you just drink coffee like a normal person?'

'I do. Sometimes it's not enough.'

'Your teeth will rot.'

'So my mother tells me.' He put down the can and grinned. 'And you sound just like her.'

His colleague slapped his arm, then pointed at the three computer screens in front of them. 'Ready to start again?'

'Go for it.'

Resting his chin in his hand, Gavin's gaze flicked from one screen to the other, a casual sweep of the images that went some way to keep him alert and his mind open to any anomalies that might appear.

He knew Laura was doing the same, the pair of them having already spent two hours of their morning in the observation suite watching the camera footage from Brian Melgren's garage forecourt.

It was quieter in here, now that the previous night's cell inmates had been processed and moved on.

A door slammed somewhere farther along the corridor, and a sardonic smile formed on his lips as heavy footsteps passed the room.

It was quieter than the bedlam of the incident room upstairs, at any rate.

Laura yawned. 'Wish we were looking at the town footage instead. That bloke at the garage could've filtered these recordings, couldn't he?'

'I guess we should just be grateful he kept it all in the first place.' He checked his watch, then his eyes found the screen once more. 'But at least we've got the visitor logs from the storage place to narrow this down. We'd be here until next weekend otherwise.'

'True.' She sighed as the recording stalled. 'Okay, onto the next file. This one's from the Easter weekend.'

'Seems like a lifetime ago,' Gavin grumbled. 'And it was warmer than it is now.'

'Tan fading, is it?'

'Very funny.' He leaned closer. 'Melgren didn't open that Saturday. He said he and his wife managed to get a last-minute break in Copenhagen at half price through to the following Wednesday. You can speed up the footage, too – Angus didn't sign in that day until one thirty.'

They sat in silence for a moment, watching a steady stream of visitors to the storage units in vehicles of different shapes and sizes.

'Looks like everyone had the same idea about having a spring clean that weekend,' Gavin murmured.

'Angus didn't seem to stop too long on his other visits, did he?' Laura glanced at her notes. 'And that one we just saw was back in February. Do you think it's unusual how long he left it until this next visit?'

'Not really. I mean, if he was a bit of a hoarder anyway, he probably just stuck stuff in there and forgot about it. It's not like he was going back to check on it, from what this logbook suggests.'

'How many more visits after this one?'

Gavin glanced down, then froze. 'Just the one, the day before he died.'

'Hang on, look.' Laura paused the recording. 'That's Angus, isn't it?'

On the screen, a battered-looking dark-coloured removals van had pulled up to the entrance to the storage business, and as it crawled to a standstill, the man in the driver's seat looked across at the garage.

'He doesn't look happy,' said Gavin.

'Why isn't he driving his car? Whose van is this?' Laura restarted the recording at its normal speed and they watched as the van crawled forward until it no longer blocked the entrance, and then the driver got out.

'I can't see the licence plates at this angle, but there might be access to other CCTV cameras along the road. I'll have to check.'

'Who's that with him, Gav?'

'I don't know, but he's built like a brick shithouse, isn't he?'

He eyed the stocky man who stood at the rear of the

van talking with Angus, the man's biceps bulging from a cut-off T-shirt, his shaven head glistening under the bright sunlight as if he was sweating.

Another car crawled up to the entrance, then turned into the storage yard and disappeared from sight. The man jerked his thumb over his shoulder and Angus scurried through the gates, returning five minutes later with a pallet trolley.

Gavin swallowed, his heart thudding. Despite the energy drink, his mouth was dry, and he held his breath.

On the screen, Angus trundled the trolley over to the van's rear doors.

The other man flung them open and climbed inside, the van rocked on its suspension for a moment and then a large object came into view.

'That's the wardrobe, the one Preston was found in,' Laura blurted.

The two men shuffled the wardrobe onto the tail lift, and then Angus hit a button on the back of the van to lower it.

After another two minutes of shuffling and angry gestures from the other man, the two men wobbled the wardrobe through the entrance gates to the storage yard.

'Why not drive the van into the yard first?' said Laura. 'It would've saved them some effort.'

'There are cameras there, remember.' Gavin nodded at the van on the screen. 'Whoever that is driving the van knew that, but didn't know that the files aren't kept for any length of time. He didn't want the licence plates to be seen.'

'I can't see any rental company logos on it anywhere, can you?'

'No, so either it's the driver's vehicle – or they borrowed it.'

Fifteen minutes later, the two men returned, got into the van and drove away.

'Preston was already in that wardrobe, wasn't he?' Laura stopped the recording and spun her chair around to face him. 'You could see they were struggling with the weight of it, and it was only a cheap piece of furniture.'

'I think so, yes.' Gavin leaned back and stared at the blank screen.

'But Harriet's report said the weight of his body pinged open the wardrobe doors once that box was moved out of the way. There was nothing wrong with the doors when they moved it just now, was there?'

'I think Preston's weight must've shifted when they put the wardrobe in the unit and then boxed it in.' He sighed, and tossed his pen onto the desk. 'But did Angus know Preston was inside? Or was he just doing the other bloke a favour?'

'Some favour, Gav.'

THIRTY-NINE

Kay flicked through the printed-out stills from the garage CCTV footage, and chewed her lip.

Gavin and Laura stood patiently beside her while her mind worked, their faces drawn from staring at the computer screens for so long.

'Did Angus's kids have any idea who this is?' she said eventually, pinning the photos to a second whiteboard that had joined the first at the front of the room.

'We went over to Richard's earlier to show him those, but he didn't recognise him,' said Gavin. 'Same goes for Alana. They also had no idea whose van that might be.'

'What about CCTV from other angles along that stretch of road?'

'It's been requested, guv, but given it's a weekend...'

'We'll be lucky to see it before the middle of the week.' Kay sighed. 'At least we've got another lead to work on. What else are you planning on doing?'

'I was going to give Ian a hand with some security recordings that came in from one of the other retailers next to where Katrina worked,' said Gavin, scrubbing his fingers across his spiky hair. 'They had to get permission from their head office in Newcastle before releasing it to us.'

'I'll have Kyle help him with that – you need to get some rest so after we're done here, I don't want to see you until Monday. That goes for you too, Laura.'

'Will do, guv, thanks,' said Laura. 'I thought I'd ask some of the uniformed lot to go through Alec Mingrove's bank statements this afternoon to see if they can spot a pattern like the one Amanda identified.'

'Good plan. Before you go home, can you draft a statement to go out to local charities that deal with gambling addiction, food banks, that sort of thing, warning them that we believe we've got a new organised crime outfit targeting vulnerable people?' Kay crossed to her desk, the two detectives in her wake. 'Be careful how you word it – I don't want them to link it to our investigation but we have to make sure we're being proactive. The last thing we want is more people falling victim to whoever's behind these murders.'

Laura nodded. 'I'll do that, then email it to you once it's done.'

'Thanks. Right, I'll catch you both on Monday.'

Kay turned back to her desk, which was currently hidden under a pile of meeting minutes from Headquarters, four new budgetary reports that required her review and signature, and a pile of crumbs from a half-eaten apple Danish pastry.

She bit back a groan.

All she wanted to do was focus on hunting down and

apprehending a killer, but it seemed her superiors had other ideas for her weekend.

Picking up the pastry, she shoved it between her lips then picked up her tepid mug of coffee and her notebook and headed back to the whiteboard.

The coffee and notebook were placed on a desk beside it while she nibbled at what would have to constitute her lunch, her gaze taking in the notes and photographs that had been collated.

'Who the hell are you?' she murmured between mouthfuls, eyeing the bald man in the photograph. 'And how did you know Angus?'

'Talking to yourself again, guv?'

She glanced over her shoulder at Barnes's voice. 'It helps. Have you ever seen this bloke before?'

Her colleague peered up at the board. 'Nope. Can't say I have. Is he a new person of interest?'

'Yes. Gavin and Laura spotted him outside the storage place over the Easter weekend helping Angus with that wardrobe. I've seen the footage, too – given the way they were struggling with it, we're assuming at the moment that Preston's body was already inside.'

Barnes whistled under his breath. 'So did Angus know…?'

'Or was he set up?' Kay dusted off her fingers and reached for the coffee. 'According to the records from the storage unit, the next time Angus went there was the day before he died.'

'But Harriet's report confirmed that the body hadn't been disturbed since being placed in the wardrobe. Angus couldn't have opened the door, found out what was inside and then closed it again. We'd have been able to tell.'

'Maybe he was told about the body, went there to see for himself, but changed his mind when he got there.'

'Or he knew, and agreed to hide it.'

'There's that, too.' Kay drained the last of her drink and picked up her notebook, flicking through the pages. 'Have we got anything yet to suggest whether Angus knew Preston – or Katrina for that matter?'

'Not yet. I can have another word with Richard Zilchrist if you want?'

'Gavin already spoke with him earlier to see if he knew our mystery man. He doesn't.'

Barnes nodded at the photograph. 'Angus wasn't that active on social media, but he might've belonged to some sort of social club, or drank regularly at a particular pub, something like that. We've already exhausted the betting shop he frequented in town, and they've told us Angus always went in on his own. Richard said when we first spoke to him that his dad had stopped drinking at his regular hangout, which the landlord corroborated, but he must've gone other places before he started to run out of money, right? He and Preston might've crossed paths somewhere.'

'It's worth a shot.' She gave the whiteboard a final sweeping gaze. 'I'll have uniform start on that while you're working through the new camera footage.'

FORTY

'This desk wasn't designed for two of us.'

Kyle grinned at the senior detective beside him. 'It's cosy, I'll give you that, Sarge.'

He turned back to the bank of screens, eyes flitting between each one while Barnes slurped a mug of tea and picked at the remains of a chicken salad.

On the monitors, a grainy image of Katrina Hovat walked into view and headed towards the retail shop where she had once worked.

She looked diminutive, bundled up in a chunky cardigan that she hugged around herself, her head lowered while she spoke on her mobile phone.

She stopped before she reached the double glass doors, ignoring the fact that they opened automatically in expectation, and instead turned her back on the store and seemed to be arguing with someone.

'Have we got the records for that call from her mobile provider, Sarge?' Kyle asked.

On the screen, Katrina paced back and forth, her hand

remonstrating with whoever was on the other end of the phone.

'Hang on.' Barnes put down the can and then flicked through a list of numbers. 'Yes, here. One of the banks by the look of it – it's for their debt collection team based in Leeds.'

Kyle blew out his cheeks. 'Hard to think she was dead a day after this. She didn't stand a chance against them, did she? I mean, there's nothing to her.'

'Not if that bloke who was driving the van with Angus was involved, no.'

The two men fell silent as Katrina finished her call, paused for a moment as if to collect her thoughts, then strode into the retail shop.

Reaching out to fast forward the recording, Kyle watched as a steady stream of customers passed in and out through the front doors, some appearing moments later with carry bags laden with bargains, others struggling with some of the larger items before wrestling them into the back of their cars.

He shuffled in his seat, risking a sideways glance at the man beside him.

Barnes had always been someone he had looked up to, ever since he had started his career with Kent Police and it wasn't as if the man held back with his opinions, so…

'Sarge? Can I ask you something?'

The detective sergeant's eyes remained on the screen. 'Sure.'

'Do you think I should apply to take the detective exam?'

Barnes turned to him and raised an eyebrow. 'Maybe. What's brought this on?'

'Philip and I were talking about it before he was killed – we were both going to sign up. I've been thinking…' He broke off, looking at his hands. 'I think I need to have something to focus on like that. Something to get my teeth into, you know?'

The older detective smiled, his attention now back on the recording. 'Then I think it'd be a great idea. To be honest, I'm not surprised you want to do it. You've come a long way since you were a probationer, and I know Kay speaks highly of you.'

'Thanks, Sarge.' Heat rose to Kyle's cheeks, and then he gave a slight nod. 'All right. I'll put my application in next week. Then—'

'Here she is.' Barnes sat up straighter. 'Must be on a break or something.'

'I took a look at the statements from the shop. Her manager – or supervisor, I can't remember – said in the last weeks of her life she was making more phone calls than usual,' Kyle replied. 'Look at the time stamp. It's only nine forty-five.'

'She's back on the phone again, look.'

They watched as Katrina huddled against the side of the building, tucked away behind a display of large garden pots, the phone to her ear.

'It's another credit card company she's calling,' said Barnes, jabbing his finger at the phone records.

Then, just over a minute later, a woman in a matching uniform shirt marched out of the store and beckoned to her, her manner impatient.

'That's one of the supervisors,' Barnes murmured. 'I recognise her from when we spoke to Katrina's manager.'

Katrina trudged in after the other woman, the doors sliding closed behind them.

They spent the next half hour stopping the recording, noting the times that Katrina reappeared. The last of the outside displays were hauled in by two other workers as Katrina left work for the day.

'Okay. That's that, then.' Hearing the disappointment in his own voice, Kyle reached out to stop the recording.

'Wait.'

He froze as Barnes pointed at the screen.

A woman, taller than Katrina due to the heels she was wearing, had approached her and was now gesturing at her aggressively.

'Who's that?' The detective sergeant took the mouse from him and enlarged the app window. 'I don't recognise her, do you?'

'Whoever she is, she's not happy about something.'

'Is she a customer do you think?' Barnes slipped on his reading glasses, trying to angle his head to get a better look.

Kyle went through his notes, then shook his head. 'I don't recall seeing anyone dressed like that walking into the shop today.'

Tucking his glasses back into his pocket, Barnes folded his arms and leaned back in his chair as the woman finished speaking and stalked away. 'Start it again. Look at the way Katrina's just standing there.'

'She looks shocked.'

'No, she looks terrified.'

––––––––

'What do you think?'

The noise in the incident room had reduced to a low murmur of voices while Kyle held the phone to his ear and turned a soft felt football between his fingers, tossing it up in the air while he waited.

A deepening sunset was bathing the carpet next to his feet, the noise from the traffic outside changing as shoppers and tourists left town for the day and the streets grew quieter in the time before all the pubs and nightclubs would get rowdy.

He bit back a rueful smile as he recalled his early days patrolling those same streets, dealing with the aftermath.

A polite cough on the other end of the phone interrupted his thoughts.

'Umm, I don't think it's going to be possible, not with the angle or quality of this recording,' said Andy Grey. 'There's no way we're going to be able to improve on what you've got here, not without the picture pixelating completely. Certainly not in a way that you're going to be able to get someone to lip-read what they're saying, in any event.'

'Fuck it.' Kyle threw the ball onto his desk, where it bounced off the keyboard and hit a pen tidy beside his computer. 'I thought we might've had something then.'

'Sorry I can't help.'

'No, that's all right. Sorry to interrupt your weekend.' Kyle replaced the receiver and quickly scrolled through the new emails that had appeared.

'What did he say?' Barnes wandered over, two small pizza boxes in his hand. 'Here you go.'

'Thanks, Sarge.' Popping open the lid, he lifted out a slice and sank his teeth into it, the warm cheese and pepperoni sending his taste buds into overdrive. 'He says it can't be done.'

'Bugger.'

'Yeah, I said something like that.'

They ate in silence for a while, each of them lost in thought.

''Night, Sarge.'

Barnes nodded to a passing uniformed constable, then turned his attention back to his pizza. 'There aren't any more outstanding files covering that car park, are there?'

'No. That lot from the other shop were the only ones we were waiting for.' Kyle suppressed a belch, and took the last slice, biting back a yawn. 'And I cross-referenced the other files while you were out getting these – I can see them both in one other shot from that furniture place next door, but when they finish speaking, that woman walks around the side of that block of units and isn't seen again.'

Barnes closed the lid of his pizza box and stood it next to the rubbish bin by the desk, the fatty aroma still clinging to the air. 'So she must've driven away, but out a different way from the main exit.'

'I thought that too. But there aren't any camera angles.' Kyle swallowed the last of his pizza and wiped his fingers on a paper napkin. 'So we're screwed.'

He looked up as the incident room door swung open and Kay strode in, a cloud crossing her face.

'Guv,' said Barnes. 'Everything all right?'

'Uniform spoke with Richard Zilchrist,' she replied. 'He suggested Angus might have occasionally socialised with members of his old golf club, but that turned up nothing. When the team went over there, it transpires Angus cancelled his membership weeks ago and hasn't been seen since. They even checked the visitor logs. Nothing.'

She leaned against the spare desk beside Barnes and then stared at Kyle's screen. 'Who's that?'

He waited while Barnes updated her, and watched as a flicker of interest turned to increasing alarm.

'Did anyone at the shop where Katrina worked recognise her?' she said.

'We've spoken to the manager there, and the supervisors,' said Barnes. 'They all say they don't.'

'And to be honest, the way she's dressed… she doesn't look like a customer,' Kyle added.

'What about Katrina's social media? Anything there?'

'Nothing that we could see in her friends or followers, no.'

'Can you print that out and put it on the board ready for Monday's briefing?' said Kay. 'There won't be one tomorrow because there's hardly anyone available on the roster.'

'Will do, guv,' said Barnes.

'We could go through all of our victims' social media profiles again tomorrow,' said Kyle, seeing the frustration in the detective inspector's face. 'Even if she isn't listed as a friend or follower, she might appear in a photo with one of them.'

'Good thinking. Do that.' Kay pointed at the screen. 'When was this taken?'

'The Friday afternoon she was killed,' said Barnes. 'According to our timeline, Katrina went from here straight to the Brassicks' house.'

'Well, whoever she is, we need to find her, and fast. She's possibly the last person to see Katrina alive.'

FORTY-ONE

The first tendrils of heat were rising off the asphalt car park as Kay paused beside a wooden bench and re-laced her training shoes.

Behind her, over by the small café that serviced visitors to Mote Park, an older man on a motorised sweeper cut back and forth, his brow etched in concentration while his head bobbed to whatever music he was listening to under the council-issued ear defenders.

A squirrel shot out from the base of a hawthorn bush at his approach, scampered across the dirt fringes of the parking area, then bolted up a convenient oak tree before disappearing from sight.

Beyond the car park, the lazy stirrings of a town waking to a bright Sunday morning began to reach Kay, the occasional swoosh of traffic along the A20 carrying across to where she stood.

After stretching her hamstrings and swinging her arms to loosen up the muscles, she raised her hand in greeting to the council worker, double-checked she'd locked the car, then set off at a comfortable jog.

Usually, she would have run here from the house but in the circumstances she planned to go straight to the incident room via the showers at the police station and try to work her way through all the reports she was expected to send to Headquarters tomorrow.

There was simply too much to do, too many loose threads amongst the murder investigation.

Kay exhaled as a gentle slope led her across open grassland towards the lake on the northern edge of the park.

Following the left fork, she felt the incline flatten out, and then picked up her pace.

To her right, the lake stretched out the length of the park, its waters replenished by the River Len as it worked its way through the county towards the larger Medway.

Ducks paddled happily towards her, then turned their backs as they realised she had no food while a pair of swans dipped their long necks and foraged under the water.

'Morning.'

She nodded in reply to the passing pair of male runners, unwilling to break her stride now that she had settled into a comfortable pace. Their voices disappeared into the distance as they continued their conversation, while Kay elongated her steps and followed the path around to the right.

A jumbled collection of pedal boats with prows in the shape of swans were moored to a concrete pier, bobbing on a gentle breeze that carried across the water and feathered her bare arms before she passed a quiet cove where an old Labrador paddled happily while its owners looked on.

The path began to rise again now, the circular route giving way to open space as she emerged from under a willow tree canopy and back to the parkland overlooking the lake. Seeking out a route that took her along the eastern edge and farther away from the town centre, she wiped sweat from her brow and tried her best to ignore the aches that were beginning to pinch at her calves.

She could feel it now, the tension starting to ease in her shoulders, her heart rate pulsing with every metre she ran, and her mind turned back to the investigation.

If she wasn't careful, her superiors at Gravesend would soon begin scrutinising her actions to date, wondering why there hadn't been a breakthrough despite hobbling her with inadequate staffing to achieve one.

It was a balancing act, all of it.

Especially when her team were already overworked.

She recalled their dogged determination, their desperation to find whoever was fuelled with such a rage to tear apart so many human lives.

Not just the lives of their victims, but those who remained as well.

Kay began to pump her arms as she turned a gentle curve and powered past the domed stone temple that overlooked the grassy expanse, heading back towards the car park.

Her nails dug into her palms.

Was she guilty of expecting too much from her team, perhaps?

Had all the demands from Headquarters relating to

budgets, rosters and the next six months' worth of personnel changes clouded her judgement?

Because they had missed something, somewhere, she was sure of it.

Two people were now connected to the murder enquiry, and yet they knew nothing about them.

Starting with the woman who was seen berating Katrina outside her place of work, and then the man who helped Angus move the wardrobe into the storage unit.

Kay reached her car, panting while she unlocked it and reached inside for a stainless steel water bottle in the middle console. Gulping a quarter of it, she leaned against the door while her heart rate returned to normal and gazed back across the trees that dotted the park, her mind wandering.

Her thoughts froze as she watched the café manager unloading four boxes from the back of a hatchback car, the woman huffing under the effort. The boxes were stamped with the supplier's logo and courier labels were stuck all over the outside, the brown packing tape glistening as it caught the light while she worked.

After taking another sip of water, Kay put the bottle down and then leaned over and rested her hands on her knees.

She breathed deeply while the oxygen gradually worked its way through her tired body, and a smile began to form.

Perhaps the paperwork could wait.

Perhaps she would spend today being a detective, not a manager.

FORTY-TWO

'Thanks for picking me up.'

Kay swung her bag into the footwell of the pool car and strapped herself in as Barnes pulled out into the lane once more.

'No problem. Good to have an excuse to get outside when it's like this.' Barnes poked his sunglasses back up his nose and turned onto the main road. 'Where do you want to go?'

'The storage place. I phoned ahead – Will Clyborne's working today and I want a word with him.' Kay flicked through her notes, reading the hurried scrawl she had made before showering after her run. 'I want to see if he knows the bloke Gavin and Laura saw helping Angus with the wardrobe.'

'They're due back in tomorrow, guv.'

'I know.' Kay bumped her fist on the door sill while they waited for the traffic lights on the A20 to turn green. 'But it can't wait.'

He frowned. 'Are the vultures circling?'

'Not yet,' she said, unable to suppress a smile at his reference to their superiors at Headquarters. 'Sharp will hold them off for a bit longer – he hasn't forgotten what it's like yet. But they'll come, Ian. They'll come.'

'And you don't want them taking over.'

'No, I don't. I owe it to Katrina, to all of them, to find out who the hell's responsible for their deaths. And then I'm going to make sure they're put away for a very long time.'

'We're doing our best, guv.'

'I know you all are.' She exhaled as the lights turned and he accelerated away. 'But I feel like I've been swamped with being a boss, not a detective lately.'

He grinned. 'Ah, so that's what today's all about. You're just jealous of the rest of us.'

'Dammit, is it that obvious?'

———

'Did Gavin and Laura see that bloke on any other footage?' said Barnes as they walked towards the pokey little office that served the storage company.

'Not from the recordings we were given, no.' Kay squinted against the bright sunshine that dappled the concrete hardstanding. 'But I was wondering whether he might recognise the van, or if we show him a photo of the man they saw…'

She paused as he raised an eyebrow. 'I know, it's a long shot.'

'Nothing ventured, guv.' He pushed open the door and stood to one side to let her enter the office first.

Will Clyborne peered around a customer at the desk and gave a slight nod. 'Be with you in a moment.'

Kay turned away and faced the window, her gaze wandering over the line of units stretching away as far as she could see.

Until a few years ago, the site had been left derelict after an old manufacturing company had ceased trading, the area separated from the road by a dilapidated barbed wire fence that only succeeded in keeping nothing out and serving as an eyesore.

She had been as surprised as many other local residents when the nationwide storage company had bought the site, demolished the decaying warehousing and planted a series of stacked shipping containers in their place.

Given the number of cars that were passing through the entrance gates today though, trade was doing well.

The door to the office slammed shut on its automatic closer and she glanced over her shoulder at Will.

'Busy?'

He rolled his eyes and moved from the counter. 'I wish. That was another tyre-kicker. I've had more of those than real customers since that bloke's body was found.'

'It happens, unfortunately,' said Barnes. 'They'll lose interest eventually.'

'What about your usual customers?' Kay asked. 'Have you lost many?'

'No, but that's probably only because most of them can't be arsed to find somewhere else and then move all their crap.' Will grinned. 'Anyway, what did you want today?'

Barnes pulled out a still from the security footage that

showed the large bald man next to Angus Zilchrist. 'Do you recognise this man on the left?'

'Nope. That's the one who rented the unit who's standing with him though, isn't it? I recognise him from another photo one of your lot showed me last week.' His eyes widened. 'Holy shit – is that the wardrobe that dead bloke was found in?'

'We believe so, yes,' said Kay. 'Which is why we're keen to speak to him.'

'I'll bet you are.'

'This photo was taken in April. Can you confirm who was working in here the same day?'

'Sure. Come over here while I check the system.'

Kay waited patiently while he scrolled through the company's schedules, only to be rewarded with a perplexed frown.

'Looks like it was just me that day,' said Will. 'Beth, who sometimes helps me out, was on holiday that week. And I do remember I had two customers clearing out units so it was bloody busy. That's probably why I don't remember seeing them move that wardrobe. It explains why they were parked out on the road too, because there were at least four removal trucks parked in here at one point. I remember that much. Bedlam, it was.'

'And you're absolutely sure you haven't got any cameras along the street that you've got access to?'

'We don't, no – that corrugated fence stops anyone getting inside, especially with the razor wire along the top. Only myself and the two other full-timers have the code to the gate.'

Kay swallowed her disappointment as Barnes shoved

the photograph back into his pocket and managed a small smile.

'Thanks for your time.'

'Fuck it,' Barnes murmured under his breath once they were outside. 'And I got Dave Morrison to double check – there's definitely no CCTV facing the street at any different angles so we can't get a clear look at that van's licence plate.'

Walking through the open gate, Kay paused on the pavement as a steady stream of traffic went past. 'And it wasn't picked up on any cameras on the main roads out of here?'

'No, so that means they probably cut through the side streets.' Barnes grimaced. 'Mind you, two cameras were broken and waiting for a maintenance crew that week, so…'

'Christ.' Kay bit her lip. 'All right. There's one more place I'd like to go today but while I'm driving, can you phone the incident room and have a team head out to Angus's old drinking hole and the golf club to see if anyone recognises this bloke?'

'Uniform could do that tomorrow, guv.'

'We can't wait that long, Ian. I'm worried we might find ourselves with another victim by then.'

FORTY-THREE

Kay rolled up her sleeves and wandered across the retail car park, her jaw set.

The rattle of metal shopping trolleys across asphalt filled the air, the occasional wail from a bored toddler mixing with the stressed voices of parents trying to usher older children out of pet supply stores before they managed to fall prey to pleas for a rabbit or guinea pig.

A young couple bickered outside the bedding store, the woman trying her best to balance three white fluffy cushions in her arms while a bulging carry bag swung from one of her wrists as she hurried after her exasperated boyfriend.

Pausing underneath the overhang from the bedding store, Kay turned until she faced the staff car park and looked up.

The camera that had caught Katrina Hovat arguing with the mystery woman was positioned above her, its lens catching the mid-afternoon sunlight.

A spider web covered in ages-old leaf litter clung to the

bracket mounted on the back of it, and Kay curled her lip at the sight of the grubby lens.

'Is the footage from this one, Ian?'

'Yes.' He pointed farther along the block of units. 'The other two are under the eaves along there, see?'

'So this is where that woman disappeared to after speaking with Katrina…' Kay wandered around the corner, casting her gaze over a shallow line of industrial-sized recycling bins. 'How often are these emptied?'

'Weekly. Uniform managed to go through the last lot before the contractors got here.' He kicked at a loose stone and glared as it tumbled away. 'They didn't find anything.'

She looked up. 'What about this one over the service door?'

'The angle was wrong – I took a look myself. Whoever she is, she kept her head turned so the camera didn't catch her features properly.'

Kay continued past the bins, eyeing the overflowing cardboard and plastic packaging that had been stripped from various items of stock, then turned her attention to a low hedge border of hornbeam and jasmine.

A gap had been hacked through the middle of the hedge to a pavement that bordered a service road, and she paused for a moment, eyeing the different entrances to other businesses.

There were no CCTV cameras in sight.

'Bugger.'

Barnes swore under his breath as he pushed past the straggly plants, freeing his trouser leg from a persistent thorn, and then joined her.

'She could've gone anywhere from here,' said Kay,

jerking her chin towards the end of the road. 'That road heads into town or out to the M20 the other way, and we don't even know what she was driving.'

'If she drove.'

Kay shook her head. 'I can't imagine her walking, can you? She didn't seem like the sort of person who'd walk here. Not in the heels she was wearing in that footage, anyway.'

'I'll work with uniform first thing in the morning to find out if any staff members in the shops along here recognise her.' Barnes attempted a hopeful look, and failed. 'We'll give it a go, anyway.'

A crawling sensation of frustration crept over Kay at the realisation that despite her best intentions, she was facing the same problems as her team. Whoever had accosted Katrina had disappeared without a trace.

'This was a waste of time,' she murmured. 'We lost her the moment she walked around the corner of this building, didn't we?'

'It was worth a look, guv,' said Barnes. He frowned as his phone began to vibrate in his pocket. 'It's Kyle.'

Kay moved closer as he answered it, putting it on speakerphone.

The young police constable didn't hang around.

'Sarge, I'm at the golf club – the one that Angus Zilchrist used to belong to. There's a bloke here who reckons he knows the man in the photograph, the one who was moving the wardrobe with Angus.'

———

Twenty minutes later, Kay hurried through the glass double doors and into the airy members' lounge of an expansive golf course on the fringes of Maidstone.

A mahogany reception desk swept around the left-hand side of the room while a number of leather sofas and wing-backed chairs surrounded a low table in the middle of the space.

She spotted Kyle Walker sitting on one of the sofas beside a man in his late seventies who appeared bemused by the sudden attention.

The police constable rose to his feet as she approached, nodded to Barnes and made the introductions. 'Guv, this is George Lamplighter.'

Kay didn't waste any time and gestured to the photograph that lay on a low table beside a leather-bound lunch menu. 'I take it you recognise the man on the right in the photograph. Who is he?'

'I'm not sure,' came the reply. The man tugged at his earlobe. 'But as I was telling your colleague, I do remember seeing Angus speaking to him out there in the car park a few weeks ago. We agreed to meet up to play a round one morning – it's usually quiet here on Sunday like it is today, and every now and again we'd play a game and then have lunch. They do a lovely carvery.'

'When was this?'

'The fifteenth of May.' The man straightened under Kay's scrutiny, then pointed to Kyle. 'I showed him the calendar on my phone.'

'Okay. What happened?'

'It looked like they were arguing about something. I remember that Angus turned away from me, but not before

I saw him go pale. Sort of like he'd had a shock. The man spoke to him in a low voice – I couldn't hear what was being said.'

'How long were they talking for?'

'No more than a couple of minutes. When he walked off, Angus just stood there for a moment doing nothing. Then he seemed to make a decision, and walked back over to my car.' Lamplighter looked down at his hands. 'I was embarrassed for him really, so I just pretended I was still getting things out of the back of my car. He tried to make light of it, but I could tell he was pretty rattled.'

'Did Angus say who he was?'

'Not a name, no. He just said he was someone he knew in passing and that there'd been a misunderstanding about something, that's all. He changed the subject after that, and I didn't want to push it.' Lamplighter gave a shy smile. 'I did thrash him that day though – his game was completely off.'

'Did he seem like he was having trouble concentrating?'

'He was all over the place. And before you ask, yes, that was unusual for Angus. It was a shame too – that was the last time he was here.'

'He never played again?'

'He cancelled his membership the next day.'

FORTY-FOUR

Kay jabbed a pin into a fresh copy of the woman's photograph from the CCTV recording and took a step back from the whiteboard.

Over her shoulder, a steady stream of officers poured into the incident room, a full contingent of them joining the others now that the weekend was over and a new roster had begun.

Such was their eagerness to return to the investigation and find the killer that a few were making last-minute adjustments to their shirt sleeves or removing cycling helmets while making their way to their desks, keen to begin the morning briefing.

Dave Morrison ran a hand over hair still wet from a shower while he spoke in a low voice to Nadine Fenning, both officers looking refreshed after some time off – although as Nadine joined Kyle beside the coffee machine Kay could hear the young probationer commenting on the amount of updates from the HOLMES2 database she would have to fight through in order to catch up.

Kay turned away, waiting while Barnes corralled the team towards her.

'This is taking too long,' she muttered, glaring at the second image showing the mystery man beside Angus Zilchrist. 'And we still have nothing, and we still don't know who these two are.'

'Guv, uniform have already made a start over at the retail park to see if anyone in the shop where Katrina worked recognises that woman, but so far they've had no luck,' said Barnes. 'They're currently working their way around the other units as those shops open.'

'Thanks, Ian.' She sighed. 'I'm not holding out a lot of hope though.'

'Debbie said she heard that Sharp was going to be here later today.'

She forced a smile. 'Don't worry, I'm not letting him take over this one yet. Yes, he's coming here for an update, but it won't be his decision to put a third party in here. That will come from someone higher up.'

'How long do you think we've got until they do that?'

'Not long.' She glanced over his shoulder as the last of the team took their seats. 'Okay, let's make a start.'

Gavin and Laura took their usual positions to one side of the gathered officers, as their eyes roamed the whiteboard while they tried to work out what they might have missed over the weekend. Kay gave them a brief nod, then took the prepared agenda from Debbie and cleared her throat.

'For those of you who weren't here over the past two days, I'm afraid we haven't had much progress in your absence. We have spoken to another witness who plays golf at the same club where Angus Zilchrist used to go, and he confirmed that the man who appears in the camera footage with Angus when they moved the wardrobe into the storage unit was also seen at the golf club. Unfortunately the club doesn't have any footage available, because their system works on four- to six-week rotation and we just missed it.'

A collective groan carried towards her, and she battened down the urge to respond with a sarcastic comment.

She reminded herself that her officers were as frustrated as her, and that those who had not yet been rostered a day off were exhausted.

'What our witness was able to tell us is that he saw Angus and that man arguing, and that Angus was quite shaken afterwards. Timing-wise, this happened only a short time before Angus died so it does make me wonder if their argument contributed to his ongoing health problems relating to stress, or maybe it was when Angus was informed about exactly what was in that wardrobe.' She paused, turning her attention to the next photograph. 'In addition, this woman was seen accosting Katrina Hovat the day she was killed.' Kay paused and rapped a knuckle against the new photograph. 'You've all been sent copies of the up-to-date images, and you'll have links to the relevant witness statements that have been collated over the weekend in HOLMES2.'

Placing the agenda to one side, she crossed her arms and gathered her thoughts for a moment before speaking once more. 'Before we continue, I'd like to dispel some of the rumours that are probably doing the rounds this morning. It's typical in an investigation like this that has gone on for several days without a breakthrough that a senior officer is brought in to audit the progress to date. This is perfectly normal, and not something to be worried about. Any review is not a reflection of your work, it is simply a means to ensure that we haven't missed something critical along the way. I understand that Detective Chief Inspector Devon Sharp is heading over here from Headquarters later today. To my knowledge, he is not taking over this investigation – yet. To that end, if he does ask you any questions regarding our enquiries please ensure you help him wherever possible. Our overarching priority is to find out who killed Katrina, Preston, and Alec.'

She watched while her officers shuffled in their seats, cast sideways glances at each other, and then turned their attention to her once more.

'Right, with that out of the way, let's take a look at what we need to focus on today. First of all, welcome back Gavin and Laura – Gav, looks like you managed to catch the sun again so thanks for making the rest of us look like shit.'

Pausing while the laughter subsided, she ran her gaze down the agenda. 'I'd like you both to go back through the CCTV footage we've gathered on Alec Mingrove and see if either of these persons of interest make an appearance. I'd also like you to speak with Edwin and Lisa Moore to see if they recognise either of them. It's too much of a coincidence that these two people turn up just before Katrina and Angus die.'

She paused when Laura muttered under her breath, the

detective constable's face wearing a baffled expression. 'What is it?'

'I just wondered why on earth she of all people might've been speaking to Katrina.'

'Do you know who she is?'

'Yes.' The younger detective blinked, then looked at Gavin. 'It's Jackie Nithercott, isn't it?'

Kay frowned. 'Jackie…?'

'She turned up at Headquarters after we spoke with her husband, Duncan,' said Laura. 'You know – Stephen Brassick's boss.'

FORTY-FIVE

'Do you want to interview her here, or at Headquarters?'

Gavin's question broke the silence as Kay paced the carpet at the front of the incident room.

The administrative staff and uniformed officers filtered back to their desks as her detectives waited patiently beside the whiteboard while she took stock.

Laura's revelation had caused a flurry of activity at the end of the briefing, with checks on social media revealing nothing to suggest that the woman knew Katrina Hovat, or what might link the two of them.

'I think we'll try to interview her at home,' she said eventually, stopping beside Barnes and eyeing the photograph once more. 'There's a danger here of us jumping to conclusions given the lack of immediate evidence to suggest that there's anything going on between these two.'

Laura cleared her throat and gestured at Gavin. 'We could speak to her, guv. I feel bad that I was off yesterday – we've lost even more time on this now, haven't we?'

'You can't think of it like that,' Kay said reassuringly. 'If you were working tired, you might not have made the connection at all. It is what it is. Having said that, no – I think Barnes and I should speak to her. If she *is* somehow connected to all this, I don't want her associating our interview with the one you conducted with her husband.'

'What are you thinking, guv?' Barnes frowned. 'Either she was threatening Katrina in that footage, or she was pissed off at her about something. There's no escaping that.'

'I know,' Kay said. 'Don't worry, this chat will just be a preliminary one.'

'To find out if she knows Katrina?' Gavin asked.

'No. To find out if she's going to lie to us.'

————

The drive over to Eynsford from the Maidstone police station only took forty minutes but within that time, Kay had sought out Amanda Miller and pleaded with the financial accountant for more of her time, as well as arranging for DCI Sharp to be met by Gavin when he arrived to brief him about the latest developments.

As she put her phone away and looked out of the car window, she started to formulate the questions she would ask Jackie Nithercott.

'How do you know she'll be in?' said Barnes, slowing as a tractor pulled out from a gated field and trundled along in front of them.

'Laura found a regular charity meeting on Jackie's social media page that she goes to every Monday morning.

She's one of the trustees so I'm guessing she'll be at home prior to that.'

'So she'll be late to the meeting.'

'If she doesn't answer my questions, yes.'

Barnes smirked, indicating left as they entered the village and followed a narrow winding road.

Moments later, he slowed outside a large modern detached house shielded from the lane by a towering privet hedge, the driveway gates wide open. Passing between matching brick gateposts, Barnes parked beside a smart SUV outside the front door.

Kay buttoned her blazer jacket, then reached out to ring the doorbell before pulling out her warrant card from her bag.

A few seconds passed, and then the door opened and the woman from the CCTV footage peered out.

The sound of a vacuum cleaner carried from somewhere within the enormous house, the distinct scent of fresh furniture polish offsetting the aroma wafting from an ornamental pot next to the door that was full of geraniums.

'Jackie Nithercott?' said Kay. 'I'm Detective Inspector Hunter, and this is my colleague Detective Sergeant Ian Barnes. May we come in?'

'I, um… What's this about?'

Kay gave a saccharine smile. 'If we could step inside, Mrs Nithercott. This will only take a minute or two, I'm sure.'

'Oh. Okay.' Jackie pushed the door open a little further, then moved out of the way as they stepped over the threshold. She gestured towards the back of the house.

'Best go through there. My cleaner is still here at the moment, so we'll speak in the kitchen.'

'Not a problem,' said Kay. 'Do you have a regular cleaner?'

Jackie waved her hand over her shoulder dismissively as she led the way. 'Only every two weeks. My husband insists that I have some help around the house. I feel guilty about it, but if she wasn't here, I wouldn't be able to dedicate so much of my time to charity.'

'That makes sense,' said Barnes. 'Is she from an agency, your cleaner?'

'Yes. That one in Maidstone called "Maid By Us". Why do you ask?'

Kay ignored the question, and instead cast her gaze around the kitchen they had just entered.

Boasting a modern array of equipment, the granite worktops sparkled in the sunlight that filtered through double patio doors opening out onto a paved patio area. A vase of lilies stood on the worktop beside a freshly brewed pot of coffee, and a pile of unopened letters had been propped against an overflowing fruit bowl.

Jackie brushed an imaginary speck of fluff from her blouse, then crossed her arms and leaned against the sink. 'Okay, what did you want to ask me? I've got a trustees meeting in half an hour, and I can't be late.'

'I'd like to show you a photograph,' said Kay, pulling out the captured image from the CCTV camera. 'Can you confirm this is you?'

Jackie frowned in response, but took the photograph and stared at it for a moment.

Eventually she held it out, but Kay ignored it.

'Can you confirm that's you?'

'It might be, yes.'

'Yes or no, Mrs Nithercott? It's very important.'

Jackie took another look, then nodded. 'Yes, that's me.'

'What were you saying to the other woman?'

'I can't remember. When was this taken?'

'A little over two weeks ago.'

'Well, there you have it,' said Jackie, exasperated. 'If you knew how many people I meet on a daily basis with my charity work…'

'Her name is Katrina Hovat. She was found dead at Stephen and Penelope Brassick's house two weeks ago. She was also employed by Maid By Us.'

'Oh my God, *her*? I had no idea…' Her eyes widened as she looked at each of them in turn. 'What on earth has that got to do with me?'

'Where were you, on the Friday two weeks ago between the hours of five and nine o'clock in the evening?'

Jackie's eyes hardened. 'Right here, Detective Hunter. Duncan was on his way back from the City and I had arranged for us to have dinner at the gastro pub down the road from here. I met him at the train station at seven thirty and we walked into the pub not ten minutes later.' Jackie picked up her phone and flicked through the apps until she found what she wanted, turning it to face Kay. 'It was our anniversary you see, so we asked one of the waiters to take our photo.'

Kay bit back her disappointment as the woman put her

phone away and instead pointed at the photograph. 'Can you tell me what was going on here?'

Jackie exhaled. 'She damaged the paintwork on my car, the silly bitch.'

'Oh?'

'I don't usually shop there.' The woman's lip curled. 'Not my sort of place, obviously. But I was driving past the retail park and realised we were running low on kibble.'

'Do you have a dog?' Barnes looked around the room.

'She's in the living room. She doesn't like strangers – we got her from a rescue centre three years ago, and God knows what happened to her in the past, but she doesn't like men in particular. We don't take any chances – the last thing we want is to be accused of being irresponsible owners.'

'Fair enough.' Barnes nodded. 'Very admirable of you.'

'When did your car get damaged?' said Kay.

Jackie snorted, jabbing her finger at the photograph. 'As I was coming back with the dog food, I saw *her* next to my car. The silly thing was, I'd parked out on the service road rather than risk getting hit in the car park because that can happen can't it? And then *she* walks past swinging her handbag and clips the door mirror with one of the metal clasps. I mean, she must've been daydreaming or something – or on drugs I think. She managed to scratch the paintwork. Anyway, she didn't stop or anything so I put the dog food on the back seat and followed her back through the gap in the hedge there. She was wearing a uniform-style polo shirt from that cheap homewares shop.'

'What happened next?'

'I called out to her, and you could see straight away she knew I'd realised what she'd done. She tried to make some pitiful excuses, but then I said I'd get your lot onto it. That's when she started swearing at me.'

'You threatened to call the police?'

Jackie dropped her gaze, twisting the wedding band on her finger. 'I know that was naughty of me, but I didn't know what else to do. I wasn't really going to call the police. I just wanted her to pay for the damage. Duncan was already cross with me because I'd managed to back the car into one of the neighbour's walls last month. It was an accident – it's a stone wall and some of the bigger stones stick out more than others, but it cost quite a bit to fix – the car, not the wall. There was nothing wrong with *that*. It's solid flint in most places. I didn't want to tell him that the car had got damaged again.'

'What did she say to you?' Kay eyed the photograph, trying to imagine the conversation while she listened.

'Well, that's just it. She threatened me, Detective Hunter. She took a photograph of me and said she'd put it on social media if I didn't leave her alone. I was shocked – I couldn't have that, not with all the charity work I do, so I let it go. I left as quickly as I could and drove home.'

She shivered. 'Look, I'm sorry she's dead, but she was utterly horrible to me. She scared me.'

FORTY-SIX

Laura looked over the top of her computer screen as the incident room door swung open and Kay and Barnes walked in.

A steady hum of activity filled the room, the investigative team trying to split their time between each of the three murder victims and other ongoing cases that still required their attention on a daily basis.

After two weeks, any lasting effects of her holiday were well and truly a distant memory and she covered her mouth as an enormous yawn seized her.

She lowered her gaze as the two senior detectives walked past her desk, guilt nagging at her consciousness that she had been the one to provide any sort of breakthrough in the case, but a day later than needed in the circumstances.

The door to DCI Sharp's old office remained shut, with he and Gavin closeted in there for the past hour while her colleague explained what the team had been doing for the past twelve days.

It opened when Kay reached her desk, and Laura watched while she spoke to them both in a low murmur before leading Sharp towards the whiteboard.

Huffing under her breath, she turned her attention back to the screen and resumed typing up her notes from speaking with Richard Zilchrist that afternoon.

Neither he nor his sister had recognised the man seen at the storage unit with Angus and, when asked in confidence, confirmed they had never met Jackie Nithercott either.

While she had been out doing that, Gavin had sat with Kyle Walker to review the CCTV images from Alec Mingrove's last hours..

Then Sharp had walked in, announcing that there would be a review of the case after all.

Gavin had shot her a look of horror before accepting Sharp's invite to provide an update.

He didn't have a choice, that much had been made clear.

Laura cringed inwardly, glad that her colleague had to be the bearer of bad news, and not her.

'How did it go?' she said as he sank into the threadbare chair at his desk.

'All right, I s'pose.'

'Did he say who the new DI is?'

'No. Just that he's very ambitious.'

Laura's top lip curled. 'I'll bet. Anything to topple the guv off her perch, eh?'

'Can't happen.' Gavin stopped typing and gave a sideways glance. 'Right?'

'But we haven't got anything, Gav,' she hissed. She

waved at her screen. 'Debbie and her team have cross-checked everything this afternoon. There's no missing information, nothing overlooked. This investigation is one of the cleanest ones I've ever seen.'

'Except we haven't arrested anyone.'

Laura fell silent, his words cutting into her desperate optimism.

'Gavin, Laura – could you join us over here?' Kay called. 'Bring what you've got on Jackie Nithercott as well.'

When they joined the senior officers, Sharp pulled his mobile phone from his jacket pocket as it buzzed loudly. 'I'm going to have to head back to Gravesend. Look, before I go, all of you should know that bringing in a third party to review your work isn't a reflection of your efforts. It's a common occurrence, and often a fresh pair of eyes can help identify an angle that hasn't yet been considered. Don't take it personally, all right?'

Laura cleared her throat. 'We don't take it personally, guv, but it *is* frustrating. If we'd just had a few more bums on seats…'

Barnes held up his hand before she could go any further. 'DCI Sharp's well aware of the staffing issues, mark my words. And he's right – this is simply a process, that's all.'

'However, your concerns are duly noted,' said Sharp kindly. 'I know you take this sort of thing personally, but that's what makes you good at your jobs.'

'Not good enough,' muttered Gavin.

'No one's superhuman,' said Sharp. He winked. 'Even me.'

That raised a polite laugh, and then Kay turned her attention to Laura.

'What did you pull together about Jackie?'

'There's nothing in the system to raise a flag,' she replied, flipping open the manila folder in her hand and sifting through the printed reports. 'I ran DVLA checks, social media searches through her posts for the past two years, and nothing looks wrong there. I also phoned that gastro pub she mentioned to you, and they confirmed the table booking two weeks ago. Apparently the chef even made a special dessert for them because they're – in the owner's words – "valued regulars".'

'So her alibi checks out for Katrina's death,' Sharp said. 'What about the social media – anything amongst that to connect her to the other victims, or to the other persons of interest you've identified?'

'Nothing, guv,' said Laura, closing the file. She could feel the heat in her cheeks. 'Unless we can get authorisation for credit history checks and the like, I don't know what else I can do.'

'And we won't get authorisation for those without due cause,' said Kay.

Sharp checked his phone once more, then eyed them all. 'You've got until Friday before Tess Bainbridge, the Assistant Chief Constable, signs off on the review. Do your best.'

Laura watched him leave the room, then turned back to Kay. 'I hate to say it, guv, but this sucks.'

'You're not wrong there.'

'What do you think, guv?' said Barnes. 'Do you think

Jackie was telling the truth about that business with Katrina in the car park?'

Kay sighed. 'I don't know, Ian. There's something going on here, something that connects our three victims and Angus Zilchrist, but I'll be buggered if I can see what it is.'

The detective sergeant grinned. 'Only one thing for it, then.'

'What's that?'

'Pub. I'm buying.'

Kay gave a tired smile as Gavin's face lit up. 'Well, how could we resist an offer like that?'

FORTY-SEVEN

Police Sergeant Ellis Hughes cricked his neck, rolled his shoulders, and then turned his attention back to the computer screen in front of him.

The custody suite was relatively quiet tonight, with only a man brought in for being drunk and disorderly currently residing in cell four, and another who had tried to start a fight outside one of the less salubrious taverns in town booked into cell six.

The rest of the cells were empty, and hopefully would remain so for the remainder of his shift.

Hughes eyed the thick security door that led through to the car park, then took a swig of tepid coffee from a chipped white ceramic mug at his elbow.

At ten thirty, it was still early. The pubs would start to close in another thirty minutes or so, and then everything could change.

Not necessarily for the better, either.

Hughes's fingers pecked at the keyboard, his eyes darting between the charge sheet that had been completed for their last temporary visitor and the screen. Beyond the raised desk, a young police constable glared at the unwashed individual slinking beside a corkboard displaying a range of health and safety posters, her radio emitting a faint crackle from its position on her vest before she reached up to turn it down.

'Haven't you finished that yet?'

Hughes raised his gaze and stared at the flea-bitten man, who was dressed in scruffy jeans and a thin multicoloured jumper with gaping holes in the sleeves. 'The only reason this is taking so long is because you've got such a long career, Mickey.'

The man emitted a raucous laugh, exposing rotten teeth amongst gaping holes where the rest had fallen out. 'Don't mean no harm, me. I needed to take a piss.'

'Well next time use a public toilet instead of the bus shelter in Jubilee Square,' quipped the constable, rolling her eyes. 'Honestly, Mickey – I've got better things to do than deal with you every week.'

Hughes shook his head, pressed a sequence of buttons and then turned to the printer behind him, dragging out the page while it was still warm. 'Right, I've printed all the details out for your court appearance. Make sure you get someone to read this for you, and make sure you turn up. Otherwise the magistrates will fine you for a non-appearance as well.'

Mickey's bottom lip drooped as he folded the page. 'I told you I just needed to take a piss.'

'That's all very well, but you can't keep going around whipping out your todger in public,' replied Hughes. 'Maybe one day, you'll remember that.'

He watched the man stumble out through the front door, and then turned to the constable. 'How many times is that now, Tara? Four? Five?'

She sighed in response. 'I spoke to the people at the shelter about him last week. He isn't well, Sarge. Some sort of kidney infection, I think. The problem is, he keeps forgetting to go to his hospital appointments that they make for him.'

Hughes tutted, reached into a drawer and pulled out an aerosol deodorant, sprayed it liberally around the desk, then glanced up as Tara's radio blipped to life.

She confirmed her attendance to Force Control then shot him a wry smile. 'And that's me off again. Marcus'll be pissed off – he was hoping to get something to eat before we got another shout.'

'Here, take these.' Moving to a side cabinet, he pulled out a handful of muesli bars and shoved them across the desk to her. 'It'll keep you both going.'

Tara grinned. 'You're a legend, Sarge.'

She hurried out to the car park, the secure door slamming shut in her wake, and Hughes exhaled.

Behind him in the custody suite, he could hear the drunk singing an old hit from the 1980s, his words slurring through the cell door.

The man who had been in the fight was surprisingly quiet, perhaps regretting his earlier temper.

Or maybe not.

Hughes checked his watch, and decided he would give it another five minutes before checking on them both.

Headlights streaked across the glass of the exit door as another patrol car swung into the car park, the electronic whirr of the security barrier vibrating against the wall, and Hughes braced himself for another round of paperwork and high emotions.

You never knew who was going to be brought into the custody suite.

He frowned when he heard voices on the other side of the door, and then the familiar buzz of someone's security card against the panel reached his ears and it opened.

A male constable fresh out of training college led a young woman in her twenties over to the desk, her eyes downturned under a ragged fringe. As he removed her cuffs, she rubbed at her wrists, and sniffed loudly.

Her clothes were old, but clean – a baggy dark-coloured sweatshirt over skinny black jeans, her feet enclosed within black ankle boots.

Her bottom lip trembled when she gave her name.

'Sophie… Sophie Anderley.'

'Ms Anderley was arrested after breaking into the laundrette out towards the Aylesford Road,' said the constable. 'The owner was in the flat upstairs and heard someone smash the glass to the back window and called triple nine. He overpowered her before she could escape. Luckily for him, she wasn't carrying a weapon of any kind.'

'I… I didn't mean to,' said Sophie, a fat tear rolling over her cheek. 'I need the money.'

The constable sighed. 'She had the takings from the desk drawer on her. Five hundred and thirty quid in tens and twenties. The owner said he doesn't normally lock the drawer because he typically gets the banking done before it gets to that much but he's been too busy today. It's all the cash from customers wanting to exchange the notes for coins.'

Hughes turned to his computer screen and then looked at the woman. 'Is that your full name?'

'Yes. No middle name.'

'Date of birth?'

He went through the preliminaries, then nodded to the constable. 'Okay, let's see what else she's got in her pockets.'

The constable turned Sophie to one side and asked her to do as Hughes requested, his tone firm but gentle.

Out came an older model mobile phone, a folded up five-pound note with a felt tip pen streak across one corner, and a single key on a crinkled leather fob.

'Is that it?'

She nodded. 'Please, you have to let me go.'

'You do understand you've been arrested for breaking and entering?' said Hughes incredulously, updating the initial report. 'You won't be going anywhere for a while.'

'But you have to.' Sophie's eyes widened as she looked at the constable beside her, then back. 'They'll kill me if I don't pay them back by Friday.'

Hughes felt his heart lurch, his hands frozen in mid-air above his keyboard. 'What did you say?'

FORTY-EIGHT

The melodic chink of the stainless steel spoon against a well-worn ceramic mug rang out through the small kitchenette, the aroma of freshly brewed coffee doing little to alleviate Kay's fatigue.

She had only stayed for one small glass of wine, leaving her colleagues at a pub on East Street to relax over another round, their insistence that she remain falling on deaf ears.

Recalling the disappointment in their faces at Sharp's words that afternoon, she had marched back to the incident room an hour ago and had spent the time since reviewing the investigation's history.

Walking back to her desk, she saw her mobile phone display light up and smiled at the familiar name on the screen.

'How are those hedgehogs doing?' she said.

'They're looking guilty about your dry-cleaning bill,' Adam replied. 'Working late?'

'Only for a bit.' She rubbed at her temples. 'I thought I

might get another hour in while it's quiet. Are you out early in the morning?'

'I'm not due in to the surgery until nine. I'm on standby tonight, though, so don't panic if I'm not here when you do get back. I made some pasta earlier, so heat it up if you're hungry. I'll bet you haven't eaten today.'

She grinned, her stomach rumbling in response. 'I've been a bit busy.'

'I knew you'd say that.'

She could hear the smile in his voice, then looked up as the door opened and Ellis Hughes peered in. 'I've got to go. Love you.'

She took one look at the police sergeant's face and reached out for her notebook and a pen. 'Are you okay?'

'I don't know. I might have got the wrong end of the stick, but a woman has just been brought in after being arrested for breaking and entering.' He jerked his thumb over his shoulder. 'She said something about that if she didn't get the cash takings from the laundrette where she was caught, that "they" would kill her – her words, not mine.'

The hairs on the back of Kay's neck frazzled with energy. Pushing back her chair, she gestured to the door. 'What are your first impressions? Do you think she's telling the truth?'

'She doesn't come across as the sort of person who's done this before. She certainly hasn't been arrested before – she's not in our system and she wasn't familiar with the routine like some of the others that come in here.' Hughes led the way down the stairs. 'She's well spoken, and… I don't know… I just get the feeling that she's more afraid of whatever or whoever is out there, rather than what's happening to her in here. Almost like she's in shock.'

'Hang on.' Kay paused next to the door leading through to the custody suite, stood to one side and peered through the reinforced glass.

Hughes had left the woman in the custody of the constable who had arrested her, and now she sat with her head in her hands on one of the plastic chairs that were bolted to the floor.

The uniformed officer looked bored while he re-read various posters on the wall that he had no doubt seen a hundred times before.

'What's her name?' Kay murmured.

'Sophie Anderley. Gave an address out past the Tonbridge Road and said it's her sister's place.'

'Okay. I want to interview her formally. Can you get someone else to manage the desk while you sit in on that?'

'I'll see who's around. Give me a minute, guv.'

'No problem.'

He brushed past her, and she paced at the bottom of the stairs until he stuck his head around the door and beckoned to her. 'All set, and I've had her taken along to interview room two.'

When Kay walked into the room, she was taken aback by the woman's appearance.

On closer inspection she looked half-starved, with prominent cheekbones devoid of colour and her sweatshirt looked like it was hanging from her slim frame.

The woman's eyes widened as Hughes eased himself into the chair opposite her and started the recording equipment, then watched Kay with unease and picked at a ragged fingernail.

'Sophie, I'm Detective Inspector Kay Hunter, and I believe you've already met my colleague, Sergeant Ellis Hughes. We're going to record this conversation, and you need to be aware of your rights so let's begin with that.'

Kay recited the formal caution, then sought confirmation of Sophie's address.

'Why did you break into the laundrette tonight?' she asked, opening her notebook to a fresh page.

'I-I needed the money,' Sophie murmured.

'You'll need to speak up so the recording can hear you,' said Kay.

'I needed the money.' The woman sighed, and brought a shaking hand to her eyes, wiping at them with her sleeve. 'I didn't have a choice.'

'Can you tell me what you mean by that?'

'I can't. They'll kill me.' Tears rolled off Sophie's cheeks and plopped onto the table's dimpled surface. 'Just like they did to Katrina.'

Kay's heart lurched, her mouth turning dry. 'Who, Sophie? Who's been threatening you?'

The woman shook her head in response.

'Okay, we'll come back to that. Why do they want to kill you?'

'Because... because I had to borrow some money. I couldn't get credit anywhere because I didn't have any work.'

'How did you find out about these people?'

Sophie swallowed, gulping back a fresh torrent of tears. 'She found me. She must've overheard me at the benefits office or outside the women's refuge or something. Then she approached me outside the post office after I'd tried to get some money out, and said she could help me.'

'When was this?'

'At the beginning of the year.'

'And do you mind if I ask how much you borrowed?'

'Three thousand pounds.' Sophie's hands trembled as she clasped them together. 'I owed some money on my heating bill, and my old flat mate did a runner after damaging a shower screen so I had to pay that off before I could get back my lease deposit.'

'And you're living at your sister's house now, is that correct?'

'Yes.'

'These people who you say have threatened you, what can you tell me about them?'

Sophie shook her head. 'I can't. I told you, they'll kill me.'

Kay paused, glanced at Hughes, then took a deep breath. 'Sophie, listen to me. These people are extremely dangerous, you know this. You know what happened to Katrina. We also suspect they're responsible for two further murders we're investigating.'

A shocked gasp emanated from the woman and she reared back on her chair. 'That's not true.'

'It *is* true, Sophie, and we need to stop them,' Kay said firmly. 'If we don't, I'm concerned what will happen to you – or your sister. Do they know where you live?'

Sophie nodded mutely.

'Please,' said Kay. 'Tell me what you can about them. Before it's too late. Before they hurt someone else.'

Sophie reached out and gripped the side of the table with both hands, her eyes downturned for a moment.

Eventually, she took a deep breath and met Kay's gaze. 'I only know her first name. Rosalind.'

Kay forced herself not to breathe a sigh of relief, and instead turned her attention back to her notebook. 'Okay, what can you tell me about Rosalind?'

'She's… normal, I suppose. Average height, a bit taller than me. When I've seen her, she's wearing suit trousers and either a blouse or a vest top underneath a jacket. Not a matching suit jacket though – something more casual, like a coloured blazer or a padded jacket back in the winter.'

'That's great, Sophie. What about hair colour?'

'Blonde, but it's bleached highlights rather than all over. Dark roots, but she seems to let them grow out a bit.' Sophie shivered. 'Brown eyes, really dark. Thin lips.'

'What's her last name?'

'I don't know – she's never told me.'

'When you've seen her, is she always on foot, or does she drive a car?'

'She walked up to me that first time.' Sophie leaned forward and folded her arms. 'There's a man who drives her. A silver car. Rosalind sits in the back, never the passenger seat. The back windows are smoked so you can't see inside.'

Kay looked up and tapped her pen against the page. 'Do you think there's anyone else inside the car?'

Sophie shook her head. 'I don't think so.'

'Tell me about the man.'

'He's scary. Bald, or at least he shaves his head. Bigger than me. More like your height,' she said, nodding at Hughes. 'He wears a dark jacket and jeans, and looks like he works out.'

'All muscle and brawn across the shoulders perhaps?' Kay said.

'Yeah, exactly. Mean eyes.'

'Any tattoos, or any other features that make him stand out from most of the bouncers I know around here?'

A small smile formed on Sophie's lips at Kay's remark, and then she shook her head. 'Not that I've seen, but like I said, he's always wearing a jacket so he might be covering up tattoos.'

'What about accents? How do each of them speak?'

Sophie frowned. 'He doesn't speak much. She's got – I don't know, I suppose you'd call it a middle-class accent. Not like mine.'

'Is there anything else you can tell me about the car?'

Pausing for a moment, Sophie's gaze roamed to the ceiling, then back. 'It smells nice, when she opens the door I mean. Not a new car smell, but something like perfume. Maybe one of those air freshener things, you know? But not pine. Something nicer.'

'And what about this Rosalind woman and the man you've seen with her? Anything else you can tell me about them?'

Sophie shook her head.

'Would you recognise them again if you saw them?'

'Absolutely, yes.'

Kay pursed her lips, then opened the manila folder she

had brought with her from the incident room, and pulled out a photograph of Jackie Nithercott.

'Is this the woman who threatened you?'

Sophie frowned. 'No, I've never met her. Who's she?'

Disappointed, Kay tucked the photograph away, ran her eyes down her notes, then sighed. 'Okay, Sophie – you've been a great help, thank you. Sergeant Hughes will take it from here, but I will make sure your assistance is noted when your case is sent to the magistrates' court.'

Sophie's mouth dropped open, realisation in her eyes. 'I'm still being charged?'

'You were arrested for breaking and entering tonight,' said Kay softly. 'Yes, you're being charged.'

As she left the room behind Hughes, she could hear the woman sobbing softly.

Walking back along the corridor, she texted a message to Barnes to pick her up early the next morning.

'Guv, what are we going to do about her?' said Hughes. 'If you're right about this, she's in danger.'

Kay heard voices, then watched as Sophie was led away to the cells. 'Once the paperwork goes through on the breaking and entering charge, we'll have to release her until she appears in court, so that's no good if she's telling the truth and someone *is* after her. However, we can keep her here for thirty-six hours before charging her, so let's do that. Make sure she's comfortable, get some food inside her for goodness sakes – she looks like she hasn't been eating enough – and keep your ears open in case she says anything else that might help us identify these people.'

'Will do.' Hughes glanced over his shoulder as a cell

door slammed shut, the noise vibrating off the plasterwork walls. 'Anything else before you head off?'

'Yes. Call her sister as soon as you can. Find out if there's somewhere else she can stay for a few days, just in case.'

FORTY-NINE

'Did you get any sleep last night, guv?'

Barnes locked the pool car, then followed Kay across to the back door leading into the police station.

'Not much,' she admitted. 'I think it was past midnight by the time I'd finished talking to Sharp.' She took a moment to savour the warm sunshine bathing the brickwork, then turned to her colleague. 'We're close, Ian. I can feel it. Something's going to give.'

'It needs to,' he said ruefully, following her into the foyer and up the stairs. 'We're running out of time, and – I don't know about you – but I'm worried if this Sophie is being threatened by the same people who killed our three victims, then they're going to panic the moment they find out she's been arrested. Who knows what they might do then?'

'My thoughts exactly.' Kay shoved open the incident room door, led the way over to the whiteboard and called over the rest of the team.

Shrugging off her jacket while they took their seats,

she gratefully accepted a takeout coffee cup from Laura, then took a moment to gather her thoughts.

The following hours would take all her leadership skills to guide the officers in front of her, and make sure every step they took would withstand scrutiny from both her superiors and the Crown Prosecution Service.

She looked up to see Barnes give her an encouraging wink, then launched into the briefing.

'Last night, a woman called Sophie Anderley was arrested for breaking into a laundrette here in town,' she said. 'When interviewed, she provided information that may link her to the people responsible for murdering Katrina Hovat, Preston Winford and Alec Mingrove.'

An explosion of voices filled the room as the assembled uniformed officers turned to each other, and Gavin spluttered on his energy drink.

'Hell of a way to open a briefing, guv,' he managed, beating his chest with his fist.

She smiled. 'I thought that would get your attention. Okay, listen up everyone. Sophie's statement is in the system so you can read through it after this briefing but essentially, she's confirmed that she was approached out of the blue by a woman who offered to loan her three thousand pounds. It sounds like she was overheard at the benefits office, or perhaps at the post office while speaking to one of the staff at the counter. The information Sophie gave included the details of a silver saloon car that's used by the people enforcing repayments – the woman who threatened her and a man who drives the car.'

Kay paused to take a sip of coffee, the caffeine only highlighting how tired she felt. 'Tasks for this morning, then. Laura, I want you to take another look at Jackie Nithercott's social media and see if anyone matching the description Sophie gave for the woman who loaned her the money makes an appearance. Obviously take into account hair colour changes, given the fact it seems that she dyes her hair.'

'Will do, guv.'

'Gavin, I need you to work with a team of officers to re-review the CCTV footage already identified as showing our victims in the days before their murders to see if you can spot this silver car that Sophie mentioned.' Kay flipped through her notes. 'Next, Kyle – I want you to speak with Sophie to find out the date she was at the post office, and then if she can recall that or a close approximation, get onto the post office and obtain their security footage. See if you can spot this woman and track her down.'

She waited while the constable jotted down the task without questioning her. 'And yes, I know that sounds impossible but we have to cover every aspect of this. Somewhere along the line, one of these people will have made a mistake. Next, where's Dave?'

'Here, guv.' The older constable raised his hand at the back of the group.

'Chances are, when these people find out that Sophie isn't going to make the deadline to pay they're going to go around to her sister's house. I'm going to head over to Headquarters after this to wrangle getting a surveillance team on the place, but I need you to arrange a watch on it in the meantime. Hughes has spoken to Sophie's sister, and she's made arrangements to stay with friends outside of Maidstone for a week, so she's safe. Given that our suspects appear to be escalating in their violence, we might get lucky if they're determined to find out where Sophie is and turn up there while we're on watch. Advise the team to take precautions though – we know full well what they're capable of.'

Kay waited until Dave Morrison had caught up with his note taking, then turned her attention to the rest of the team. 'Sophie's arrest has given us an opportunity. Something's happened in the past few weeks to make these people panic – it makes no sense killing the people they've loaned money to, so why is it happening? Why now?'

She lowered her notes and eyed each of the officers in turn as she spoke. 'I need every one of you to give your full attention to this investigation. I know you've got others that are taking up your time but mark my words – if we don't get some answers today, we may regret it.'

Laura held up her hand. 'Do you think Headquarters will take over sooner than the end of the week, guv?'

'No,' said Kay. 'I'm worried someone else will die.'

FIFTY

Gavin drummed his fingers on top of the printer and shifted from foot to foot as it whirred to life.

An uneasy atmosphere filled the incident room, with Kay's words ringing in his ears while he plucked out each page as it appeared, impatient to return to his desk.

He could hear the desperation in his colleagues' voices, in the way they snapped at each other before apologising, and the lack of banter from the small kitchenette off to one side.

Phones rang, murmured conversations were kept brief, and when he glanced over his shoulder, everyone looked as tense as he felt.

They couldn't let another victim die.

'Finally,' he muttered, snatching out the last page and crossing to his desk.

Sifting through the various documents in his hand, he gathered up his laptop and a half-finished can of soft drink before hurrying into one of the spare meeting rooms along the corridor.

Kicking the door shut, he took a moment to savour the quiet, then laid out the pages on the laminated table that took up the centre of the room and glared at them.

Something had been niggling at him since he'd been woken by Leanne's alarm at four o'clock.

It was here, somewhere, he was sure of it.

He pulled out one of the chairs and leaned forward, rubbing at his temples. 'Okay, Piper, *think.*'

So much had happened since Katrina Hovat's mutilated body was discovered by Mark and Estelle Hastings-Jones that his thoughts tumbled over one another.

The first document he turned to was the transcript of the video interview he and Laura had conducted with Penelope and Stephen Brassick.

In it, they had stated that Katrina had been working for them through an agency since January. He read through the witness statement from the cleaning company next, his frown deepening with each page. He had already identified two different payments going into Katrina's account, one from the cleaning agency and the other from the part-time job at the retail store, but something didn't match up.

The next document he selected was a list of guests Penelope and Stephen had accommodated in between their trips to New York over the past six months.

Eyeing the dates, he traced those back to the payments Katrina had received from the agency, then lowered the pages.

'But Penelope said she went there weekly when they were at home,' he murmured. 'So where are those payments?'

Growling under his breath, he shoved the documents to

one side, opened up his laptop and logged into HOLMES2. Scrolling as fast as he could, he found the witness statement he sought, and read his notes once more.

When interviewed at Northfleet HQ, Duncan Nithercott had been adamant that there were no issues with Stephen Brassick's work.

And yet…

'Found you.'

When asked by Laura if he socialised with Stephen Brassick, he confirmed he didn't – except that both their wives got on well with each other at events. In fact, he'd elaborated further, citing that he was glad they didn't for fear of them fuelling each other's love of antiques and shoes.

And yet…

Only yesterday his wife, Jackie, had insisted that her altercation with Katrina had been nothing more than an argument over a scratch to her car.

And yet…

When they had interviewed Duncan at Headquarters, he seemed surprised when his wife turned up despite making a joke about the fact that she had been shopping.

Gavin froze, stunned by the reality in the pages before him.

Why *had* Jackie Nithercott turned up at Northfleet that morning?

———

'Laura!'

Gavin called out to his colleague as he walked into the

incident room, then apologised to the young administrative assistant he almost collided with in his haste to reach her.

'Why the stampede?' his colleague said, an amused smile in her eyes.

'Whatever you're working on, drop it. This is urgent.' He waved the copy of Duncan Nithercott's statement at her. 'I think there's something here, and we missed it.'

'What do you mean?' Laura's face paled.

Gavin slid her computer keyboard towards him, scrolled through HOLMES2 and then pointed at the images of Penelope Brassick and Jackie Nithercott. 'Remember when we interviewed Duncan, he said he and Stephen never socialised outside of company events? He then went on to say their wives got on well, but sort of hinted that they both had voracious shopping habits.'

Laura snatched the statement from him, skimming the pages. 'He also said that Jackie doesn't work, so she's dependent on him for money isn't she?'

'Right, but I got the impression he isn't completely aware of what that money gets spent on.'

'He said "antiques and shoes". Nothing wrong with that.'

'Unless she's not spending the money on antiques and shoes. What if she's spending her money on people?'

'But he said she's involved in charity work, so that would make sense.'

'I…' Gavin paused as his colleague's words sank in. 'I know that, but what if… what if she's been lending her money to some of the people she's come into contact with via her charity work?'

Reaching into a tray beside her keyboard, Laura picked

up another document and waved it at him. 'This is Sophie Anderley's statement. She doesn't mention anything about going to a charity for help.'

'Kay didn't ask her. No one was focusing on this angle when she interviewed her last night.'

Laura peeled his fingers from the mouse and took over, opening another window. 'Okay, so let's see what charities Jackie works with. If she's that involved, then there's got to be something on social media or one of the local news sites.'

They found a report on the *Kentish Times* website ten minutes later.

'And look who's in the photo,' Gavin murmured.

Penelope Brassick and Jackie Nithercott were dressed in cocktail dresses, wide smiles aimed at the camera while they raised champagne glasses, a third woman at Penelope's elbow.

None of the women's names appeared under the photograph, the caption instead only providing a generalised description of donors enjoying a fund-raising gala.

Laura scrolled through the accompanying article, then sighed. 'This article doesn't mention Duncan or Stephen.'

'So maybe the wives were socialising at this event without their knowledge?' said Gavin. 'Especially if Stephen was overseas at the time.'

'And you think they're more than just casual acquaintances as Duncan suggested?'

'Exactly.' He pointed at the screen. 'Print that out, then come with me.'

Two minutes later, they were waiting outside interview

room one when a bemused custody sergeant appeared, his hand gently guiding Sophie Anderley towards them.

Quickly dispensing with the formalities, Gavin took a moment to calm his breathing, then raised his chin and watched the woman in front of him.

She was tense, but certainly had more colour in her cheeks this morning than when her photograph had been processed last night upon being charged.

'Sophie, I'm going to ask you some questions in relation to another investigation, and I need you to remember that you are currently under caution. Do you understand?'

'Yes.'

'Did you approach any charities for help or advice in the lead-up to or after you borrowed that three thousand pounds?'

Confusion flitted across the woman's face. 'Yes, but what's that—'

'Please, just answer the question.'

'I did, yes. There's a new-ish one, quite local, that offers help to people who need legal advice, financial advice, that sort of thing.' Her lips curled. 'They were pretty useless though – I was told my circumstances didn't warrant financial assistance under their remit or something like that, and sent packing.'

'Did you meet Rosalind before or after approaching the charity?'

'After. Why?'

He unfolded the news article and placed it on the desk in front of her. 'Do you recognise anyone in this photograph?'

Sophie swallowed, and then her finger traced the woman on the far left of the image. 'This is Rosalind, the one I told the other detective about last night.'

Gavin heard the muffled surprise from his colleague, but kept his attention on Sophie. 'Anyone else in that photograph look familiar?'

'This woman, but only because that other detective asked me if I knew her. I don't. Who is she?'

'Jackie Nithercott. Does the name sound familiar?'

'No.'

'What about the woman in the middle?'

'No, sorry.'

'Interview terminated at nine forty-five.'

Ignoring Sophie's shocked expression, Gavin shot from the room, Laura in his wake.

Pausing by the door leading through to the stairwell, he dug out his mobile phone, flicked through his notes and then dialled a number.

It was answered after two rings.

'It's DC Gavin Piper, Kent Police. I need to speak to Duncan Nithercott. Now.'

FIFTY-ONE

When Kay returned from Northfleet and followed Barnes into the incident room, she was astounded at the number of officers who were gathered in small groups, each working frantically at a computer while Gavin dashed between them.

A late afternoon downpour soaked the windows, misting up the panes and obliterating the view across the town, creating a dullness that sapped at the overhead lights and gave everything around her a muted tone.

She reached out and stopped Debbie as the uniformed constable hurried past. 'What's going on?'

Shifting a pile of folders in her arms, the woman jerked her chin over her shoulder. 'Gavin's managed to get Stephen Brassick on a plane back here this afternoon. We're trying to liaise with a team nearer Heathrow to meet him off the plane and bring him in for questioning.'

'What the hell—' Kay peered over Debbie's head, saw Gavin looking her way, and beckoned him over. 'Gav? A word?'

Barnes headed over to their desks, wheeling over an extra chair for the detective constable while Laura scuttled over to the photocopier, no doubt creating some distance between her and whatever fallout might be heading her colleague's way.

Kay waited until Gavin joined her, then marched across to where Barnes waited, patting the back of the chair as the younger detective sat down.

Taking a deep breath, Kay watched his face for any signs of contriteness, then gave up. 'All right. Explain to me what's going on.'

'First of all, guv – sorry.' Gavin leaned forward, his expression earnest. 'But I didn't think this should wait until you were back here, and I couldn't get through to you at Headquarters. I was also worried that if my theory is correct, Penelope Brassick might pose a problem if we had to try and extradite her from the States.'

'Extradite her?' Kay tried and failed to keep her surprise from her voice, then looked up as Laura sidled closer. 'Exactly what have you two been up to while I was out?'

She listened while the two detectives explained Gavin's theory, then took the printed out newspaper article from him and peered at the photograph.

'Bloody hell,' she murmured, before passing it to Barnes.

'The thing is, guv – when we started out with Katrina's death and interviewed Duncan Nithercott and Stephen Brassick, there was an element of the investigation that considered whether her murder was a message to them,' said Gavin. 'We were so focused on whether the Brassicks were the ones being threatened indirectly that once we eliminated the military angle, we didn't consider that their wives might somehow be involved.'

'Have you spoken to the charity?'

'About twenty minutes ago,' said Laura, her shoulders relaxing a little as she warmed to her subject. 'One of the directors was able to meet with us at their offices in the High Street at short notice…'

'Although she was pretty persuasive about her request,' Gavin grinned.

'Go on,' Kay urged.

'Well, the director told us that Penelope Nithercott has been a trustee for three years and attends all their social events,' Laura continued. 'But he also said that – how did he put it, Gav?'

'Her contributions were less than salutary,' he finished. 'Basically, she started out being generous with her donations but they've dried up over the past year or so. Now they have to ask her if they need her to contribute something other than her time. And her time, like Laura said, is mostly only given when there's a social gathering involved rather than actual help.'

'Especially if there's a journalist within a whiff of it,' said the younger detective, her cheeks dimpling.

Kay eyed them both, then shook her head in wonder. 'Okay, so tell me what this has to do with coercing the Brassicks back from the States. And how on earth did you manage that anyway?'

'I asked Duncan Nithercott to recall Stephen under the guise of an urgent business meeting that had to be held in London in the morning. Luckily, the Brassicks were due back in a couple of weeks anyway so it won't come as too much of a surprise to them that he wants them back earlier.' Gavin's gaze dropped to his hands. 'I *may* have also suggested to Mr Nithercott that it was in his best interests to help us.'

'Like how?'

'Apparently, Duncan's been secretly planning to divorce Jackie. In his words, things haven't been too good between them lately.' He winced. 'I said we'd try not to involve him in any criminal proceedings if we could help it.'

Kay stared at him. 'And if we can't help it?'

'The Brassicks are already in the air, guv.' He checked his watch. 'They should land at Heathrow in just over six hours.'

She craned her neck and looked across the incident room, ignoring the stony expression that Barnes wore.

No doubt her detective sergeant was wondering the same as her – whether to strangle the younger detective, or applaud his audacity.

'Who's picking them up?' she said.

'That's the thing. We were trying to get someone from the Met to assist,' said Gavin. 'But that's proving difficult, and I can't get hold of anyone with the authority needed at Gravesend or Dartford.'

Kay turned back to him, unable to keep the smile from forming. 'Best you two get a move on if you're going to coordinate with airport security before they get here, then. The traffic on the M25 will be a bitch at this time of the day.'

He blinked, frozen to his seat for a moment, then sprang into action. 'Right, guv. Thanks, guv.'

Laura trotted after him, their voices fraught as they grabbed car keys, jackets and backpacks and hurried from the room.

When Kay turned back to Barnes, he was grinning.

'You've got to hand it to him, guv. That was good work.'

'It was,' she said. 'And Headquarters are going to love him for it – as long as he's right.'

FIFTY-TWO

Kay watched Barnes pinch the bridge of his nose, then rummaged in her desk drawer and found a packet of paracetamol.

'Here,' she said, tossing the bubble pack towards him and shoving a glass of water across the desk. 'You've been doing that for the past ten minutes.'

'Thanks, guv.' He popped two capsules in his mouth, swallowed the water, and then rubbed his jaw. 'About time I got my eyes checked again, I think.'

'Feeling your age?'

'It'll catch up with you,' he retorted, unable to keep the smile from his voice. 'And no, I'm probably just spending too much time hunched over this computer screen.'

She peered beyond Barnes to the clock on the wall, then the time displayed in the corner of her own screen.

'What time did the flight land?'

'An hour ago. They'll have been rushed through passport control and they were travelling business class, so it won't have taken them long to reach the exit.'

'What are the traffic reports like?'

'Not too bad for this time of night. The usual congestion at the junction with the M23 but apart from that, they should be here any—ah, here you go.'

Kay turned as the door opened and Gavin and Laura hurried in, their faces fatigued from the frantic rush to the airport.

'How did it go?' she asked.

'We split them up at customs,' replied Gavin. 'Both of them were read their rights, and as soon as they gave us the details of their solicitor we arranged for force control to get in touch with them. The first one's just arrived downstairs and says his colleague's not too far away.'

'Who's representing them? Anyone we know?'

'A City-based firm, guv. I haven't dealt with them before – they're based in Shoreditch. The bloke downstairs is one of the partners, Bernard Crossley. His colleague, Diane Higgsworth, is a junior partner.'

'Bloody hell, they've brought the big guns with them,' said Barnes, then turned his attention to Gavin. 'Best hope you're right about all this.'

'So do I,' came the muttered reply.

'Too late now.' Kay rose and pulled a stack of manila folders towards her. 'Okay, while you two were chauffeuring Mr and Mrs Brassick back here, we've pulled together briefing packs for each of you. Laura, you'll be interviewing Stephen with Barnes, and myself and Gavin will interview Penelope. Gavin, you're leading this one given the circumstances.'

She slapped one of the folders into his hands. 'Good luck.'

———

When Kay walked into the interview room with Gavin in her wake, Penelope Brassick shrank back in her chair and clutched a cashmere cardigan tighter around her chest.

Despite her seven-hour flight and subsequent arrest, her hair and make-up was immaculate, and after her initial reaction she quickly recovered and turned her attention to her solicitor, who murmured under his breath.

Having soothed his client, he pulled a business card from his suit pocket and handed it over to Kay. 'Bernard Crossley.'

'Mr Crossley, thanks for coming at short notice. Shall we proceed?'

After seeking confirmation of Penelope's name and address and reciting the formal caution, Gavin opened the evidence folder and spent the next few seconds reviewing his scrawled handwriting.

Kay waited patiently, her pen poised over a fresh page in her notebook and silently hoping her colleague's hypothesis was right.

After all, it was the only one they had.

After a while, Gavin looked up from his notes and slid out the newspaper article.

'Tell me about your friendship with Jackie Nithercott,' he said.

'Jackie?' Penelope ran her tongue across her top lip, then glanced at the photograph in the middle of the page. 'We're just passing acquaintances. Our husbands work together, but you already know that.'

'When was the last time you saw Jackie?'

'Well, we've been out of the country since April so I suppose it must have been back in March. We were all at a party the company held after the AGM to celebrate that year's results.'

'Do you mean the company your husband, Stephen, works for?'

'That's right.' Penelope's mouth almost formed a smile. 'They're quite generous in that respect. Even the receptionist was invited, although you'll appreciate we didn't mingle with the admin staff.'

'This photograph was taken last year at a charity event. Was that organised by the company as well?'

'No.' Colour rose to the woman's face. 'That was an event organised by a charity that Jackie's involved in. Fundraising and the like – you know, trying to raise their public profile.'

'If you're just passing acquaintances, why were you there?'

'I… um…' Penelope's shoulders stiffened, and Kay saw her shoot a sideways glance at her solicitor. 'I suppose she must've invited me.'

'Do you often accept invitations from people you hardly know?'

The woman looked up. 'It was for a good cause.'

'How much did you donate that night?'

'I can't remember – you said yourself, it was last year sometime.'

'Nothing,' said Gavin, his voice flat. 'Our team spoke with the charity's head office earlier today, and they confirmed they've never received a penny from you.

Which to me sounds like defeating the purpose of the exercise, wouldn't you agree?'

Penelope said nothing.

'Why did you go?'

'Jackie said it'd be good for networking.'

'Networking for what?'

Penelope exhaled. 'I don't know. Look, she phoned me out of the blue and said it'd be fun. We could get dressed up, and have a night out without having to listen to our husbands talk about bloody hostile takeovers and who's representing who at the next arbitration hearing or whatever. It made a nice change, to be honest.'

'Have you socialised with Jackie Nithercott since?'

'Once or twice.'

'Where?'

'At another gala event just before Christmas, and then one in February which was a bit rubbish to be honest.'

'Do you socialise with Jackie outside of these events?'

Kay saw Penelope give her solicitor a sideways glance and purse her lips in response.

Gavin leaned forward and jabbed his finger on the photograph in the article. 'Who's that standing next to you?'

'I-I'm not sure.'

Kay's eyes narrowed as she watched the woman fidget in her seat.

To his credit, Gavin managed to stifle the snort that escaped, but his incredulousness was evident.

'I don't believe you,' he said. 'So I'll remind you, you're under caution and this is a triple murder investigation in which you're currently implicated. So, I'll ask you again. Who is this woman?'

A single tear escaped, and Penelope wiped at it, emitting a loud sniff as her face crumpled.

'It's Jackie's sister, Rosalind. And it's all their fault.'

FIFTY-THREE

Kay waited until Gavin had recovered from Penelope's response enough to turn to her for direction.

She gave him a slight nod, then eyed the woman in front of her.

Before she had a chance to proceed though, Penelope emitted a trembling sigh.

'I was afraid they'd go too far,' she said. 'But killing Katrina like that… in my home…'

'Who killed Katrina?' asked Kay.

In response, Penelope looked at the newspaper article, then shoved it back towards Gavin as if it were diseased.

'Rosalind, I'd imagine. I don't think even Jackie could do something as evil as that.' Penelope brought a shaking fist to her mouth. 'Oh God, what have I done?'

Kay gave her a few moments to compose herself, then edged forward. 'Take us back to the beginning. What's been going on between the three of you, and how did it start?'

'I wasn't lying about how we met,' said Penelope.

'Jackie and I often bumped into each other at company events. I think it was back in June last year that we found ourselves at a bar ordering gin and tonics at the same time and she turned around to me and said that if she had to drag herself around after her husband any more, she'd lose the will to live.'

'Were they going through a bad patch?'

'Yes, and it was getting worse.' Penelope shook her head sadly. 'They should never have got married, to be honest. Thank God they don't have children.'

She paused while her solicitor leaned over and murmured in her ear, then gave a slight nod and faced Kay once more. 'We met up for lunch about a week later, and Jackie told me that she wanted to leave Duncan but couldn't afford to. She said that she didn't work and relied on him for money. He gave her a monthly allowance to do whatever she wanted with.' Penelope stared at the table between them and picked at a hangnail. 'She could've been describing my own marriage. I think that's what resonated with me. I mean, even when I travel with Stephen I'm usually stuck in whatever apartment the company books us into – and shopping only occupies your time for so long, believe me.'

Kay said nothing, waiting as the woman took a paper tissue from her solicitor and dabbed delicately at her reddening eyes.

Eventually, Penelope continued.

'I'd been thinking of a way to leave Stephen but didn't have the confidence to try it – and I didn't have the contacts. So when Jackie told me she was helping out with that charity to get her out of the house, I… I suggested to her that there might be a way to use our allowances to make some extra money and build up a nest egg. Or an escape fund, I suppose.'

'So you targeted vulnerable people who were already in debt, and loaned them money illegally, is that correct?'

Penelope nodded. 'Yes.'

'How much interest were you charging them?'

'Twenty-two percent.' The woman glanced up. 'It's still cheaper than some of the credit cards out there, and they'd never have been able to borrow from a bank anyway. We were helping them out.'

Kay swallowed to try and counteract the dryness in her throat. 'How many?'

'I don't understand.'

'How many people did you loan money to?'

'I don't know for sure. You'd have to ask Jackie. She's better at paperwork than me.'

'Guess.'

'Maybe fifteen, eighteen since July last year.'

A stunned silence met with her words, and even Bernard Crossley visibly shrank back from his client at the revelation.

'What changed?' said Kay. 'Why was Preston Winford murdered?'

'I'm not sure,' Penelope whispered. 'I wasn't here when it happened. Stephen had been asked to speak at a conference in Atlanta and we were away that weekend. When I came back, Jackie said one of the clients – that's what she called them – had defaulted on his repayments three weeks in a row, and another hadn't paid anything for two months. She said they wanted to scare the old man into coughing up what he owed, but…'

She broke off, fresh tears rolling over her cheeks. 'Oh God, I didn't mean for any of this. It went wrong. That's what Jackie said. I believed her at first, but then…'

Kay looked down at her notes, her heart rate accelerating as she seethed at the woman's words. 'I take it from what you've said that Angus Zilchrist was the one who hadn't paid Jackie for three weeks, and Preston Winford's debt was two months overdue?'

'Yes.'

'So tell me – what went wrong? They cut Preston Winford to pieces and shoved his body into a wardrobe. To me, that suggests someone thought very carefully about what was going to happen to him. It wasn't an accident.'

Penelope turned to her solicitor. 'That's not true. They said he suffocated.'

Biting back her anger, Kay watched while Gavin opened one of the other folders beside him and slipped another photograph across the table towards Penelope.

'That's what happened to Preston Winford,' he spat.

Bernard Crossley edged farther away from his client, averting his eyes from the grisly image.

'How many of those victims have you killed?' Kay said eventually.

Penelope's eyes widened. 'None! I haven't harmed anyone. I told you – I wasn't even in the country when this happened, Detective Hunter, and I can assure you I had no idea what Jackie had planned.'

'Why is her sister Rosalind involved?'

'I don't know. That was Jackie's idea about six months

ago.' She shrugged. 'Maybe Christmas time. All I know is that in early January, Jackie changed her mind about all of this. She said things had deteriorated so much between her and Duncan that she had to leave him sooner rather than later, and so that meant getting all the money back that we'd loaned—'

'And the interest I suppose?' said Kay.

'Yes. She needed everything in order to be able to leave him and rent somewhere while the divorce was going through.' Penelope leaned forward. 'You can understand that, can't you? She was desperately unhappy.'

Slipping more photographs from the folder, Gavin laid them out on the table.

Penelope sobbed silently while Kay named each of the victims in turn.

'Who told Angus Zilchrist what was in the wardrobe in his storage unit?'

'Jackie, I think. She figured blackmailing him with that knowledge would make him pay up. And then he died of a heart attack because of the stress I suppose, and she didn't get any of the money anyway – from either of them.' Penelope clutched at her cardigan. 'And that's when she said Rosalind had a plan to get the rest of the money quickly. Duncan isn't a nice man, Detective Hunter. I think Jackie was worried what he'd do if he found out she was planning to divorce him. She had to get away.'

'Tell me about Rosalind.'

'She's absolutely mad. As is that bloody husband of hers.'

'What does Rosalind do? Apart from butchering innocent people?'

Penelope exhaled, her gaze scanning the images. 'She used to work for a cosmetic surgeon in London. All I know is that something happened a few years ago. I'm not sure what but something went wrong and both she and the surgeon were struck off the register. She couldn't find a job after that, although I think Miles was earning enough to support them both.'

'Miles? Is he her husband?'

'Yes.'

'What does he do?'

'Private security, things like that.'

'Did he provide the security system at your house?'

Penelope nodded.

'Speak up for the recording, please.'

'Yes. Miles installed our security cameras and everything. I didn't know they were planning on using it against us though, I'm telling you the truth.'

'How did you meet Katrina?'

'Through the agency we use to get cleaners in when we're expecting guests.'

'Was that the only time she cleaned for you?'

Penelope bit her lip. 'No. We were talking one day and she told me she was struggling to get by but hoped that her main job would have a full-time opening coming up soon. That was back in early February. One thing led to another so I told her Jackie could loan her some money to help her out. I said she could do the cleaning for me when I was at home to help pay it off. I was trying to help her, I swear.'

Sickened by the woman's excuses, Kay pointed at Katrina's photograph. 'What on earth did she do to you?'

'I told Jackie last month that I didn't want to be a part

of this anymore. I couldn't. Not after that man was killed. They went too far. But Rosalind said I didn't have a choice because Jackie needed the money back and they had to scare people into paying it back. I was terrified that she'd hurt me. Then I got a phone call from Jackie earlier that week – she must've been at the charity's offices or something because I didn't recognise the number. She told me she was leaving Duncan that weekend and needed somewhere to stay until she sorted herself out,' Penelope said, her face blotchy from crying.

'What did you do?'

'I gave her the latest codes for the house. And afterwards, after they… they killed Katrina, they sent me a link to that video. And Jackie told me if I ever told anyone about our loan scheme that they'd kill me next.'

FIFTY-FOUR

Kyle Walker ran his finger under his collar and grimaced as sweat prickled at his neck.

The bulky stab vest he wore clung to his chest and spine, digging into the flesh above his hips and weighing on his broad shoulders.

Both patrol cars were parked five minutes away from the house identified as being rented by Rosalind and Miles Kirwen, and his superiors were taking no chances.

The team had been instructed to wait until final checks about the Kirwens had been made, along with any associates who might be living at the property and add to an already highly charged arrest.

Kyle glanced around at the other three officers who stood next to the cars, stretching their legs and talking in low voices, their soft banter belying the adrenaline that coursed through the air, sending the hairs on his neck tingling in anticipation.

Beyond the lay-by where the cars were parked was an abandoned bus stop, the old torn timetable hanging through the broken plastic display case and the perspex weather shield panels removed to stop vandals breaking them. On the opposite side of the road, a row of large semi-detached houses faced them, the curtains pulled – although he noticed a twitch at one every now and again.

A faint scent of hibiscus carried on the warm evening air towards him, bringing with it a fragrant memory of a holiday in balmier climes over a year ago.

Before all of this.

Before his colleague, Philip, had been accidentally killed during a hostage situation.

Before his shift found him here, drenched in sweat and wondering if this time it was his turn.

Mouth dry, he rested his hand on his radio while the latest commands from the control room were relayed, then caught Dave Morrison staring at him.

'All right over there?' said the older constable. 'How're you doing?'

'I'm okay,' he rasped, then cleared his throat. 'I'm fine.'

'We won't take any chances, don't you worry.' Dave stuck his thumb over his shoulder towards the other two constables. 'These two are just as experienced as us, and we've just received authorisation from Headquarters to use tasers if we need to.'

Kyle nodded in response, unwilling to open his mouth in case he only managed a pitiful squeak, and then Dave's attention was taken by a fresh set of commands spewing from his radio.

He clenched his fists, digging his short nails into the soft flesh of his palms, and exhaled.

The counsellor that Kay had recommended was good, he'd give her that.

The breathing exercises helped, although he realised that until now he had relied on them less over the past few weeks.

The familiar count of six breaths in, eight out soothed him, edging away some of the fear that enveloped him.

'Right, here we go.' Dave lowered his radio from where he'd been talking. He beckoned the other two officers closer, then looked at each of them in turn. 'We're to assume that both suspects are armed and know their way around a knife so we're not taking any chances. We've received confirmation from the landlord that the back door of the property leads into a garden that has no access. Beyond the back fence is another property and that one leads out to the main road. Control have another car over there out of sight in case one of the suspects does a runner. All four of us are going through the front door. Me first, then you, Kyle. Steve, you're with me – we'll take Miles Kirwen and if we need additional help then you can step in, Tom. We'll use the cars to block theirs in, which is parked in a private lay-by directly in front of the terraced houses. Any questions?'

Kyle shook his head while the other two constables murmured their understanding, and then Dave led the way to their car.

He paused when he started the engine and glanced across. 'Ready?'

'As I'll ever be,' Kyle muttered. 'Let's do this.'

His head rocked back as Dave accelerated, and he reached out for the door sill to steady himself as the older constable took the junction at speed, the lights from the other vehicle flashing across the upholstery as it followed in their wake.

Within minutes, they shuddered to a halt outside an ugly line of terraced houses.

Pushing through a dilapidated gate, Kyle followed Dave up a short path bordered by overgrown grass and an abandoned washing machine, the sound of heavy footsteps behind him a welcome accompaniment as the other two officers joined them.

Dave's fist hit the door with such force that Kyle wondered if they'd need to bother breaking it down, and then angry voices filtered through the thin window glazing and a light flickered to life in one of the upstairs rooms.

Then there was shouting, thundering footsteps, and he suddenly wanted to throw up.

He took a step back, careening into Tom, who uttered a confused grunt before shoving him in the back as Dave kicked down the door.

With no choice but to follow, Kyle stepped over the threshold and into the Kirwens' house.

Dave was already making his way along the hallway towards the back of the house, shouting at the top of his voice to Miles, Steve at his heels.

Kyle paused at the bottom of the stairs for a moment, then turned to Tom. 'She's still up here.'

They raced up the treads, the smell of cigarette smoke and stale body odour washing over him as he reached the landing, just in time to see a door slam shut on his left.

'She's locked herself in the bathroom,' said Tom.

'God knows what she's got in there. We'll have to break it down.'

'Wait, she might have a knife.'

'Exactly. I'm worried she'll use it on herself.'

With that, Kyle aimed his size twelve boot at the side of the door handle and lashed out with as much force as he could muster.

The thin panelling split on impact, and with one more kick the lock twisted and the door popped open.

Pushing away the remnant wooden template, he rushed forward.

Rosalind Kirwen was bending over the bath, her hands shaking as she held a knife to her thigh.

Kyle lunged as she turned towards him, her eyes widening as a ragged scream escaped.

FIFTY-FIVE

Kay rubbed at tired eyes and leaned against the cinderblock wall outside the back door to the police station.

Beside her, Gavin scrolled through the emails on his phone, his face haggard.

Neither had spoken since terminating the interview and arranging for Penelope Brassick to be charged, and now Kay closed her eyes and inhaled the warm air that lifted her hair from her shoulders and gently flapped the paperwork under her arm.

She blinked at the sound of the door opening to see Barnes and Laura emerge, both of their faces grim.

'Stephen Brassick categorically denies having anything to do with his wife's scheme,' said the detective sergeant. 'And he's washed his hands of her, to put it politely. He's also agreed to provide full access to any and all financial records to show the money he paid to Penelope on a monthly basis, and any phone records we need. It turns out he pays her mobile phone bill too.'

'Thanks,' said Kay. 'Do either of you get the impression that he's lying about his involvement?'

'I didn't,' Laura replied. 'Honestly, I thought he was going to throw up at one point.'

'What about you two?' said Barnes. 'Did Gavin's theory hold up?'

'It did.' Kay smiled. 'And we've got enough information from Penelope to arrest Jackie Nithercott – we've sent a uniformed patrol to pick her up, as well as her husband.'

Gavin looked up from his phone. 'Guv, Rosalind and Miles Kirwen have been traced to an address in Leybourne, too. Control sent over a couple of cars to arrest them fifteen minutes ago.'

'Okay, thanks.' Kay checked her watch. 'Given the timeframe, I'd like to get all of these interviews done tonight. Do any of you have a problem with that?'

'Not me, guv,' said Barnes. 'We can only hold Sophie for another few hours unless you're going to get Sharp to authorise another twelve, and if you want to keep her safe…'

'Exactly my thoughts, and nor do I want any other victims of this illegal money-lending scheme to be put in danger. The sooner we can do these formal interviews, the better. I've asked Hughes to corroborate what we've learned so far with Sophie as well to better understand how victims were being targeted. Plus we can ensure we have something to give Headquarters in the morning with any luck.'

'That'd be good.' Laura stepped forward. 'Count me in.'

'I'm staying, guv,' said Gavin, and then blushed. 'I mean, it's sort of my fault you're all working late tonight anyway.'

'And don't think we're going to let you forget that.' Laura grinned. 'It'll be fine, as long as you don't fade on us. When was the last time you had something to eat?'

'Oh God, don't mention food,' said Kay, then turned as the security barrier whirred upwards and three patrol cars swept into the car park. 'Looks like our guests have arrived.'

Her stomach lurched when Kyle Walker emerged from the first car, the lights from the other vehicles catching the blood streaked across his cheek as he walked towards them leading a handcuffed woman, her dark eyes blazing.

'Are you all right?' she managed.

'Mrs Kirwen decided to lash out, guv,' he said grimly. 'She caught me with one of her talons.'

Rosalind peered up at him, her eyes hooded. 'More's the pity I didn't have a knife.'

Kyle gave a faint smile. 'I may have persuaded her to drop it.'

'Nice work. Okay, go and book her in.'

She moved out of the way as one by one, Miles Kirwen, Jackie Nithercott and a stunned-looking Duncan Nithercott were led past, then turned to her small team of detectives.

'Right, Gavin and Laura, I need you to interview Miles Kirwen first, then Duncan Nithercott. I want to know everything about Miles's so-called security business. God knows how many other houses he's able to break into around here, or who else he might've threatened. As for Duncan, see what he knows about Jackie's relationship with her sister. Barnes, you're with me.'

She wrenched open the back door in time to see Rosalind being led away to the first of the interview rooms, then paused as Gavin and Laura accompanied Miles Kirwen to another.

Jackie Nithercott stood with her head bowed, rubbing her wrists as the duty sergeant spoke to her in a low murmur while ensuring each item of her jewellery was taken from her and recorded into the filing system. Her husband stood a few paces from her, his jaw set while he glared at the back of her head.

Then there was movement from the internal door leading to the cells, and Hughes emerged with Sophie Anderley.

'I'll take her upstairs for now,' he said. 'It's getting crowded down here.'

'No problem,' said Kay, then turned to follow Barnes. 'We'll be up later. Can you—'

'You bitch!' Sophie screamed.

Kay spun around, taking in Sophie's anguished features and the way she strained against Hughes's grip, then looked at Jackie.

The woman had turned pale, and she swallowed as the uniformed sergeant coaxed Sophie away, leading her towards the stairs.

'Wait.' Kay hurried over to them. 'Sophie, what's going on? Do you recognise her?'

'No,' Sophie gulped. 'But it's her, I know it. That woman out there. She's one of them.'

Kay crossed her arms, her tone patient. 'If you don't recognise her, how can you be so sure?'

'Because I remember. It's that perfume she's wearing.' Sophie wriggled free from Hughes and gave them both a defiant look. 'It's the same smell that was inside that car I told you about.'

FIFTY-SIX

A shell-shocked Jackie Nithercott stared at Kay and Barnes when they settled into the seats opposite her.

While Barnes started the recording equipment and recited the formal caution, Kay looked for any sign of remorse in the woman's eyes.

Instead, all she saw was a burning resentment that grew with every passing second.

'Jackie, when we interviewed you yesterday, you informed us that on the night that Katrina Hovat was murdered, you and your husband were celebrating your wedding anniversary at a pub. You also stated that you had no idea who Katrina was when you accosted her the day before that in the car park outside the shop where she worked,' Kay began. 'Do you wish to change anything in your previous statement to us?'

'No.' Jackie lifted her chin defiantly. 'I do not.'

'But you did know her, didn't you?' said Kay. 'Because you identified her through your so-called charity work as a perfect target for your illegal money-lending scheme.'

Jackie blinked, then crossed her arms over her chest. 'I've got no idea what you're talking about.'

A predatory smile crossed Kay's lips. 'Unfortunately, we have your friend Penelope telling us something completely different. In fact, Penelope has been *most* helpful in setting out exactly how the scheme got started.'

'Not only that,' said Barnes, sliding a print-out of a DVLA record across the table to her, 'but given that one of your victims has just identified you and the car you drive as the same one Rosalind Kirwen and her husband have used when threatening people, we can also assume that you were an accomplice to Katrina's murder, as well as the murders of Preston Winford and Alec Mingrove.'

'Unless you're able to tell us *exactly* what the hell has been going on,' Kay finished. 'What's it going to be, Jackie? As it is, we're going to be asking for the maximum custodial sentence for you. Especially as our forensics team are, as we speak, processing your car. Do you think they'll find evidence to show Alec Mingrove was inside it before he was killed? What about Preston Winford? Was your car used to transport his body as well?'

'I don't know!' Jackie wiped at the spittle that escaped the corner of her mouth, then turned to her solicitor. 'I want a deal.'

Kay chuckled. 'I don't know what TV programmes you've been watching, but it doesn't work like that around here.'

'Especially when we have your accomplices under arrest and being interviewed, and enough evidence to charge you alongside them,' said Barnes. 'This interview is just a formality in the circumstances. We don't need a confession to charge you.'

'But we would like to understand what the hell has been going on,' added Kay.

The solicitor mutely gestured to his client that he concurred, then leaned across and murmured in her ear.

Kay watched impassively as the woman's face paled even further, and then raised an eyebrow as Jackie turned back to them.

'I'd like to change my statement,' she gulped. 'I was mistaken when I last spoke to you.'

'Tell me what really happened,' said Kay. 'From the beginning.'

Jackie sniffed. 'When I first met Duncan, it was great. I thought the world of him, really I did. He was already doing well in the City by then. We met at a cocktail event one evening. I was working at a graphic design company and sourcing new clients, and I think his company was looking at negotiating the buy-out of one of the marketing agencies that was attending. I didn't think anything of it when he asked me to sign a pre-nuptial agreement when we got engaged. It seemed fair.'

Her top lip curled then. 'Little did I realise how cold he could be, and how controlling. I made excuses for his behaviour for a while, telling people that he wasn't great in social situations or that he was only ruthless because that's what he was used to at work. Believe me, that gets exhausting after a while. So I decided over lunch with Penelope one day that I'd leave him.'

'When did you and Penelope first meet?'

'At one of Duncan's company events a few years ago. I wasn't lying about that, detective. But about two years ago, we started meeting up for the occasional lunch or evening drinks, especially if she wasn't travelling with Stephen while he was overseas, or if Duncan and he were holed up over a weekend trying to negotiate some deal or other.' Jackie looked down at her perfectly manicured hands, flexing her fingers. 'I mentioned to her that I wasn't happy, but that I couldn't leave because of the pre-nuptial. If I left, I'd have nothing. That's when she suggested I loan out the money he gives me as a monthly allowance, so I could squirrel away the profit and build up a nest egg.'

'How did you target your victims?'

Jackie winced. 'I prefer to call them clients.'

'I don't care what you prefer,' Kay hissed, fanning out the photographs taken at each of the crime scenes. 'This is what you did to them.'

'No, no that wasn't me!' Jackie shook her head. 'That was all Rosalind's fault. She and that stupid husband of hers. It was their idea.'

'Why? What did any of these people do to you?'

Jackie took a deep breath. 'Nothing. They were just… just a way to make the money I needed, that's all. They came to the charity's office in town for help. Angus was the first one. He was so desperate for money, I think he'd have agreed to anything.'

'What did you say to him?'

'I overheard him when he was talking to one of the counsellors. It wasn't difficult – the offices are old, and the walls are paper-thin.' She paused and glanced around her. 'Not like this. You can hear everything from the next room if you're quiet.'

'Go on.'

'I waited until he left, then made some excuse about being late for a dentist appointment and followed him.' Jackie choked out a laugh. 'I found him outside the betting shop, debating whether to go inside. Honestly, you'd have thought he'd have known better. I knew the charity's counsellor wouldn't loan him any money, not with his track record, so I made him an offer he couldn't refuse. Three hundred quid there and then, with another four thousand two days later. He nearly ripped my hand off taking the cash from me.'

'Did he pay you back?'

'Some of it, yes. To start with.' Jackie's face took on a look of wonder. 'That gave me the confidence to help more people. And slowly, week by week, my little nest egg started to grow. I could see a way out of my bloody marriage at last.'

'When did it go wrong?'

Jackie frowned. 'When I found out Duncan was having an affair with his executive assistant.'

'Why not just divorce him?' said Barnes. 'Surely you'd have grounds?'

'I would, except there's a provision in the pre-nuptial agreement that I get nothing if the marriage deteriorates after twelve years. There's a no-fault clause, even if the bastard cheats on me.' She wiped her eyes. 'I'd never have signed the fucking thing if I knew he'd turn out to be like this. I just had to leave him as soon as possible.'

'So you decided to recall all the debts?' said Kay.

'Yes.'

'How?' Kay sifted through her notes. 'According to Penelope, you've loaned money to over a dozen people.'

'Easy,' said Jackie, a twisted smile cutting through her tears. 'I set Rosalind after them.'

FIFTY-SEVEN

Kay was taking no chances with Jackie's younger sister, especially after seeing the damage the woman had done to Kyle's cheek.

Two officers were posted outside the room while a duty solicitor met with Rosalind, and would accompany them when they conducted the interview.

Meanwhile, Kyle sat on a chair in the custody suite dabbing at his face with an antiseptic wipe while Hughes stood beside him, a fresh dressing from the first aid kit in his hand.

'Make sure you get your tetanus shot and some blood tests done,' said Barnes, his face grim while he watched the young constable stick the plaster to his jaw. 'Just in case.'

'I will.' Kyle loosened his stab vest and gave a weary sigh. 'I'm just glad I managed to disarm her. I really think she would've used that knife on me.'

'Is she suicidal?' said Kay. 'I heard Tom say she was about to cut herself when you broke into the bathroom.'

'I think it was a bluff to get us closer, guv. I don't think she had any intention of coming quietly.'

Barnes whistled under his breath. 'What about the husband, Miles? What've you found out there?'

'I can help with that.' Laura appeared at the door, her face wan. 'We've just taken a break from interviewing him but it turns out he's got a juvenile record for almost killing another boy in a fight at school when he was thirteen. That's why we couldn't find it on the system – it's a sealed record. When he told us, it was almost like he was proud of it.'

Kay sighed. 'Jesus. How the hell did he get into the security game, then?'

'He talks a good talk,' said Gavin, joining Laura and handing her a glass of water. 'He was released when he reached eighteen, and put whatever he'd learned in prison to good use. According to him, he started out working for an electrician who took on "troubled boys" – his words, mind – and saw a gap in the market for installing security systems. Given the sort of people he was hanging around with in prison, he was a convincing salesman.'

'It's a long way from installing security systems to torturing and killing people,' said Barnes.

'Dave's been taking a look at the laptop we seized when we arrested them,' Laura said. 'His search history's full of paramilitary videos, bushcraft skills, and so on. There's some other stuff too but he says he's leaving that for Andy Grey's team at Headquarters. From what he said, it's pretty nasty, guv.'

Kay shivered, recalling Andy's comments about the

number of staff he was losing due to stress. 'Anything else you want to tell us before we interview his wife?'

'They met six years ago at a friend's party in Rochester,' said Gavin. 'Although I think the only thing they have in common is a violent streak.'

'Has he admitted to anything?'

'Only to driving the car when Sophie saw them, so far.' Laura drained the water and gave Hughes a grateful smile as he took the empty glass from her. 'We'll head back in there and ask him about that wardrobe he put Preston's body in next.'

Kay watched the two detectives walk back to the interview rooms, then glanced at Barnes. 'What do you think?'

'I think we're all going to have nightmares for a few weeks, guv.'

————

The two uniformed constables trailed into the interview room after Kay and Barnes, taking up position beside the door and keeping a keen eye on the woman who sat at the bare plastic-covered table.

The duty solicitor appointed to represent her had positioned his chair as far away from his client as possible but now reluctantly dragged it closer, ready to begin proceedings.

After starting the recording and ensuring all the formal introductions were properly captured, Kay quietly sat for a moment while Barnes laid out each of the victims' photographs in front of Rosalind Kirwen.

The duty solicitor blanched at the images, but to his credit recovered quickly and lowered his gaze to his legal pad, his pen writing furiously across the page.

'Rosalind, I want to start by asking you whether it was your idea or someone else's to torture and kill these people?' Kay said.

'Jackie said she wanted to give them a fright.'

The woman's voice had an underlying musicality to it that made Kay wonder whether she had enjoyed what she had done, and whether she would have continued her killing spree if it weren't for Gavin's hunch about Jackie Nithercott.

There was no denial, no histrionics, and no remorse in her response.

There was only a coldness that seeped from the woman's pores and crept across the table to where Kay sat.

'Are you close to your sister?'

'I'd do anything for her.'

'There's a big jump from giving someone a fright to doing this to them,' said Kay, tapping the photograph of Katrina's broken body. 'Why did you torture her? What had she done to you?'

'She needed to be taught a lesson,' Rosalind said, her tone bored now. 'They all did.'

'Why?'

'Because they broke their promise to Jackie. They said they'd pay her back.'

'And they were, weren't they?' Kay sifted through the paperwork in front of her until she found what she was looking for. 'These are statements from Preston Winford's bank account. He was making regular monthly payments by the look of these cash withdrawals. Right up until April, which is when you killed him, wasn't it?'

Rosalind said nothing.

'Why on earth would you kill someone who was providing your sister with the money she was trying to raise to leave her husband? Because that's what was happening, wasn't it? The interest on these loans was going to be her nest egg.' Kay turned to Barnes, affecting a confused expression. 'That's what she told us, anyway.'

'Did you kill the golden goose, Rosalind?' said Barnes mockingly. 'Did Jackie send you to scare him into paying her back faster, and it went too far?'

Rosalind's gaze dropped to Preston's photograph, her jaw clenched. 'It was an accident.'

'What was?' said Kay.

'He wasn't meant to die. It was his fault. He moved, and that was that. I couldn't stop the bleeding. I only meant to cut him a bit,' Rosalind pouted. 'Jackie was really pissed off.'

'Where did this happen?'

The woman shrugged. 'Miles knows a place out near Tenterden. Deserted like, y'know? Just as well, because it took us a few days to work out what to do with him afterwards.'

'You mean the wardrobe.'

Rosalind smiled, and it wasn't pretty. 'Miles thought knowing about Preston would make the old man pay up faster, but he still wouldn't cough up what he owed.'

'Do you mean Angus Zilchrist?'

'Yeah.'

'We have a witness statement that says your husband

threatened Angus at the golf club where he played. Was that before or after Preston was killed?'

'After.' She sneered. 'Jackie was livid about him – Preston – dying, but she soon changed her mind when a few of the others started paying her back that week. That's when we noticed Angus still hadn't paid anything. She asked Miles to go and have a word.'

'Did this "having a word" include threats to his life?'

'I don't know. I wasn't there.'

'But why the wardrobe? Why put it in Angus's storage unit?'

'That's Miles all over, that is. He reckoned it'd be a laugh to insist that Angus store some stuff for us, then tell him what was really in there. I suppose he thought if he knew, he'd pay. We found some cheap furniture going for free, shoved Preston's body into the wardrobe and then got Angus to help Miles.' A cackle erupted from Rosalind. 'I didn't expect the old man to have a heart attack when we told him though. He was just meant to pay up. She was *so* angry.'

'Who?'

'Jackie, of course. Now she had two clients who'd never pay her back.' Rosalind sighed. 'And then Penelope found out.'

Kay's gaze snapped up from her notes. 'Tell me about that.'

'Oh, she was fine all the time she was telling Jackie how to make all this money, how to keep everything normal at home while she planned to leave Duncan and building her little nest egg.' The woman snorted. 'She soon changed her tune when she found out someone got hurt.

Like, what did she think was going to happen? My sister isn't a charity, y'know. Anyway, Penelope came back from the States at the end of April, found out that Jackie decided to try and get all her money back from those people, and I suppose one thing led to another…'

'What did she do?'

'She threatened my sister,' said Rosalind, edging forward. Her eyes darkened. 'And *nobody* does that.'

Kay swallowed, the woman's rage palpable. 'How did she threaten her?'

'She said she'd come to you lot anonymously. Even if it meant risking herself being found out eventually. She said that people weren't meant to die, and that we'd gone too far.'

'What did you do?' Kay found the photograph of Katrina and held it up. 'Did you torture and kill her to silence Penelope?'

'It worked, didn't it? Penelope never told you what was going on, did she? And she couldn't do anything to stop us, not once that husband of hers got sent back to the States. The stupid bitch thought she could swan back over here and start telling us what to do,' Rosalind snapped. 'Then when she threatened us, I knew I had to do something.'

'So you went to her home when you knew Katrina would be there—'

'Well, Jackie had the security code, after all.'

'Did she?'

'Of course she did. Penelope told her what it was, in case she ever wanted a place to stay when Duncan was being an arsehole.'

Kay paused for a moment, needing time to control the revulsion that swallowed her. Eventually, she reached out and tapped Alec Mingrove's photograph. 'Tell me about him.'

'I didn't like him.'

'Why not?'

Rosalind sighed, her gaze finding the fluorescent lights in the ceiling. 'Because he lied, all the time. He made a promise to Jackie and kept breaking it. He was one of the worst. I mean, even after he saw the video we uploaded, he still didn't pay up. I can't help it if people are stupid, can I?'

'What did you do?'

'We found him, eventually. I mean, what was he *thinking*, having a posh meal out when he was two months behind on his debt to Jackie?' Rosalind lowered her chin and contemplated a ragged thumbnail. 'He was taking the piss.'

'So you tortured him, and threw his body in the river. Why? Why there?'

The woman on the other side of the table grinned. 'We thought it'd get everyone else's attention of course. Surprisingly, a lot of them didn't pay up after seeing what happened to Katrina. Me and Miles figured something more public might get their attention.'

'Hell of a risk.'

'It worked.' Rosalind sat back in her chair, her shoulders relaxing. 'Only three more people owe my sister money now.'

Kay glanced at the duty solicitor, who sat stock-still,

his gaze frozen on the images before him. She could only assume she wore the same shocked expression.

'Why did you do this?' she managed, cursing as her hand shook while she turned Katrina's photograph to the light. 'Why kill all these innocent people?'

Rosalind tilted her head to one side, as if pondering the question for a moment. Then she smiled. 'I suppose I liked it.'

Kay dropped the photograph as Barnes shifted in his seat, wondering if she would ever fail to be repulsed at some of the criminals who she faced.

She hoped not.

She owed it to their victims.

FIFTY-EIGHT

Kay lifted the last of the manila files from her desk and dropped them into an archive box at her feet, rubbed the base of her spine with her knuckles, and then glanced over her shoulder at voices from the corridor.

Barnes appeared first, his tie already askew despite the early hour, closely followed by Gavin and Laura and the distinct aroma of savoury pastries.

'The café had a special on, guv,' Gavin grinned, passing her a greasy paper bag. 'Figured you hadn't bothered with breakfast this morning, so there you go.'

'Thanks.' Kay unwrapped the sausage roll and took a bite. 'Did any of you get much sleep after you left here?'

'A couple of hours,' said Barnes. 'I couldn't stop thinking about Sophie, and how lucky she was. A few more days, and...'

Laura shuddered. 'Don't, Sarge.'

'That was good work with the lead, Gav,' said Kay, before licking crumbs from her fingers.

'Just a lucky break,' replied the detective constable with a shrug, before he took a swig from an energy drink can.

'Bollocks.' Barnes finished his food and tossed the wrapper into the bin beside Kay's desk. 'That was more than luck.'

Kay swallowed the last of the sausage roll and wiped her hands. 'What've you lot got on today?'

'I'm going to head over to Northfleet and meet with Andy Grey,' said Laura. 'I'll let him know we've charged all three women plus Miles Kirwen, and I'll tell him we're going to need the computers analysed before the CPS get antsy. Are those the files going over to them?'

'Some of them. I'll need you all to finish your reports by Friday, please.' She turned to Barnes. 'Aren't you due at court at ten?'

'Yes, but it's a clear-cut one, guv. I should be back by one, latest.'

'Okay, I'll catch you before you go. Gav, can I have a word?'

Kay watched the other two detectives drift away to their desks, then turned to Gavin with a smile. 'We need to have a talk.'

He lowered the energy drink and stared. 'Something the matter, guv?'

'Not at all. Come on – Sharp's old office will do.'

Threading her way between the desks, Kay smiled. The nervous energy emanating from the younger detective was palpable, but she didn't want to speak to him in front of the others.

Not about this.

'All right,' she said, closing the door after him and crossing her arms. 'When are you going to apply for a promotion?'

'Eh?'

'Come on, Gav. You've got detective sergeant written all over you, and have for some time.'

'I-I don't know, guv.' His brow creased. 'I suppose I see what you and Barnes have to deal with and I wonder if I'm ready for it.'

'Oh, you're ready all right. What if I told you there's a sniff of a rumour about a DS role coming up here in Maidstone? Would that convince you?'

'What about Barnes?'

'I'm not letting him go.' She smiled. 'I've already spoken with Sharp and told him there's enough workload here for the two of you. This investigation has proven that.'

Gavin looked down at his feet and blew out his cheeks before his gaze returned to hers. 'To be honest, guv, I've been wondering whether I should speak to you about a promotion.'

'And here we are.' She cocked her head to one side. 'Just don't get any ideas about disappearing to Northfleet just yet, okay? I need you here.'

He shot her a lop-sided grin. 'Don't worry. I don't think Leanne wants me over there. She'd never see me, right?'

'Right.' Kay gave a theatrical shudder and opened the door, waving him back into the incident room. 'Besides, imagine the commute. And there are no cafés nearby. No decent pizza, either.'

'I'd fall apart, guv.'

'Probably. You're starting to look too thin anyway.'

He laughed, then paused beside the dilapidated photocopier. 'Thanks, guv. I'll keep an eye out for the vacancy alert in my emails.'

'And if I hear anything in the meantime, I'll give you a heads-up.'

'Deal.'

He threw a mock salute her way before crossing to his desk, immediately turning his attention to his phone as it began to trill.

'Everything all right, guv?' Barnes sidled up to her, jerking his chin towards his colleague. 'Did you have a word with him?'

'I did, and I think he's ours for now. Especially if that DS role comes up here.'

'Good to know.'

They turned at raised voices from outside and crossed to the window to see Rosalind Kirwen and her sister Jackie being led towards a security van.

Both women were handcuffed, Jackie's hair mussed up from a night in the cells while Rosalind thrashed her shoulders under the grip of a burly uniformed officer.

Behind them, Penelope Brassick followed mutely alongside a female officer who guided her towards the prison transport vehicle.

'Good bloody riddance,' murmured Kay.

'When shall we three meet again?' Barnes cackled.

Kay groaned, placed her hand on his arm and steered him towards the door. 'If you're going to start quoting Shakespeare at me, I'm going to need another coffee.'

THE END

ABOUT THE AUTHOR

Rachel Amphlett is a USA Today bestselling author of crime fiction and spy thrillers, many of which have been translated worldwide.

Her novels are available in eBook, print, and audiobook formats from libraries and retailers as well as her website shop.

A keen traveller and accidental private investigator, Rachel has both Australian and British citizenship.

Find out more about Rachel's books at: www.rachelamphlett.com.